Homewrecker

Koniotis Mysteries
Book Six

www.cyberworldpublishing.com

First published by Cyberworld Publishing in 2011
Cover design by S Bush © 2011
Cover photo - © Blaze86 | Dreamstime.com
E-book ISBN 978-1-921879-42-5
Print ISBN 978-1-921879-43-2

Published by
Cyberworld Publishing
Jindalee St
Toronto, NSW
Australia, 2283

Koniotis Mysteries Series

Each book in this series stands alone, but they are also all connected in various ways and form the different parts of one story.

Laughter's Echo

Salted Away

Mouflon Brigade

Amathus Armageddon

Bogus Bills

Homewrecker

Homewrecker

Koniotis Mysteries Book Six

Gina Drew

Caitlyn's map of Cyprus showing the places mentioned in this book:

Cape Kormaktiki

Kyr

Morphou
Bay

Lapithos
Karmi

Ayia Irini

Sisklipo
Philia

St. Hilarion
Cast.

M E S A

Gunyel

Morphou
Karavo Pasi
Soli
Vouni

Elda

Makedoni

Polis

Skouriotissa
Kallana

Galata

Kakopetria

Kykko Mon.

Mt.
Olympus

Troodos

Platres

PAPHOS

Omodhos

Khiro

Kouklia
(Old Paphos)

Episkopi Curium
Pissouri

Aphrodite's Rock

LIMASSOL

Kolossi
Cast.

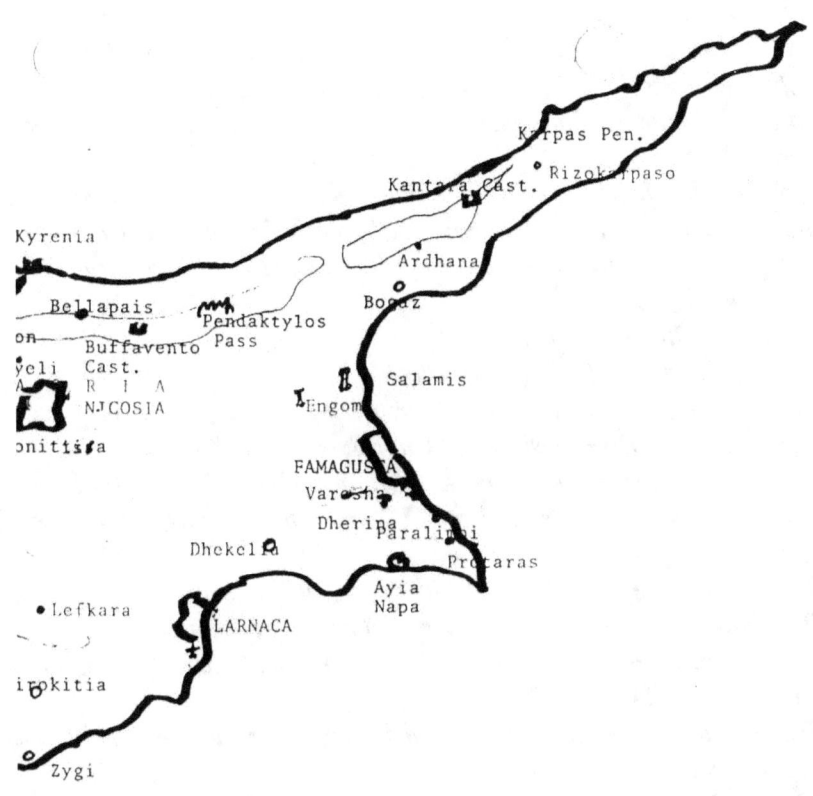

Kyrenia

Bellapais

on

ýcli Cast.
Λ   R I A
    NICOSIA

onittia

Pendaktylos
Buffavento Pass

Karpas Pen.

Kantara Cast.   ° Rizokarpaso

Ardhana

Bogaz

Salamis

Engom

FAMAGUSTA
Varosha

Dherina
Paralimni

Dhekelia   Protaras

Ayia
Napa

• Lefkara

LARNACA

irokitia

Zygi

7

Primary Characters

Sarah Bristow—*U.S. Army Research Lab director*
Stuart Claymore—*Head of the UNICIS computer lab division*
Assadollah Egdal—*New prime minister of Iran*
Lala Hatan—*Turkish Cypriot vice president of the Federated State of Cyprus (FSC)*
Inga Hartzel—*Managing Partner of the Hartzel-Wegner arms merchant firm*
Trevor Hawkins—*British illustrator and spy*
Irene—*Takis Koniotis's aunt, and the Koniotises' nanny and housekeeper*
Chrystalla Ioannou—*Greek Cypriot president of the Federated State of Cyprus (FSC)*
Ahmad Jallud—*Cypriot chief of police*
Leila Jallud—*Wife of Ahmad Jallud*
Nabil Jallud—*Damascus copperware merchant; uncle of Ahmad Jallud*
Ahmad Koniotis—*Twin son of Caitlyn and Takis Koniotis*
Caitlyn Spencer Koniotis—*American archaeologist in Cyprus and Dean of Archeology at the Eastern Mediterranean University; wife of Takis Koniotis*
Eric Koniotis—*Twin son of Caitlyn and Takis Koniotis*
Takis Koniotis—*UN secretary general for security affairs*
Ellen Larkin—*Director of the UN International Crime Investigations Service (UNICIS)*
Irina Lukenov—*Mother of Uri and Pavel Lukenov; common-law wife of Sergey Stepanov*
Pavel Lukenov—*Assistant to the Hartzel-Wegner firm general manager; son of Irina Lukenov and younger brother of Uri Lukenov*
Uri Lukenov—*Executive of the Zurich office of the Piccard Shipping company; son of Irina Lukenov and brother of Pavel Lukenov*
Joseph MacAlister—*American commander chief; U.S. president's nephew*
Demetris Mattas—*Publisher of the Cypriot newspaper* Semerini
Holst Meinhart—*Mercenary soldier*
Gerhard Mueller—*Agent of the Hartzel-Wegner arms merchant firm*
Ginger Patterson—*President of the Patterson Solar Systems company*
Andre Piccard—*CEO, Piccard Holdings*

Frieda Piccard von Meisse—*Manager of the Zurich office of the Piccard Shipping company*

Maria Solonos—*Cypriot interior minister*

Isma'il Safari Shah—*New ruler of Iran*

Sergey Stepanov—*Hartzel-Wegner general manager*

Brigadier James Tymes-Smith—*Episkopi British Sovereign Base commander*

Dr. Andriko Visiliou—*the chief of the Cypriot Archaeology Department*

Ann Wynette—*Head of U.S. Embassy Nicosia Secret Service office*

Chapter One

Sometimes in hindsight, as when an archduke was felled by an assassin's bullet in Sarajevo in 1914 or when the Japanese city of Hiroshima disintegrated beneath the first delivered atomic bomb, the exact instant of time at which the earth is retilted on its axis can be identified. Just such a moment occurred at 10:02 PM on a late June night in 2014 when the lights went out in Tehran, Iran.

It was not that the Iranians were not prepared for a significant event. Indeed, they and the whole world had been watching for nearly eight months with various shadings of glee and trepidation as the thirty-five-year-old religious fundamentalist regime of the ayatollahs lost steam and started its inevitable slide into rejection and oblivion. Thus, when the Be'sat power station in the southern, industrial section of the city suddenly flickered off, this act that pitched Iran's capital city into darkness served to mark the release of a collective sigh across the city, country, and world that automatically registered in the minds of all as the heralding in of a new era. Little did anyone know at the time just how momentous that change would be.

At the beginning of the ayatollahs' innings, when the supposedly unassailable Pahlavi dynasty of Mohammad Reza Pahlavi succumbed to the opposition, under the unlikely leadership of the exiled Ayatollah Khomeyni in 1979, nobody would provide odds that would give an Islamic fundamentalist regime in Iran even two years in power. But as late as the summer of 2013, however, the same odds makers would not have backed the suggestion that the fundamentalists would be out of power within the next decade.

It had been oil that had enabled the Pahlavis to maintain their place as one of the richest of the world's royal families. And it had been control of the same oil that had permitted the Islamic fundamentalists to maintain their place in the world, while thumbing their noses at the Western economic powers, and to export their own form of religious extremism and hatred. However, it had also been the oil—or rather the plummeting value of that oil in the regime's last decade—that had caused the demise of the ayatollahs.

When some elderly tinkering British inventor on the small Mediterranean island of Cyprus happened upon the formula for harnessing and conveniently storing solar energy for later use in a constant power supply, the power days of Iran and of all the other nations whose economies and influence had depended for a century on the reservoirs of liquid fossil fuels buried beneath their national territory were marked. In retrospect, therefore, perhaps the first retilting of the earth's political axis in the twenty-first century wasn't really indexed to the night the lights went out in Tehran in 2014 but to this earlier solar energy storage discovery by a shy little man named John Patterson.

The change of power in Tehran had been inevitable when it became obvious that the regime had lost its economic foundation when the price of oil fell dramatically. This was the point where the technopowers, which included the industrialized nations as well as corporations far wealthier and more powerful than many industrial nations, switched to stored solar power for their energy generation. Freed of the stranglehold of the Iranian oil barons, the long knives of the opposition forces within Iran were unsheathed and flashed in unison.

First the Azadegan, the paramilitary "freedom fighter" group committed to the restoration of the monarchy, combined with the Paris-based National Movement of Iranian Resistance that had grown to be the largest movement in opposition to the Islamic government in Tehran in spite of its own inability to decide on a desired government form. Then, when the opposition forces curled around the political spectrum to pick up the support of the Forqan, the far rightist, extreme Islamic fundamentalists who opposed all political involvement by religious leaders, the die was cast.

Even the Iranian military forces, which had somehow managed to remain cohesive, professional, and resilient during the reign of the ayatollahs, were able to read the picture and retired to their barracks, just as they had done when the shah lost his mandate, to accommodate to the inevitable, whatever that might be.

The inevitable, just as happened when the Pahlavis moved from titular monarchs to benevolent despots, was brokered on this warm night in June by an American. And, although it brought back to power a royal dynasty—this time with a republican constitution that looked suspiciously like that of the United States—it was not the Pahlavis who were returning to the Peacock Throne, as they had done with the help of the American swashbuckler Kermit Roosevelt. Rather, it was the Safavis, who had ruled much earlier, for over two centuries, from the golden Persian era of the sixteenth century, who were regaining the reins of power.

Tehran was pitched, not unexpectedly, into total darkness at 10:02 PM on June 22nd, 2014. For six minutes the city held its breath. All traffic, both vehicular and pedestrian, stopped, as if the Be'sat power station had provided all energy in the city. Silence reigned for those six minutes. And then, as if spontaneously, torches were lit and chanting commenced on the campuses of Tehran University on the Enqelab main drag in the central city, of the Shahid Behesti University just north of the International Trade Fair grounds in the city's northern suburbs, and at Edam Sedeq University to the east of the major north-south street, the Bozorg Rahj-E-Shahid Doktor Chamran.

As if on cue, traffic started up again and bolted for the safety of home. Even those who had not been headed for home at the time redirected their automobiles or their steps—at least those who were not part of the "spontaneous" movement to effect the change of power.

Unfortunately, not all of those who had been out on the streets that night moved fast enough for cover. At 10:23 PM mobs of "students" poured forth from the grounds of three universities and ran amok in seemingly random and uncoordinated havoc—only seemingly—in the city's streets. Within minutes, the Emam Khomeyni, Shadid Raja', and Savaneti and Suktegi hospitals were swamped with business.

It had seemed that the cutting of power to the city had unleashed an uncontrollable monster, long suppressed and thirsting for blood. However, the darkness and well-planned random violence were merely screens for the movement of three relatively small, but surgically inserted, commando groups that, ironically, crept out of the supposedly empty American embassy compound on Ayatollah Taleqani Street and swiftly set out in three different directions, along avenues that had been

15

effectively cleared just moments before by the cleverly preprogrammed rampaging of the armed "students."

It had been the humor of the plan's mastermind, the brilliant Joseph MacAlister, the not-so-distinguished nephew of a distinguished American president and the uncle of a distinguished U.S. president-to-be, that had led to the use of the derelict American embassy compound as the center of the operation to put the Safavis back in power. The compound had remained abandoned and left to rot since the Iranians signaled in 1980 their intent to flaunt the rules of international diplomacy and invaded the embassy compound, took the American diplomatic community into brutal captivity, and paraded their bound and blindfolded prisoners in front of the world's cameras until the moment of the change in presidential administrations in Washington, taking credit, of course, for a "forced" change of power in Washington.

By 11:04 PM, almost exactly on schedule, the "student'" rampage ended as quickly and dramatically as it had begun and its instigators melted into the alleys of the moaning city. The three small commando forces were in place.

The force that had moved northwest from the American embassy compound had reached its assigned spot in the radio and television center just south of the International Trade Fair grounds as the Be'sat power station flickered back on, as suddenly and as effortlessly as it had blacked out an hour previously. The new team of telecasters at Tehran Domestic Radio and Television was fully scripted and dressed to go on the air at 11:15 PM to announce the supposedly bloodless transfer of power to the legitimate government of Isma'il Safavi Shah and Prime Minister Assadollah Egbal, which had already been recognized by the European Union and the United States. The very fact of the news broadcast itself took no one in Iran by surprise, although the names of the new leaders caused their full share of gasps, especially among the country's history buffs.

A second commando group sped in a southeast direction from the American embassy compound. The unit was composed solely of Azadegan irregulars, who had been carefully compartmented and separated by Joseph MacAlister and the other American assistants who the deep coffers of the rabidly nationalistic American multimillionaire former oilman, turned computer chip tycoon and failed U.S. reactionary presidential candidate had provided for the project. Their goal was the Shahid Motahhar Mosque, to which the entire fifteen-ayatollah ruling Islamic Revolutionary Council had retired in what they had thought was complete secrecy two days earlier to contemplate and to try to pray away the crumbling of their control and of their very lives.

After the three groups had split up at the American embassy, Joseph MacAlister and Isma'il Safavi Shah were never to hear from the Azadegan group again. That was, of course, the enunciated plan. Coincidentally, they were never to hear from any of the fifteen ayatollahs who had been on the last Islamic Revolutionary Council either. That had not been part of the enunciated plan, but it certainly caught no one by surprise—except, of course, in public posturing.

MacAlister himself led the third group, which went due south from the embassy compound and which was ceremoniously greeted on the steps of the Golestah Palace by an army of servants that had quietly taken up residence there the previous day and had worked through the night to welcome MacAlister's group. Isma'il Safavi Shah, the great friend of the European Union and the United States, who had already won many industrial concessions from an important American business leader that would put Iran back on the road to economic prosperity, was home. Following a short, televised meeting between the new shah and his prime minister, Assadollah Egdal, with the American director of this touching and "impromptu" little scene lurking properly in the shadows, the shah went to bed, the prime minister went to work, and MacAlister and his happy little band trundled off to Ghasr Prison, where the Intelligence network of their mentor had told them they could find a vast underground vault containing very interesting files.

Of everything that had happened this night, it would be the contents of those files, not the dramatic show of the will of the people in the return of the ancient Safavid Dynasty to the Peacock Throne or the suppressed reality of the brief bloodletting of the university "students," that was destined to rock the world. And this change of direction in world affairs could have been—but would not be—traced back to the delayed effect of the musing two decades previously of quiet little John Patterson.

* * * *

At the same moment that Iran Domestic Radio and Television's new, well-scrubbed, Western attired, and perkily smiling newscasters went on the air, some nine time zones to the east, a small group of ultimately affected administrators and business visitors were, without knowing that their world had changed, finishing up an amicable lunch in a lush, but falsely lighted tropical atrium cafe deep inside a mountain in the United States' southern state of Virginia.

Although not particularly considered a national secret, few knew about the U.S. Army Research Lab. It had been constructed in the late 1990s in one of the minor, but still impressive and extensive cavern systems just outside the sleepy little town of Luray, in the Blue Ridge Mountains, barely an hour and half by auto to the southwest of the center of the nation's capital, Washington, D.C. Once isolated, now, in the year 2014, it stood well within the perimeter of the city's ring of suburban bedroom communities.

The lab's long-time director, General Sarah Bristow, was justly proud of this facility. She had commanded the building of it herself. It had been her labor of redemption. Having been brought home in partial disgrace twenty years earlier from a defense attaché posting to a Mediterranean island country as one of her country's senior women army colonels, where she had become unprofessionally and emotionally embroiled in a major spy scandal, General Bristow had had to work her way back into the good graces of her country. She had done so—and had done so with flying colors—by taking over the development of a new high-tech army research lab.

It had been Bristow's idea, for security, safety, and cost-effectiveness reasons, to construct the facility inside a network of caverns. Although the cave complex that was chosen was large, it was dwarfed in size and impressiveness by the nearby commercially developed Skyline and Luray caverns and it was largely—although not completely—located under land owned already by the federal government, so there had been no opposition to Bristow's innovative proposals. In the two succeeding decades, Bristow's operation had flourished, as had her reputation for creative planning and solid organization. The various research areas were located in isolated cavern areas, protected from each other by tons of solid rock. Here experiments on esoteric substances and devices that were being considered for weapons and defense system-related production could be conducted in nearly complete security and safety—and far from the prying eyes of the curious public and even more curious media establishment. Gone were the days of superpower political espionage, to be replaced by the days of strict public scrutiny and less understood and controllable international terrorism and crime. Bristow's facilities plan had proven to be ideal to handle the modern world pressures.

Her designs had also taken high prizes for environmental excellence. In the administrative, break, and food service areas of the complex, at the compound's center, Bristow had used modern environmental biotech methods to develop the sense of a tropical garden. Workers were thus able to work for long periods of time, even when the snow was piling up at the facility's entry and the wind was whistling through the pines on the mountain slopes overhead, without suffering from the sensation of being trapped underground.

On this late June afternoon, General Bristow, who was entering her last month of active duty, which had already been extended twice in the interests of the government but which, alas, could not be extended for a third time, was personally conducting a tour for a representative of the Swiss defense systems brokerage firm of Hartzel-Wegner. Sarah wanted her last month on the job to be a banner month for lab contracts, and the deal being discussed with Hartzel-Wegner for night-vision photo-optic devices would put the lab's statistics over the top. General Bristow didn't normally conduct these tours herself and the lab didn't normally push so hard on a sale, but the meeting of her goals meant everything to Bristow.

As the general was leading the visitor and his assistants toward the night-vision photo-optics lab, she was a tad more informative and open than she normally would have been—and certainly more talkative than one of her trained, highly security conscious briefers would have been. Even the act of taking the Swiss visitors to the lab area went beyond the lab's normal rules. They usually were not permitted beyond the display rooms in the installation's central core.

"And what goes on in these corridors off to the left and right?" Herr Mueller was asking to keep the conversation going as they approached the photo-optics lab.

"Oh, we're working on laser-sighting devices off to the left here and triggering devices for low-altitude rocket launchers off to the right, and we just passed the lab where we're developing a streamlined, light-weight gas mask. But it's all very hush, hush, of course," the general gushed amicably, her charm channel turned to its highest level.

"But that all sounds so dangerous," Herr Mueller commented. "We're so far from the central core now. Aren't your workers afraid of being trapped back here by an explosion or a gas leak?"

"Well, we try to keep our experimentation on such systems to a small scale here. We have test ranges elsewhere for the more dangerous procedures. And, of course, we don't actually have to go all the way back to the core from here to escape in the case of an emergency."

"I think you must be joking with me," Herr Mueller responded in heavy Germanic tones that sent a bolt of apprehension through Bristow. She wasn't losing him, was she, she thought in panic.

Then, with overriding concern for her sale, she quickly interjected: "Oh, no indeed. It is highly confidential, of course, but we do have escape towers to the surface located in the various corridors. That door over there, for instance, goes up the mountain and opens very close to the Beaverbrook Lodge site on the Skyline Drive that runs across the mountain ridge above us. We could not have constructed this lab without escape plans that met federal regulations."

The group swept on to the photo-optics lab, where the visitors spent very little time before declaring they were very impressed with quality control and were ready to sign a contract. In the few days remaining to her at the lab, a triumphant Sarah Bristow was only able to remember how masterfully she had handled the Hartzel-Wegner visitors and how easily she had gained their trust. Maybe she would go into defense contract brokering herself following her belated, but forced retirement. With her obvious talents she knew she would be a natural saleswoman.

* * * *

Within moments of shutdown of the Be'sat power station, the Syrian ambassador to Iran was fully aware that he had run out of time. From the balcony of his flat on Enqelab near the grounds of Tehran University, he had heard the roar that had gone up on the campus following the six minutes of deafening silence and had seen the well-masked but a little too obvious, to one of his experience, movement of the "students" toward specific areas of the city. He was a brutal realist. He had had to be to get to the level he had reached in the Syrian administration. As soon as the precision of the dramatic changes in the streets four flights below him had sunk in, he knew that he had lost the race.

Perhaps if his superiors had trusted him and had been more explicit about what they had needed, he could have beaten the clock. But that too had only been an illusion. He had known that it would only be a matter of a few days. Damascus had refused to believe that. But they were the ones who had deluded themselves.

He was here, on the ground. As soon as he had not been able to make an appointment with a single member of the Islamic Revolutionary Council two days previously, the ambassador had known that the regime was in its death throes.

He had sent his own agents out to try to find the location of the sensitive files Damascus had demanded that he find and destroy, but they had not been successful. And how could they have been successful if they didn't know what they were looking for beyond "scientific files that would compromise the Syrians."

When Damascus had called earlier today and said that a team of "friends" from the Hizballah Islamic revolutionary movement in Lebanon would be arriving under Lebanese diplomatic cover to take over the search, the ambassador had realized both that the issue was much more serious than he had been led to believe and that he was now screwed to the wall no matter how the events unfolded. He also knew, and had known all day, that the Hizballah team would arrive too late, if they were able to enter the country at all, which, in fact, thanks to the computer network of the highly acclaimed United Nations International Crime Investigation Service—UNICIS—they ultimately were prevented from doing. But by the time the team was picked up at Isfahan port, the Syrian ambassador no longer had any interest in their activities.

He had no place to go, no place to hide—either from the new Iranian regime or from his own government. If the files Damascus sought were even half as damning as they appeared to be, his cause was lost. Even the activities he had openly engaged in with the council's ayatollahs were enough to guarantee him a painful and long imprisonment. Luckily, he thought, as he headed for the bottle of pills he had morosely kept in his bedroom for just such a contingency, he beloved wife had predeceased him and his children had emigrated to the teeming, protective anonymity of London many years previously.

* * * *

It was amazing how long and strong collective memories held on among the ethnic communities of the Mediterranean islands. It had been more than fifty years since the historic events in the ancient fourteenth-century Turkish ethnic village of Gunyeli on the old road north from the Cypriot capital of Nicosia to the Kyrenia Range mountain pass that descended to the ancient castle harbor town of Kyrenia on the island's northern coast. But still, it was a single community event, not personally experienced by any single living and present member of the Gunyeli community, that sprang to every survivor's mind when the ancient mosque and market at the center of what had once been a separate village but which was now just a swallowed subsection of Nicosia exploded and was reduced to a mound of fine dust.

The sleepy little Turkish village of Gunyeli had had its moment of fame in 1958, as the Greek community's terrorist organization that supported forced annexation of the independent Cyprus to Greece, the EOKA, ratcheted up its armed activity in two prongs—aimed both at the occupying British colonialists who were to give up the "good fight" and withdraw from most of the island within two years and at the minority ethnic Turkish villages that dotted the island.

Although the Turkish minority of approximately a third of the island's population had managed to live on reasonably amicable terms with the island's Greek ethnic majority for many centuries prior to the nineteenth-century arrival of British control, including a period of almost three centuries of nearly benign and absent Ottoman Turk rule, the British colonialists managed to upset the ethnic balance on the island for succeeding years. Until the advent of the British, both the Greeks and Turks had come to recognize and accept their relative status on the island, which was representative of the relative sizes of their populations. The British colonialists, however, finding that their Turkish subjects were more malleable and helpful than the Greeks, had tried to move the Turkish population from underclass to upper class (although not, of course, as "upper" as the British themselves) on the island. Thus when the Greek revolutionaries moved to rid the island of the British colonialists, they naturally thought this would be a good time to cleanse the island by forcing the Turkish population into the sea as well.

In 1958, at the height of the EOKA attacks on British installations and on Turkish settlements, a massive EOKA cleansing operation had been launched against the town of Gunyeli, then a discrete village a bare two miles north of the edge of Nicosia. However, news of the planned attack had preceded them, and the Turkish community had protected itself without the loss of a single life.

Within years the village had been enclosed in a Turkish-dominated enclave that included the northern section of Nicosia, which became solidified following the invasion and occupation of northern Cyprus by Turkish forces from 1974 to 1999, and as part of a recognized Turkish-dominated canton following the 1999 unification of the island under Cypriot rule that legally took the rights of both Greeks and Turks into account.

Old memories die hard, however, especially memories of ethnic differences punctuated with bloody pogroms. For fifteen years now, Gunyeli and its predominately Turkish residents had been protected under what was considered to be a very successful federated canton system. In just the last three years the cooperation that had developed between the Greek and Turkish elements on the island, spurred by a major earthquake on the island's eastern coast that had brought residents of all ethnic backgrounds together as Cypriots, had even attracted the favorable attention of the island's neighbors and of the world media.

However, on this June evening, at just about the same time the new Iranian shah was being introduced to his surprised subjects just two time zones to the east, the center of the village disintegrated in a noisy explosion. Immediately, the same hated and feared word, rooted in the island's bloody past, was on the lips of every Turkish resident who stumbled blindly and magnetically toward the scene of disaster.

EOKA. EOKA. That was the only explanation anyone in Gunyeli could verbalize for the disaster that had visited the center of their quiet village.

In the days to come, all of the progress that had been made in the previous decade in the forging of a unified Cypriot identity and nation was to come into question and under threat. Little did any of the Cypriots involved realize, however, that the tragedy of Gunyeli had less to do with Cyprus' rich, yet troubling, history than with events that were simultaneously unfolding in the Iranian capital city two hours to the east and in the hills of Virginia seven hours to the west.

Chapter Two

As she broke the telephone connection, Caitlyn's eyes had that pained, mournful look that had increasingly been present these past two years. How could her twin sons be so totally different?

This question had nagged at Caitlyn Spencer Koniotis's mind for much of the time since her world had fallen apart within the first year after her return to Cyprus from New York with her husband, Takis Koniotis, to live in his native island paradise.

"Paradise," Caitlyn thought bitterly as she rose and moved to look out at the nearby Mediterranean Sea from her office window. The sun was shining in a cobalt blue sky, as it nearly always was. The balcony outside her own window was encased with a cascade of white jasmine, the strong evening scent of which made late nights in her Dean of Archaeology office on the EMU—Eastern Mediterranean University— campus just north of the ancient walled town of Famagusta, almost bearable. Farther down the slope, however, toward the jagged seaside cliffs that had been created by a massive real estate-swallowing earthquake just two years previously, the view was dominated by white and ochre-colored villas with red-tiled roofs, all smothered in deep rose and magenta-colored bougainvillea offset by olive, orange, lemon, and palm trees and distinguished from each other by their individualistic and strongly hued window shutters. And what lay beyond was the azure sweep of the Mediterranean with just a glimpse toward the southeast of the sixteenth-century Venetian walls of old Famagusta—now Caitlyn's home—and the spires of the ruins of a few of its nearly four hundred churches.

Yes, a paradise, at least on the surface, Caitlyn had to admit to herself. But it was a heartache as well. It continued to be so alien and set in its ways that, after twenty years of association, she still felt foreign.

Caitlyn Spencer Koniotis had changed dramatically over the past two years, as any of her long-time friends could have told in a instant from seeing her stand at her office window. She now was thin to the point of transparency against the strong sunlight. They could also have seen the change from her once sparkling and laughing, but now melancholy eyes, or from her slightly bowed, withdrawn stance. To her friends and colleagues alike—and to much of the intellectual Western world, the beautiful, Nordic blonde, world-renowned Caitlyn Spencer

31

Koniotis had stood for nearly two decades as a model of self-confidence and scientific excellence.

Having established her international reputation for having pushed the archaeological history of the Mediterranean basin back two eras with her early work in Cyprus, she had returned to New York to take up a professorial chair of archaeological studies at Colombia University and had further enhanced her international standing. In the intervening years, she had pioneered new archaeological exploration and exhibition techniques and had been instrumental in helping to develop the island nation of Cyprus as a scientifically excellent and easily accessible showplace for studying and viewing the heritage of ancient Western civilization. Just three years previously she had reached new heights in her career when, during a lecture tour of the Mediterranean, she had simultaneously unveiled evidence that Cyprus might have been the cradle of civilization, the biblical Garden of Eden, and had announced that a first-ranked archaeological study institute would be established in Cyprus.

In the wake of these revelations, a series of articles in the *National Geographic* magazine on Caitlyn's work propelled her name and lovely face into the living rooms of the world. And a year later she left Colombia when her husband, then the United Nations Organization's top international crime fighting official, had wanted to return to his native Cyprus, and she had taken charge of establishing the archaeological institute at the Eastern Mediterranean University.

Yes, her career had been fantastically successful, and it hadn't been either her career or the aging process that had dimmed the smile in Caitlyn's eyes to the shadows of mourning. At forty-eight she could still pass for a much younger woman. Having inherited very good genes and a model's facial bone structure, age had not diminished her beauty. But the vagaries of her personal life, in particular over the past two years, had robbed her of much of the self-confidence and vitality that had once caused all eyes to turn in her direction whenever she entered a room.

Caitlyn left the window and returned to her desk, where she slumped into her chair and tried to focus on the plans for the world-famous layered time exhibit she had helped to develop a bit further up the coast on the slope above the former sleepy fishing and smugglers' village of Bogaz. One of the most significant innovations of Caitlyn's creative mind had been the development of an exhibition process, where, instead of obliterating the separate layers of archaeological history as ancient sites were excavated, the ruins from the separate important eras were lifted and displayed on separate floors of a structure built immediately adjacent to the excavation site. This innovation had revolutionized public access to ancient history and was now being employed elsewhere in the world.

What Caitlyn had been trying to concentrate on before having received her disturbing and frustrating telephone call were plans for an expansion in concept of the popular Bogaz exhibition site. Her old friend and the controller of one of the archaeological institute's major sponsors, Ginger Patterson, had become very interested in environmental matters. And, in addition to helping to clean up the environment of Cyprus and of the entire Mediterranean basin area with the profits from the Patterson Solar Systems Company, Ginger had been sponsoring studies of the ancient plant and biological environments. The plans Caitlyn was studying constituted a proposal to add exhibition halls at the side of the Bogaz layered archaeological exhibit that would provide displays of the plants and animals that predominated on the island during the archaeological periods already represented in the facility. Beyond Caitlyn's personal affection for Ginger and her appreciation for the hefty financial backing provided to the institute by Ginger's company, Caitlyn was also enticed by a plan to add dimension and interest to the Bogaz site.

The funding for all of this would come from the company that was founded on John Patterson's discovery of the secret for capturing and conveniently storing solar energy for later use. First having caught on in the world's sun belt centered on the equator and initially used to provide direct transportation and power generation energy, the company had begun to be able to economically push the energy into the far northern and southern zones of the earth and also to reduce and concentrate the packaging of the controlled energy to replace battery power. In just a decade and a half, the sun's energy had been harnessed to make fossil and mineral fuels nearly obsolete. And, although the sun's power is not infinite either, long before it would have lost its vitality and flickered out, civilization on earth would likely have become extinct and would not be in a position to decry the loss of an energy source to power its toys as most assuredly would have happened within a few generations if human civilization had remained dependent on fossil fuels.

As Caitlyn's mind wandered away from the drawings in front of her, her memory went back to the shy little British gentleman that she had met nearly twenty years previously when she had first lived in Cyprus and her husband had been chief of the Cypriot national police force's International Investigations Division. John Patterson had then been the companion of Takis's counterpart in the Turkish Cypriot police, Safa Ziya, when the island was suffering under ethnic partition. And, when Takis had been elevated to be chief of a new United Nations International Crimes Investigation Service—UNICIS—he had brought Safa Ziya with him as his deputy and John Patterson as the head of research. Years later, during the struggle for unification on the island, Safa Ziya had been killed in a terrorist attack and Patterson had ended up married to another of the

Koniotises' British friends, Ginger Hamilton, the widow of a newspaper political columnist.

If John Patterson, just the last of a long string of husbands Ginger Patterson had had over her more than seven decades, was able to foresee the future he was building for the world with his scientific discovery, he had never had time to express this vision. While his theories of solar energy storage were still only written formulas he was trying to sell to a production company, he had been murdered in Beirut—at the instruction of underworld forces that did have the vision to understand the implications of his discovery. Another company, the Cyprus-based RayGo Corporation had been marketing the technology up to three years previously, and the profits had been used to further international crime and terrorism—that is until the Cypriot police, with the help of Takis Koniotis's UN investigation unit had closed that operation down and returned control of the solar energy storage process formulas to Patterson's widow.

The thought of Takis brought a look of pain into Caitlyn's face and she instantly looked haggard. No wonder Ginger had married so many times, Caitlyn found herself musing toward her wall of awards. Nothing in life made up for having to return to an empty house and to sleep alone after eighteen years of marriage to someone like Takis. She sighed deeply and tried to return her attention to the Bogaz exhibition plan proposal.

But, it was no use; she could not concentrate. And it wasn't the perpetual pressure of mourning her years with Takis that was the primary problem here and now. It had been that damn telephone call from Eric. Caitlyn thrust the plans out of her hands, rang for her chauffeur, and headed for the door. She would go home and beat some of her Oriental carpets. They were long overdue for cleaning, and this had always been one of her most useful outlets for aggression.

She and Takis had been blessed with twin sons seventeen years ago. And, while she was carrying the boys, she had been kidnapped by a terrorist band in Cyprus in an unsuccessful effort to force her investigator husband to call off his work in tracking them down. They had named one son Eric, after the UN official, Eric Isaksen, who once had been kidnapped with Caitlyn and who had kept her spirits up during her plight, and the other son Ahmad, after the young man, Ahmad Jallud, who had saved her life by sacrificing his own safety and who was now the chief of the Cypriot national police.

The two boys had been fraternal, not identical twins, but throughout their lives people had commented on the vast disparity in their names. Although Caitlyn had never regretted honoring the men who had been responsible for keeping her alive so she could give birth to these sons, in the last two years she had begun to wonder if she had jinxed them by naming them so differently.

Until just before the time she and Takis had returned to New York from their last Cyprus visit, in 2011, their sons had both been pure blessings. They had been cooperative, friendly sons who performed brilliantly in school. With both of their parents pinned down by demanding jobs in New York City, Takis at UN Headquarters in Turtle Bay and Caitlyn at Columbia University, the painful decision had been made to send the boys to residential prep schools for their secondary education. Eric wanted to be a geneticist and Ahmad wanted to follow the law. Therefore they had chosen different prep schools and both had been in accelerated study programs.

Ahmad was about to finish his studies and would be entering the University of Virginia in pre-Law in the coming spring. He had remained a good, motivated, model child.

Eric, on the other hand, had gone off the deep end. He was the more brilliant of the two intelligent youngsters, and his academic program had actually pushed him to secondary school graduation the past summer and he had been accepted to the prestigious MIT program in the city of Boston. But he had never shown up for classes. During the previous two years, Eric had become unruly and willful. He had had girl trouble and had actually gotten a woman pregnant who lived in the town where his prep school had been located. This had started a rift between his parents that no one who had known them would ever have thought would be possible.

Takis Koniotis came from a Mediterranean culture that was paternalistic and that had very old ideas of manliness. Although Takis's marriage to Caitlyn had changed many of his views toward social customs and the relative worth of men and woman, he was Greek at his core. He thus was unable to see much of a problem in Eric's involvement with woman, and there was even an unconscious pride that Eric had taken up with an older woman—as long as it didn't lead to anything more permanent, and there had never been an indication it would.

Caitlyn, conversely, was angry and crushed. This activity had gone completely against the values she had been raised on in American society. During this frustrating period, she didn't know if she felt betrayal and anger more at her son or at the husband who laughed it off as a natural phase, more to be smiled at in a "boys will be men" way than admonished and rectified.

And then the worm dramatically turned. In this early activity Eric may have been reaching out for more attention from his parents, because, when his dalliance in town with an older woman didn't have the desired effect, he turned to recreational drugs and to petty theft. He did not, however, get caught at this until, nearly a year ago, after Takis and Caitlyn had returned to Cyprus, Takis to conduct his work through the UNICIS facility in Morphou, Cyprus, by permission of UN Headquarters and Caitlyn, on leave from Columbia, to set up the archaeological institute at EMU.

Now Eric had pushed the intolerance button on his father, whose UN position made him the world's chief crime fighter. Takis came down hard on the boy, refusing, when he had been caught on both offenses, to either talk with him or to seek leniency from the judicial system. In traditional Greek terms, fooling around, at least for the family of the boy, was just a natural maturing phase. For the girl, of course, it was still a stoning offense. But criminal activity, especially theft of any sort, was a black spot on the honor of the entire family and could only be erased by ostracism of the offender.

It had been left to Caitlyn, motivated by the mother's love, which ultimately made her blind to even her own value system, that had taken her back to New York to stand by her unyielding, belligerent son through his ordeal, sentencing, and probation. Takis had not even called during this whole process, and, unable to fully appreciate the deep values of his own ancestry that had kept him at bay, Caitlyn's heart had hardened toward her husband.

It had not helped when Eric had inexplicably refused to criticize his father's lack of involvement during this period and had belittled his mother's attempts to understand and relate to him. And it had crushed Caitlyn when, on one early morning, Eric had simply walked out of their Manhattan apartment with Caitlyn's jewelry box under his arm and Caitlyn had seen the letter from MIT withdrawing Eric's university acceptance.

Although she had waited for for several weeks for Eric to return or call, she eventually heard through Ahmad that Eric didn't want to return but planned to travel on his own for awhile.

Caitlyn then gave up and returned to Cyprus. But she didn't return to the Koniotis home in the shadow of the Acropolis outside of the Venetian walls of Nicosia, the Cypriot capital between the Troodos and Kyrenia mountain ranges on the island's central plain. Instead, she moved close to her own work, to a restored Turkish-style house within the old city walls of the eastern harbor town of Famagusta.

As her institute driver delivered her to her door in the late afternoon and she entered her compound, the soothing sounds of running water began to work magic on her nerves. Located in a narrow street in the town's old Armenian quarter, Caitlyn's two-floored house formed an "L," with the long side toward the street, and the short side forming one side of a small patio garden with a gurgling fountain in the middle. The other two sides of the garden were enclosed by neighboring structures. Most of the ground floor of the house was open and functioned as a summer living room, opening onto the garden through Moorish archways. To the left of the entry door from the street, however, there was a small study that had once been the gatekeeper's room and at the far side of the "L" was located a guest room and bath. A circular stone stairway rose from the covered patio area and ended at another formal entry door in the building's upper story.

A living room, with small windows toward the street and large, balcony glass doors within Moorish arches toward the garden took up most of the side of the house toward the street. There was a kitchen tucked into the corner where the two wings met, followed by a dining room, and by Caitlyn's bedroom and bath, located over the guest room. There weren't many rooms, but they were large and had high ceilings and all looked out over the enclosed garden and its happily dancing fountain. Caitlyn kept her own sports coupe in a parking area a block away, toward the center of the town. A sedan from the institute drove her back and forth to the EMU campus, which was located just a ten-minute drive north of the walled city.

The phone was ringing as Caitlyn entered the house. It was Eric again, and her mother's love dissolved her resolve. He was in Cyprus—searching for his genetic roots, whatever that was supposed to mean to her—and he had run out of money. As with the previous call, he wasn't interested in talking to his mother about anything but bankrolling his adventure. Caitlyn could hear a woman's voice in the background, and she started to flush.

But then something inside her melted. Her life was already a mess, and this was her son. If he was here and in need of money, he would probably get into some serious trouble if she didn't help him. It was one thing for the son of a prominent Cypriot and international crime-fighting official to get messed up with the law in New York. It was quite another thing for that to happen here in Takis's home country. She agreed to send him money and asked him where he was, to discover that he was in the Troodos mountain resort of Platres, once a British colonial hill station where the families of officials were sent to escape the summer heat of the capital.

"I will transfer the money to your worldwide computer account as soon as you hang up. You can access it at the Cyprus Bank in Platres. Of course I would like to see you and, since you have reached me both at the office and here at home, you obviously know where I am, and I presume I'll see you when you are ready. And, Eric . . . are you listening, Eric?"

"Yes, mother," Eric responded in almost civil tones, the money not yet having been transferred.

"Your 'genetic roots' aren't in Platres, they are down in Nicosia at the Acropolis home. I think you should connect with your father and try to make up."

Eric swallowed his "so should you" first response and just mumbled something he hoped his mother would take for agreement.

When he disconnected, he turned to the bank's ATM, which was immediately adjacent to the telephone he had been using and impatiently jammed his bank card in the machine. He

43

continued jamming it in until Caitlyn's transfer went through. All of the time he kept brushing off the hands of the girl he was with—a woman, actually, who was a good ten years older than he was—who couldn't seem to get close enough to him. This was understandable, even though the woman herself was a flaxen-haired knockout. Eric had grown into an identical copy of his father at a young age. Takis had been an Apollo-like standout with black eyes and curly hair, olive complexion, and god-like physique, even when contrasted with that of most Cypriot men who, as a group, were blessed with the highly reputed southern European attractiveness. Only Eric's flashing eyes and belligerent stance separated him from the generally good-natured appearance and languid movements that marked his father's Greek ancestry.

While Eric was counting the cash, the young woman was pressing him with the question that she had been continually asking all morning. Where were they headed next? She hadn't shared Eric's obsession with obtaining a new bankroll. A highly accomplished artist in her own right, she had plenty of cash reserves herself and would willingly have paid Eric's expenses. But, although he knew this, he was the independent, rebellious type and wanted to take care of himself—even if that meant being blind to the thin line of difference between sponging off of your girlfriend and off of your mother.

"Behave yourself, Anita! People are watching. You've already made enough sketches here. I don't know. We can either go down toward Limassol on the southern coast—I understand there are some interesting mountain villages, like Omodhos, in that direction—or we can go down the northern side of the mountain, toward Nicosia on the central plain. One of my parents' favorite villages, Kakopetria, is down that way. I understand it has a famous, picturesque old village area artists love. What the hell . . . stop that, Nita. Keep your hands to yourself! Let's go down toward Kakopetria."

Of the two, this was perhaps the less wise choice.

Chapter Three

That was peculiar. That had never happened before. General Sarah Bristow had just been checking the computer records of the month's defense system sales at the Army Research Lab in Virginia and yesterday's night-vision photo-optics equipment sale to the Hartzel-Wegner people wasn't listed. She had even had her administrative staff check for it, and they had reported that, not only wasn't the specific sale registered, but the whole visit by Gerhard Mueller and his entourage was no longer registered in the computer system. According to the system, Herr Mueller had never visited before and the last appearance by anyone of Hartzel-Wegner was five months ago.

"Impossible," Bristow snorted into her telephone. "The sale was in the computer already last night. I checked it then."

"I'm sorry, General. There must have been some glitch in the program," the assistant politely responded. "I'll call the people at Hartzel-Wegner and have everything redocumented."

"No, that won't do," General Bristow answered coldly. If they followed this process, the sale would not be registered until after she had retired. Didn't these people understand why she had been pressing sales hard in her last month on the job and appreciate how important this was to the pride in the program? "No, no. I'll call through to the firm's main office myself and get this back into the computer now."

But when General Bristow had been connected through to the office of the firm's general manager in Lucerne, Switzerland, she found he wasn't available.

"I'm sorry, General Bristow, Mr. Stepanov is not in today. This is his assistant, Pavel. May I help you, please?"

Sarah was thrown off guard. That name had rung a bell, but she couldn't readily place it. However, strangely, she was sure that it did not have pleasant connotations. Time was of the essence, though, so she plunged on and told the general manager's assistant what her plight was.

"Ah, yes," the assistant responded smoothly. "We can certainly readily acknowledge the details of the agreement. Herr Mueller contacted us last night and told us what he had agreed to. Unfortunately, Herr Mueller will not reach our offices until two day's time, and it would be difficult to obtain his copies of the transaction before then. Would that be time enough for us to resubmit the transaction to your sales computer system?"

"Y-e-s," the general said reluctantly with one eye on the calendar. That would be time enough for the transaction to be posted on this month's sales. "I had, of course, hoped that this could be wrapped up immediately, but two days will be acceptable." She had to treat this company with full respect until the transaction was recommitted. This was a big order, and its successful conclusion was all important for her sales goal.

As she rang off, her thoughts returned to why the general manager's name had had such a peculiar effect on her. Stepanov. Maybe she had been thrown off guard because she had expected a Germanic name rather than a Slavic one for a Swiss firm. But, of course, in these days in which the European Union was solidified, there was no such thing as separate national identity in Europe anymore. It was only old fogies like her, who could remember when Europe was divided from Russia by an ideological "Iron Curtain," who remembered when there were such differences and enmities. But, wait. She almost had it and then it escaped her again. Maybe that last comment was relevant. She had once served in Europe, at NATO headquarters in Belgium. Damn, it was frustrating not to remember names from the past. She truly was past her prime, although she would not, of course, have admitted this to any of her superiors.

Ah, well, she was having dinner with one of her old buddies from the NATO days tomorrow evening in

Washington. Some sort of bash for the secretary of state, who had once been the Department spokesman, who had been her ambassador in Cyprus when she was the defense attaché, and who eventually went on to serve more than a decade as the U.S. ambassador to China. Maybe her friend would remember who this Steppish person was.

"No, 'Steppish' isn't right," General Bristow thought to herself in irritation at her fading memory capabilities. "But what was it? I'll have to write it down when it comes back to me." With that she heaved her now-bulky body from her chair and prepared to make her regular rounds of the lab area.

* * * *

"Well, would ya look at this," Joseph MacAlister whistled, as his fellow mercenaries gathered around him. "Holy moley, I guess this was worth all of the security."

"Homewrecker? They called it Homewrecker?" An exhausted Stan Hodges, bleeding from a bullet graze to his shoulder, handed the file back to his chief and slowly slid down the wall of the basement cell and onto his haunches, still holding his rifle at the ready between his knees.

The planned takeover of the Iranian government the previous night had been a piece of cake compared with what Joseph MacAlister and his small squad of American and

49

European mercenaries had encountered most of today at the Ghasr Prison.

This trip had not been part of the agreement with the new government of Isma'il Safavi Shah and Prime Minister Assadollah Egbal, and thus there had been no prior conditioning of the locale, no prior notification they were coming, and no instructions to either look the other way or stand aside as MacAlister and his men perused through the deepest secrets of a fanatical regime that had been backing international terrorism for over thirty years. In fact, MacAlister suspected that when Egbal had heard the mercenary group had shown up unexpectedly at the prison site, he had actually ordered resistance. Perhaps he wanted the old regime's secret files for himself, or, more ominously, maybe his name was mentioned in embarrassing ways in these files.

After the struggle MacAlister had had to get the files, he certainly hoped that Egbal was not mentioned in them in a compromising way. Perhaps they had not established a firm enough hold over that gentleman. But MacAlister would truly hate having to come back here again after only a short time, to enable yet another, more pro-American—or, more to the point, more pro-MacAlister's employer—regime to come to power in Tehran.

In fact, MacAlister sort of wondered why his employer even bothered with Iran anymore. Perhaps he himself was so steeped in the historical importance of petroleum that he had not seen the irrevocable winds of change that were bringing solar power to the forefront. Given very little time, the ayatollahs and the international terrorist organizations they backed probably would have collapsed under their own weight.

Given time. But now that MacAlister had reached the inner sanctum of the Iranian Intelligence apparatus and had read some of these files on the terrorist activities that Iran had, until yesterday, been backing, he could see that his employer probably had been right to push for the destruction of the ayatollahs. It didn't look like they had time on their side. In truth, he wasn't at all sure they had made it here in time.

Looking around the small room, he could tell that all of the men and women who were still standing were utterly exhausted. By the time they had reached the Ghasr Prison, the nearby Savar police station had mobilized its forces and had attempted to stop MacAlister's squad short of the prison gates. When they had gotten past the police, the prison itself had been a real bear to storm. But this fact alone had assured them that their information had been correct. While in all other parts of the city, the police authorities were now laying down their weapons and trying to fade into oblivion, only here, at this point, were the coupists meeting resistance. When they had gotten inside the prison's walls, they had noticed that there were very few prisoners. And those that they found were obviously state prisoners being held by the secret police rather than common criminals.

Once daylight appeared, MacAlister's people had hunkered down in their hard-won positions and waited for nightfall again. They had been specially trained to fight at night. When they launched their attack once more, they concentrated on the best-defended positions, knowing that these marked the way to what the police forces had been told not to reveal or to give up. Eventually, they had fought their way into this subbasement and ultimately to this small room, with its walls of files.

This was where the Harvard training of the Boston Brahman, socially the purest of the pure and the rarest of the rare, raised as presidential timber but now far from that particular forest, had once again come in handy. While at Harvard, supposedly studying politics (how to win) and economics (how to spend while seeming to save), Joseph had found that he had a knack for languages—in addition to his knack for rowdy behavior, street fighting, scheming pranks, and falling into leadership positions, of course. One of the languages he had picked up was Farsi. Most of the other mercenaries he had brought along on this little adventure also knew Farsi.

So, while the less-linguistically adept members of his band protected the perimeter, Joseph and the others, using the company names that his employer had given him, started searching through the files to find specific references.

An hour after they had started the search, they had hit pay dirt. MacAlister had been beginning to be afraid they would have to give up the hunt and clear out, as they knew they had to lift out before dawn of this day. The new government had not given them protection for any longer than that, and it had not actually proven to be fully supportive for even this long.

One of the company names the group was searching for had been the Hartzel-Wegner arms merchants, and this had proven to be the key. The file was sketchy, but it was informative enough for MacAlister to proceed, as he could now see, after scanning the file, that his employer would want him to continue the operation into another phase—and then another phase after that. Anything to stop what Hartzel-Wegner was involved in, presuming there was time to do so.

The treasure file made clear that the Swiss firm of Hartzel-Wegner had been contracted with Iranian money to bring together the parts of a long-distance nuclear rocket propulsion gun, that most of the parts had already been acquired, and that the country of destination was Syria. The code name attached to the weapon was Homewrecker. As there had been much talk in the world's press in recent months concerning the Jewish homeland of Israel, and Syria had begun to heavily renew the defenses of the Golan Heights, there was little doubt in MacAlister's mind whose home this gun was being designed to wreck. The Golan Heights was the high ridge overlooking Israel and the Sea of Galilee whose return to Syria by Israel had been one of the only manifested good-will gestures made at the nearly completed "final" Middle East settlement of nearly two decades previously. The final signing conference had opened on the Amathus hotel resort beach coast of southern Cyprus, but the agreements had broken down, largely because of the pressure of such countries as Iran but also because the conference's chair, the UN official Ingrid Bittmann, had proven to be in the employ of Lebanon and the Iranian-backed Hizballah terrorist organization.

The Israelis had already transferred the Golan Heights back to Syrian control, from whence it had been seized in an earlier Mideast war, before the talks broke down. And the Syrians had just walked out of the conference when they had gotten what they wanted.

And now, years later, it seemed they were poised to use the strategic advantage of the heights to lob nuclear rockets into Israeli population centers. The irony, MacAlister thought, was that Iran was now out of the terrorism support business. On top of that the stranglehold the Arab nations of the region had always had on the availability of petroleum was collapsing. It therefore looked likely that a genuine Middle East settlement was once again possible. That is, if the plans for the Homewrecker device had not already progressed too far to stop.

MacAlister looked around the room and gauged the condition of his people. They could use some rest, but there was no time. And they had to get out of here soon in any event.

"OK, ladies and gentleman," MacAlister announced, as he offered a supporting arm to Stan Hodges. "It's time for us to go home. This was a great job. Next stop Bahrain for a night's R&R and then I suspect it's on to Syria to save the world for democracy and American business."

* * * *

She was beginning to regret she had come into the shop from the street of copper in the souk of Damascus, the capital of Syria. It was late and she would have to leave for Beirut tomorrow. If she had not seen a prayer rug in this shop earlier in the day that had intrigued her and had captivated her mind ever since, she would not have come back—and, even having come back, she most certainly would not have stayed in this shop with this oily merchant. The girl who had been here earlier in the day hadn't been as obsequious and pushy. However, she did want the rug and the man had maneuvered himself between her and the door to the overstuffed shop in such a way that she wouldn't be getting past the big tub of lard before he permitted her to do so in any event.

The shopkeeper had been babbling mindlessly at her until their eyes met, and then he had abruptly hesitated for a moment before he had begun again, bobbing and sweating and trying to show her everything in his shop except the rug, which she had precisely indicated was the only object in this pile of junk that interested her.

The man's reaction when he had first gotten a look at her was disturbing. She did not want to be recognized here in Damascus—or anywhere outside of Beirut for that matter. But he was just an old, slimy Syrian. He probably had never been beyond the copper street of the Damascus souk in his lifetime. She was just getting jittery, as she did whenever she traveled outside of the Hizballah-controlled district of the Lebanese capital. But such trips as she had made here were necessary. At least they were necessary for the moment, and soon—very soon—she may never need to hide her face again.

No, he was probably just surprised to see a well-dressed European woman unaccompanied in the souk this late at night. And he was probably right. It probably was both dangerous and unwise for her to be here alone at night. But she had left the hotel on impulse. The rug had become an obsession, a silly obsession, as she had countless numbers of prayer rugs back in

Beirut already. But she was an obsessive woman—and what she wanted she usually got.

In any event, she had not foreseen having to deal with this smelly butterball of a jabbering machine.

In an effort to get the ordeal over as soon as possible, she didn't haggle for the rug, but threw money at the merchant and her business card, upon which she had scrawled the name of the hotel and a deadline time for delivery. She was sure she would receive the rug in time, because, as she was handing the money and calling card to the merchant, she affixed him with one of her famous "obey or die" stares. She was happy to see she hadn't lost the knack. Oh, yes, she thought, as she maneuvered around the sweating man mountain and slid out of the shop, she could tell by the way he had melted into the floor under her gaze that the rug would appear on time.

As the woman disappeared into the night beyond the shop's open front, the copper merchant Nabil Jallud produced a dirty rag from the folds of the tent he was wearing and began to mop his brow. No doubt about it, the woman had, indeed, terrified him.

Jallud took a look at the business card she had handed him. Dr. Inga Hartzel of Hartzel-Wegner at a Beirut, Lebanon, address. No indication on the card of the nature of her business.

"Inga Hartzel, in a rat's eye," Jallud spat out as he regained his courage in the solitude of his now-deserted shop.

He had seen that face before, a face that symbolized great evil. She couldn't fool him with the business card either. There had been talk in the souk, and he knew what was being said concerning the activities of this Hartzel-Wegner company. And if *this* woman was involved in that company, what he had heard was probably an understatement rather than an exaggeration.

Jallud stopped trying to mop the fear from his face and started waddling back toward the office at the back of the shop. He had state-of-the-art communications equipment back there. He had been meaning to connect with his nephew, the high and mighty police chief of the Cypriot police, for some time concerning this company. Now, when he had seen a face from the past, a face no one was supposed to be seeing again, a face that he recognized because of the newspaper articles his nephew himself had sent him to amuse an old man, Nabil Jallud knew this call was long overdue.

* * * *

Takis Koniotis staggered up the marble stairs leading to the entry door of his Nicosia home. He looked furtively from left to right to see if any of his neighbors were watching, but, thankfully, he seemed to be alone on this short little residential street just below the Acropolis hill. Good, he thought. It wouldn't do for the world's chief criminal investigator, the

United Nations under secretary general for security affairs, to be observed coming home so late half crocked and totally embarrassed.

The "half crocked" part wasn't so bad, actually. This had not been an uncommon condition for Takis in the more than a year since Caitlyn had left him—or, rather, had just not returned to him from her trip to New York for Eric's trial. And Takis's neighbors, like all Cypriots, were tolerant of a drinking habit. Takis, however, had let himself deteriorate too fast and too far since his split with his American wife. Still quite handsome at fifty-one, Takis was beginning to fill out around the middle, a direct result of his increased alcohol intake, and he was no longer taking impeccable pains with his personal grooming.

His Cypriot friends looked right through these growing blemishes, however, and tended to blame his American wife for the falling out and for its effect on Takis. Takis was being treated as a most eligible bachelor even though he and Caitlyn were just separated, not divorced, and, indeed, considering his international standing and his good looks, he probably still was one of the island's most desirable catches.

And this was what was at the root of Takis's stealthy return home this evening. His drinking wasn't the current problem. What had just happened to him had sobered him up real fast. It was his embarrassment that was disturbing him so. He was sure that anyone who saw him just now would have seen the words "infidelity" written all over him, and, although it would not have disturbed any of his very casual neighbors one iota even if they could have seen what had happened written all over his face, it was not something that Takis himself could take lightly. He still loved his wife deeply, he wanted to have her back with him, and he had no intention of giving her reason not to come back to him.

It was becoming increasingly obvious that he would have to stay away from socializing with his old friend Ahmad Jallud, the Cypriot police chief. He just didn't know how he could avoid Jallud without the latter suspecting something was wrong. Of course Takis had heard that Ahmad Jallud's wife from the Turkish mainland, Leila, was man-crazy and that she was quite enticing. He just had not realized until this evening the extremes to which both of those aspects of her personality could take a man.

Takis had gone to the Jalluds' for dinner tonight, the first time he had been the only guest at their home. The evening had gone well, and the two Jalluds were so vibrant and entertaining that he had come out of his mournful haze for the first time in many months. He also had drunk too much. During dessert, Jallud had gotten a call and had had to leave for the police station. He urged Takis to stay, however, until he had finished his desert and coffee. Like a fool he had done so. It had taken Leila no time to add a further dessert to the menu. As she had delivered his coffee, she proceeded to sit in his lap, kiss him passionately, and run her hands up his chest. Without thinking, he found himself returning the compliment, with both of them being fully aware that he was enjoying himself and was quickly becoming aroused. As soon as he had regained his senses and the alcohol had cleared from his brain, he had quickly risen, almost dumping Leila unceremoniously on the floor, and run out of the house. The husky laughter that followed him, however, had fairly obviously signaled that Leila was neither insulted nor put off by his rejection.

He was still blushing and mumbling angry words at himself as he reached the top of the stairs and could hear the tones of the telephone on the other side of the entry door. He fumbled with his door key, all the time castigating himself with curses. He had to get to the telephone. Maybe it was Caitlyn. Or maybe it was one of the boys. But, no, he thought bitterly to himself. More likely it was Leila Jallud wanting to tease him. He knew he couldn't take that. And what he was most afraid of was either that she would tell Ahmad that he'd made advances to her or, probably worse, that next time he would not fight her attraction. She was a beautiful woman, with a luscious body, and mesmerizing eyes. And he was still a man, full of vitality, and with a man's needs.

Takis stopped fumbling with the key and slid down, sitting in front of the door, waiting for the telephone to become silent. "Caitlyn. Eric. Ahmad. What has become of us?" Takis whispered to himself. He ached for the perfect family he had had and had lost, without understanding what had happened to put him in the fix he was in. Maybe it was true. Maybe these mixed ethnic marriages could never work. But he and Caitlyn had been so sure that they could make their marriage work. He had wanted it to work. He still wanted it to work. If only Caitlyn could see reason. If only Eric would clean up his act. He could not make the step toward Eric under these circumstances. It was just alien to everything he had been raised to believe. If Eric had done what he had done here in Cyprus, there would be no hope the boy could stay in the family. But perhaps this wasn't necessary just because he had gotten in trouble in America. The Koniotis clan had seemed to consider what had happened as America's fault and were prepared to accept Eric as the victim. But still, Takis could not make the first step. Eric had to make the first step. But would that ever happen?

Takis became aware that the telephone had stopped its ringing. He struggled to his feet and entered the dark, lonely house. He took a moment to note that no telephone number had been left on the caller ID, which led him to assume it probably was from Leila Jallud after all. And then he shuffled off to bed—having missed the call from his son Eric, who was not likely to think of trying again until his mother urged him to do so again, which probably would not be until the next time the boy needed money from Caitlyn.

Chapter Four

No one would have thought that she herself was pushing eighty—in age, not in speed, as she was going a good bit faster than that—as she swept past the elderly villagers near Omodhos in her baby blue BMW convertible and waved jauntily at the (other) relics of the previous century. What was more surprising than seeing the thin old lady, her long, bottle-blonde hair wafting on the breeze produced by her old reconditioned sports car, power through the curves on the southern slopes of the Troodos Mountains was the reaction of the black-swathed old Cypriot widows and hoary shepherds on the edge of the road that climbed above Omodhos. For these traditional mountain villagers, usually wary of strangers and disapproving of speeding tourist vehicles, on this occasion laughed heartily and waved back.

Oddly enough, the villagers accepted the British widow Ginger Nives-Smyth Baldwin Remington Hamilton Patterson as one of their own. For a few years and until two years previously she had actually been, in a legal sense, one of them, having moved to Omodhos following the death of her last—although, those who knew Ginger well would probably more naturally use the term "latest"—husband, the scientist and inventor John Patterson.

As an unassuming and friendly but sensitive neighbor, the more flamboyant aspects to her personality having been hidden by her quiet grieving for her recently deceased spouse, Ginger had been fully accepted by the Cypriot residents of Omodhos. There now were several non-Cypriot retirees who had taken up life in the restored inner village area of Omodhos, and Cypriots are naturally outgoing and helpful people.

But what had brought Ginger her special love and affection, not only in Omodhos but throughout Cyprus, was what she had done when it had been discovered three years previously that her deceased husband, murdered in Beirut to steal his precious scientific discovery, was the true inventor of the compact solar energy collection and storage process that loosened and was quickly nullifying the grip that diminishing fossil fuel technology had held on the progress of human development. When the elderly British widow realized that she had inherited and now controlled the solar energy process, whose power source was virtually infinitely replenishing and cost-free and which, until that time, had been used by the RayGo Corporation to underwrite international crime and terrorism, she had formed a company of her own. She had named her company Patterson Solar Systems—PSS, and she was using its profits in far different ways than RayGo had used them.

Although Ginger had entrusted the day-to-day running of PSS to a far younger friend, Andre Piccard, who also was the CEO of a large French-based shipping empire in his own right, the new and inevitable corporate demands on Ginger had pulled her back into the mainstream of life and she had, almost reluctantly, moved from the quaint village of Omodhos to a large villa high on the slopes of Cyprus's southern port city of Limassol to be closer to the heart of the operation. Limassol had long been the Cyprus base for the Piccard holdings and it was now coming back into its own as the island's commercial center following a major earthquake three years previously that had leveled the corporate center the now-defunct RayGo Corporation had been developing at Varosha, just south of the ancient walled harbor town of Famagusta at the southern end of the island's eastern coast.

Cyprus had inevitably prospered from both the technology and the jobs that the RayGo Corporation had brought to Cyprus, but most of that company's profits had been used for other purposes, some of which had been very harmful to Cyprus's interests. Now, however, through PSS and under the guidance of Andre Piccard and the inspiration of Ginger Patterson, Cyprus was benefiting fully from the solar energy storage miracle. Although Ginger had returned to an active social life in Cyprus and had moved to a large villa above Limassol, this was all financed from the considerable means she had already had at her disposal before rightful credit for the solar power technology was returned to her husband and its legal ownership and control were passed to her. Now all of the profits of her new company were being plowed back into service to humanity.

Ginger Patterson, to the amazement of her acquaintances from many years past who had remembered her as the many-husbanded ultimate party girl, had taken up with her usual intensity the struggle to meld environmental protection and enhancement with service to human developmental needs. When she had first come to Cyprus, much of its surface had consisted of desert land that momentarily flowered into a land of color and beauty following the winter rains but that then all too soon largely returned to parched, barren ground. This had contrasted sharply with the legends she had read of Cyprus having been the heavily forested reserve for the construction of the Mediterranean-dominating Phoenician fleets.

Not long after Ginger had arrived, escaping from a shadowy past in Belgium, the Cypriots themselves had launched an extensive campaign to reforest the now largely barren island, under the theory that heavier vegetation would bring more precipitation, which would restart a cycle of life that would bring

Cyprus's legendary forests back. And, to Ginger's perceptions, these theories had held true. She did sense that the rains over Cyprus had increased over the past thirty years, and Cyprus was now greener than she had remembered it to have been when she first arrived. However, the progress had only been slight, and the island's overall water needs had actually worsened because of a growing population.

Cyprus had depended almost entirely on precipitation to meet its water needs. It did not sit on any massive underground aquifer and, until very recently, it had no naturally flowing rivers to the sea that permitted irrigation of the plain from mountain run-off. In addition its climate was too warm to encourage the accumulation of snow for later, gradual run-off for controlled use. When the island experienced a heavy rainfall, most of the water ran immediately to the sea. And, although Cyprus had developed reservoirs, the construction of these had not kept pace with the rise in the population, and fully a third of the water in reservoirs was lost to evaporation in the island's warm climate. After many years of talk, two desalination plants had been built, but these had not been operated efficiently and had seemed to be more for show than effect.

Ginger had seen all of this and, like many around her, had been able to understand that water was the real control on human development in Cyprus, as it now was throughout much of the world. But, also like most of the others around her, she had drifted through life assuming the problem was too big and complex for her to help solve and that it, thus, would be best to ignore it altogether. But when she had gained the power that control over the solar energy power process had brought her, she immediately set out to apply both this technology and the profit it brought to the water and other environmental problems.

The villagers of Omodhos, and all others in Cyprus and in many of the other formerly desert areas of the world, now revered Ginger and PSS, because in just two short years she had brought a noticeable change in the environment. Now, thanks to inspired work under her direction, in Cyprus alone the landscape was greener than it had ever before been. More desalination plants, now cheaply powered by solar energy, were creating potable water for humans and plants alike from the Mediterranean's waters. Desalinized water was economically being pumped up the mountains by solar power, to be trickled back down for use in irrigating fields. Workable schemes for recycling water were about to be unveiled. PSS had funded the construction of several more major reservoirs. And a special reservoir sealant process, pioneered in Israel, had been brought to Cyprus free of charge by PSS, and applied to all existing reservoirs. Now Cyprus's reservoirs would suffer less than 5 percent evaporation loss for stored water rather than the previous 35 percent. And PSS was helping to extend the same sort of water creation and conservation techniques to other areas of the world, as well.

Thus, it was easy for the Cypriots to view the eccentric old woman who roared past them in her baby blue BMW not as yet another bothersome foreign interloper but in the same vein as the goddess Aphrodite who had risen from the sea on Cyprus's southwestern coast to bring life to the island. Ginger Patterson had brought a cheap, accessible, and clean source of energy and life-giving water to Cyprus and to the rest of the world. To the Cypriots, Ginger was the modern version of Aphrodite, and goddesses were expected to be eccentric and outrageous.

It was precisely her outrageous life Ginger was contemplating this sunny afternoon as she left sight of Omodhos and approached the formerly colonial British-style hill station that had become the Troodos mountain town of Platres. From here her BMW would top the Troodos peaks at the ski resort town of Troodos, now sporting snowy slopes most of the year round thanks to technological advances in the production and preservation of manufactured snow, and then swoop down the mountain's northern face, past the health-resort town of Kakopetria to her destination, Galata, where she was to unveil the next of the PSS water recycling projects.

Ginger had had quite a checkered past, and, as she gunned the responsive vehicle into a particularly tight hairpin curve, was now contemplating that throughout the wildly varied phases of her existence she never would have guessed her life would end this way. Now why, she suddenly caught herself, was she thinking of her life ending? In many respects she seemed to be beginning a new life, as she had done so many times previously. She was quite aware that she was being identified with the goddess Aphrodite in the Cypriots' minds—she had been openly labeled as such in the country's media, and this both amused and frightened her. But primarily it warned her that she was taking on far more responsibilities toward her fellow human beings than she had ever sought or accepted before.

Ginger had been a free-spirited, self-indulging, and painfully self-centered social butterfly in the heady years following World War II. A beauty who had had all the attributes of a runway model, who had actually done some professional modeling, and who might have turned to this as a profession if her family had not considered it a tawdry activity in contrast to pursuing title and money, Ginger had married young and wealthy, and, when that hadn't worked out, had proceeded to enter and exit marriages as frequently as a taste for change in venue and climate appealed to her.

At some point she had found herself in Brussels, married to the Remington husband, who was attached to the British delegation to the North Atlantic Treaty Organization— NATO—alliance that had been constructed in the post–World

71

War Two Iron Curtain days to keep the Russians at bay and from moving Communism further into Western Europe. A muddle-headed, self-indulging Ginger had somewhat innocently brushed against the activities of a spy ring working, quite successfully, to get at NATO's innermost secrets, and her husband had committed suicide from the mistaken belief that his wife had been far deeper involved in the scandal than she had been.

A scared and confused Ginger had than escaped to Cyprus, where she tried to establish a new life. Within a few years she was married again, to a retired British Army officer, William Hamilton. In retirement, Hamilton had become a political journalist for the island's premier English-language daily, the *Cyprus Mail*. Ginger had fled political intrigue and suspicion, grown tired of her hollow and self-indulgent lifestyle, and increasingly became aware that she had grown old. In her new boredom she and her strongly opinionated, jealous, and alcoholic new husband quickly attained a reputation within the island's expatriate community as champion scrappers. They were constantly at each other's throats, in public as much as in private, and anyone who had tried to come between them to make peace had instantly regretted having made the effort. Ginger, in reaction both to her husband's jealousy and to her unwillingness to accept that she was growing old and had lost her sexual appeal, had actively sought brief sexual encounters and affairs, which served to send her husband into more frequent jealous rages and trips to the brandy bottle.

Ginger's life and lifestyle had instantly changed, however, when Hamilton had been kidnapped and presumed dead. This shock forced Ginger to see her life as it was and to realize that she, in fact, did love Willie Hamilton. When he returned to her, she was a totally changed woman, and they had had a couple of blissful years of marriage until Hamilton died. Her marriage to John Patterson had similarly been one of mutual comfort.

Ginger's move to an active corporate life following her acquisition of the solar power process patents had marked a brand new phase of her life. She had never concerned herself with business matters before, although she took to it brilliantly, and she had never before taken responsibility for anyone but herself in the first half of her life or herself and her spouse for the past two decades. She was finding this new experience quite pleasant and empowering.

She was still contemplating how well she had taken to being a business executive many minutes after the BMW had topped the mountain ridge and started its descent down the Solea Valley. The thoughts linked up with the view, as the village of Kakopetria and its dominating mill complex came into sight. The high stone-walled building climbing up the valley's western wall reminded Ginger of that early acquaintance of hers, Eleni

Piccard, whose highly successful life as a Cypriot businesswoman and philanthropist—in her case centered on archaeology and authentic handicrafts, Ginger had, almost subconsciously, modeled her own business style on. Eleni had created a well-known restaurant and luxury hotel in that former grain storage building, and it had become the centerpiece of all of her other far-reaching business interests.

Eleni had been raised in this village, and the mill complex had been owned by her family for centuries. She had subsequently married into the Piccard shipping empire family and had brought its activities to Cyprus. Andre Piccard, the CEO Ginger had hand-picked for PSS, was Eleni's grandson. Eleni, who had kept a flat at the top of the Old Mill Inn building, had died there and was buried in the yard of the church she had built for the village on a high point along the valley wall in the southern sector of Kakopetria where it ran into the town of Galata.

Now that Ginger had consciously and directly linked her new business- and philanthropist-centered life with that of her former acquaintance, she suddenly felt close to Eleni. They had never been close when Eleni was alive, as that had been during Ginger's "bitchy" phase and Eleni was far too proper to have comfortably related to Ginger at the time. But now, seeing the Old Mill Inn just as she herself was thinking of her work with PSS and her environmental activities, Ginger's heart went out to

Eleni, who had died tragically, murdered by a former lover and under the mistaken impression even at the time of her death that her own long-missing husband and son were dead.

Ginger knew Eleni was buried in the church yard in Kakopetria, but she had never herself visited the grave. The thought hit her that she should do that. Perhaps she would do so after the ceremony in Galata. Ginger normally avoided the topics of death and graves. She had already known too much of death and, especially of tragic deaths, having lost one husband to suicide and two to murder. She couldn't really understand what was drawing her to Eleni's grave today. She truly didn't want to think of death. And right now she only wanted to think about the opening ceremony for the Galata water recycling project, the first of hopefully many PSS-sponsored water recycling efforts on the island. Ginger had worked hard on her speech and she knew this was going to be a real bang up of a day.

* * * *

Nabil Jallud's fingers hovered nervously over the buttons on the satellite telephone before he punched in the code he used to reach the scrambler satellite to attain a private connection with his nephew in Cyprus, the Cypriot national police chief, Ahmad Jallud. The Damascus copperware merchant paid dearly for his subscription to the satellite, but it returned rich dividends in his emerald smuggling business. He had heard rumors that the Syrian secret police would soon have a descrambler for this system, so he would have to start looking for another communications mode. Luckily, the underworld usually managed to move on to new systems before the authorities homed in on them. International crime always seemed to have the edge.

The merchant had had to close up his shop to make this private transmission, which was almost unheard of in the Damascus copper souk in the middle of the day. He knew he could not be closed long without causing suspicion. But it was to avoid suspicion that he had waited until the next day but then not waited until after closing. Nighttime and the early hours of the morning were the most active hours for the police searchers. They might not be able to unscramble his satellite call, but, with the right search techniques, they could have discerned that such a call was being made from his location.

After registering his code, Jallud voiced the command that would connect him with his nephew's home. It was ironic that the system he had acquired to circumvent the law was being used to help the law. But his relationship with his nephew was special, and he was very proud of Ahmad. The boy had come a long way to get to where he was, and Nabil had not always been able to help him and felt he had not done enough for him. It was with undying gratitude that the old man realized that Ahmad had not abandoned him when he had joined the police in the then-

Turkish zone of Cyprus and had started up the ladder to the top police post in the country, this even knowing what his uncle was and that he was unlikely to change.

It was with great disappointment, therefore, when the connection went through that Nabil found Ahmad was not home. It was with even greater consternation that he found himself talking with Ahmad's wife, Leila, rather than with one of the servants. Nabil and Leila had never gotten along well. Each was able to discern the weaknesses of the other, even if Ahmad was unable to do so, or was so tolerant toward those he loved that he was prepared to shut his eyes to their sins.

Unfortunately, Nabil felt that some of his information was too important not to try to pass on to Ahmad through Leila. He told her of the visitation to his shop by Inga Hartzel and who Nabil thought the woman really was. He only neglected to pass on the information from the business card she had given him, the card providing the name of her company. He had, at the last minute, chosen not to be fully informative with Leila, because she was being far too sweet and understanding in her responses. Nabil concluded that she was up to something and decided he would just have to try to get directly in touch with Ahmad some other way.

Leila tried to keep him on the line, probably sensing he hadn't told her everything and asking for more information to pass on to Ahmad, but Nabil decided he had been on the air too long and, at the sound of pounding on the steel door he had lowered across the front of his shop—no doubt by a neighboring concerned merchant, caused him to cut her short, hurriedly cover his satellite phone, and waddle toward the noise.

Unfortunately, Nabil Jallud had been a bit off on his timing of the Syrian secret police's acquisition of a descrambler for the satellite telephone system. Thanks to the help of the Hartzel-Wegner systems broker company, the Syrians already had their descrambler and, this being a relatively quiet communications time in the day, had isolated on Jallud's signal nearly as soon as he had punched in his code. The police had been very grateful to Hartzel-Wegner for procuring a system that only international criminals seemed to be able to acquire at this point. The duty officer at their communications center was very pleased, therefore, when he saw that they could return the favor to the company's president, Inga Hartzel, by passing Jallud's message on to her either at the airport or at her Beirut destination. His assumption was that she would then have a job for the secret police to do, and they would be glad to oblige. They had been building a case on this copper merchant for months, and if the local Russian mafia crowd hadn't been protecting him, he'd probably already be dead by now.

* * * *

The Syrian secret police were not the only ones trying to intercept Inga Hartzel at Damascus's airport before she boarded the airplane for Beirut. Joseph MacAlister and his squad of mercenaries had also entered Syria the previous night, not via the airport, of course, but via their own light helicopters that had been designed to hinder detection by Syrian radar. Not that the Syrians had set their radars to detect the approach of foe aircraft from the direction of Iran, which Joseph MacAlister well knew. Syria's obsession was Israel, which was located in the direction of the opposite border, and the country's military was currently preoccupied with what it thought was a secret buildup on the Golan Heights. It had no idea there might be a threat from the other direction.

MacAlister and crew had taken advantage of this and had made a mad dash from Tehran to Damascus, deciding at the last minute to bypass their R&R in Bahrain, specifically to try to stop Inga Hartzel, who they considered to be the key to a diabolical plot that was building to destroy the balance of power in the Middle East. What they had found in the vaults of Ghasr Prison had told them of the nuclear weapon delivery system being pieced together by Hartzel's company with Iranian money and for the Syrians. What the Iranian general named in those documents had told MacAlister following a bit of softening up was that Hartzel was in Damascus until today, after which she would return to the Hizballah-controlled area of Beirut.

MacAlister had a support mechanism in Syria, a mechanism which had helped his people get ticketed as legitimate travelers who were leaving the Damascus airport for various destinations that day. There was no one on the ground to help him in Lebanon. If he was to stop Hartzel quickly, it would have to be here, in Damascus, and today. He had not even taken the time to raise the general alarm concerning what he had found in Tehran concerning the Homewrecker weapon. As his people fanned out around the airport, each on the look-out for the woman who had been identified as Inga Hartzel, and each armed to take her down on sight even if this meant they would be caught, MacAlister prayed that, when he told his employers about the Homewrecker weapon, he would also be able to tell them that the key to the operation had been neutralized.

Chapter Five

Comfortably seated in a secluded corner of the VIP suite of the Damascus Airport and pampered by service suitable for the queen she was, Inga Hartzel took the time to give the young man who served her coffee and brandy a particularly critical—and appreciative—once over before she started to make her cell phone calls. She needed to check on how Stepanov was coming in acquiring the nuclear material for the Homewrecker payload, she wanted to hear whether they had been able to keep the Army Research Lab on hold concerning the missing documentation, she had to make her regular call to Cyprus for an update on the weapon, and she was beginning to worry about what was happening in Iran.

There had been a government coup, she knew. But she wasn't sure how far down it had extended and to what extent it would change things. Even if they had lost Iranian sponsorship, at least for now, the Homewrecker project was funded and was too far along to be stopped. It needed to be put into operation very soon, however. When it had performed its chosen task, the whole world would change, and Tehran would probably return to its former level of support.

Hartzel had experienced many setbacks, some very serious, in her long life, but she had also managed many spectacular successes. To see her, no one would have guessed she was in her mid seventies. A large-boned, statuesque blonde of Middle European extraction, Hartzel was a bit hefty, but her bulk was well-proportioned and she had an air of confidence and authority that made people want to salute her—which was just exactly what she wanted them to do. Although she was well into the age that most other women—and men, for that matter— were prepared to retreat to the hearth and think grandparent thoughts, Inga still strove for control and notoriety, if not fame, and she still had a weakness for cigarettes, in an age when almost everyone else was giving them up, and for young, muscular men.

Her brief flirtation, her third cigarette, and her cell phone calls completed, Hartzel turned toward checking through her papers to see how close they were to being able to implement Homewrecker. It appeared that all they needed was the nuclear material to start arriving for the bombs, the completion of the weapons testing, and the new triggering device she had sent Gerhard Mueller after. The gun emplacement itself was in place on the Golan Heights, and most of the other components were even now being assembled and tested.

They had been having trouble with trajectories because of the inconsistent recoil, but the new triggering device should solve that. Then all they needed was delivery of the nuclear warhead that was being acquired from the stockpiles that the Russians had convinced the world had been destroyed but were now held in the hands of private companies near Moscow for just such highly lucrative business deals.

She was displeased to find that Stepanov had been called away to help Mueller. She was not able to find out anything of use about conditions in Iran and only Stepanov was connected with the controlling ayatollah and had the network in Tehran to tell her how bad the situation there was for them.

In any event, it was good she was on her way back to Beirut. She had planned to reveal herself to the world following the triumph of Homewrecker, but she did not want to be exposed before then, and she no longer felt safe anywhere but her home sector of Beirut. At least she could count on the Syrians to protect her here—at least until she had delivered a complete and working weapons system. And after that had been successful, they probably would give her the key to Damascus.

Her server returned to tell her that her flight was ready to board, and, as he bent down to pick up her empty cup, she let her hand stray coquettishly to his forearm and gave him a welcoming smile that immediately froze. She recoiled in horror as her hand felt the outline of the dagger the young man had in his sleeve.

"Please do not be alarmed, Madam," the server whispered soothingly. "I offer you no harm. I am from the Syrian secret police and have been assigned to guard your person."

Inga was used to danger and thus recovered quickly from the shock. "And would the service to my person be sustainable all the way to Beirut?" she asked sweetly, her hand gripping his upper thigh as she pulled herself to her feet.

"But, of course, if Madam would like," the only slightly nonplussed bodyguard responded. A job was a job, and he had heard about this one before he had been assigned to the case.

"Madam would like very much," Inga tossed over her shoulder as she headed for the VIP lounge entrance. "See that we get adjoining seats on a dark and very quiet row. Regretfully, it is not a long flight to Beirut, but the next flight will not be returning to Damascus until tomorrow afternoon. You need not book a hotel."

The secret service agent departed the lounge ahead of Hartzel to attend to her commands, and, before she herself could get to the entry, she was being called back to take another telephone call.

"Hello, Ms. Hartzel," her contact at the secret police headquarters intoned importantly. "I am so glad we reached you before you left Damascus. Did you buy a prayer rug in the souk last evening?"

"Yes, I did. It has been delivered, thank you," Inga answered distractedly.

"I'm afraid to report, Ms. Hartzel, that the merchant who sold you that rug seemed to have recognized you and has made an international call to the Cypriot police to try to expose you. Our recording of the call indicated he did not get through to the police, however, and that he has not yet specifically identified you to his connection in Cyprus. We will ensure the merchant does not bother you further, but he may have caused you a serious problem merely by having mentioned you to the Cypriot authorities. The call was placed to the chief of police in Cyprus."

"Yes, thank you, Colonel," Inga answered coolly. "I know all about the call, and I've already arranged everything, including taking care of the merchant. But thank you for being so helpful." She disconnected before the dumbfounded colonel could think of anything to say and resumed her stroll toward the entry. She was in no hurry; she knew the plane wouldn't leave without her.

* * * *

The unifying calm that had existed in the Cyprus Federated State's Presidential Palace in Nicosia, the office of the country's executive authority rather than the residence of its president, was shattered for the first time in three years as Vice President Lala Hatan stormed out of the office of President Chrystalla Ioannou and, rather than returning to his own office in the palace, rammed his bulk into an awaiting limousine, which swept back toward his old offices in the city's Turkish sector.

In the years immediately following the delicately forged unification of the island under a bicommunal structure, the Turkish Cypriot vice president had remained in the safety of the Turkish quarter of the city, where, by law, he presided over the judicial system, while the Greek Cypriot president presided over the executive and legislative arms of government from the Presidential Palace in the Greek-dominated southern suburbs of the capital. But three years previously Turkish Cypriot vice president Lala Hatan had saved Greek Cypriot president Chrystalla Ioannou from an assassination attempt. This act, which had been captured on film by several television companies, had helped, more than any other event in the country's recent history, to bring down the barriers between the two, historically belligerent, major ethnic communities in Cyprus.

In what was more than just a symbolic act, Hatan had moved his office to the Presidential Palace, and Ioannou had carefully ensured that he was fully consulted in government matters and that the Turkish population increasingly accepted that their concerns were being seriously considered and addressed by the government.

Today, that long-developed atmosphere of good will had been smashed like glass. And in the wake of her incensed vice president's departure, Ioannou, well known for her highly successful efforts to ensure equity in the protection of all ethnic groups in the country, was left confused and crushed.

She had avoided broaching the subject of Hatan's personal acquisition of property in the Morphou Canton for too long already. Many of her detractors had said, as her public media nemesis Demetris Mattas had done so frequently and so nastily in the Greek daily *Semerini*, that she had ignored the issue for two years longer than she should have. She knew that this was not a good time to raise the issue with Hatan, but there had not been a good time in recent years, and she had reached a point that something had to be done about it.

Since before the settlement, Hatan, who was also the wealthiest businessman in the Turkish-dominated cantons, had been acquiring property in the Morphou district, now the neutrally administered Morphou Canton. The most recent statistics Ioannou had seen indicated that Hatan now owned over 50 percent of the large, but economically depressed district. This had been seen as a threat by many, especially by those Greeks who had once lived in the district, which constituted the bulk of the island's agricultural land, and who had thought that they would benefit from the country's reunification by being able to return to farming the soil of Morphou.

The environmental programs of Ginger Patterson's PSS-sponsored work were helping to relieve the negative effect of this inability to obtain land in Morphou, as these efforts were helping to make once-desert land arable again all over the island. But this work wasn't being accomplished fast enough. The vice president's hold on the land in Morphou was beginning to cause serious problems in the political unity of the island.

Ioannou had known that she couldn't make much headway with Hatan in her first face-to-face probing into the topic of what his intentions were in Morphou and why he couldn't put his responsibility to the stability of the government above his personal business interests. She had not had any idea that he would immediately blow up as he did, however.

"You want me to talk about the ownership of some land in Morphou when your Greeks are starting up the massacres of innocent Turks again?" Hatan had screamed in her face, as he waved a copy of the Turkish daily, *Kibris*, over her head.

She didn't have to be told that the paper's front page was fully devoted to the explosion in the Turkish village of Gunyeli in Nicosia's northern suburbs. And then the red-faced giant of a man had stormed out of her office—and quite possibly out of her political life—without giving her an opportunity for comment.

When she was able to regain her breath, Ioannou rose from her desk and crossed to the window. As she watched the vice president's vehicle sweep out of the palace gates and into the Nicosia traffic, she began to review recent events and Hatan's reaction to them. She was sure that the relationship she had forged with Hatan had been close and trust-filled enough that they could have discussed the explosion in Gunyeli rationally and without being taken in by the sudden hatred and innuendo that was being splashed in Greek- and Turkish-language media alike.

No, the more she thought about it, the more convinced she was that the real motive for Hatan's indignant outburst was a desire to avoid talking about his activities in Morphou. And *that* in itself made the possibilities concerning that subject even more disturbing than she had anticipated they would be. The pressures of the demands on her to keep Cyprus unified were terrifying. She was so sure that there was a real foundation of trust between herself and her vice president, and she, more than anyone else, realized just how vital good relations were between a Greek president and Turkish vice president to move the genuine forging of the Cypriot nation from the realm of the impossible at least to the land of the improbable, but discussable.

Ioannou permitted her aching head to rest against the cooling window pane. She now knew she had not been understanding and forgiving enough to her own father when he himself had held this office. The pressures were just too great. She didn't know how she could go on if the situation between the communities deteriorated any further. But she also knew that if she didn't go on, the whole system would collapse. As Cyprus had proved in its previous behavior, the alternative to the unity she was trying to forge and maintain was an unthinkable horrible and bloody chaos. She couldn't let this happen.

If Hatan had not returned to the Presidential Palace office by tomorrow, she would have to crawl to him to preserve, at least publicly, their relations. And the views of the press be damned. She would, of course, start a very private investigation into his activities in Morphou. She would have to call in her trusted and highly capable interior minister, Maria Solonos, for that. She was so afraid, however, of what Maria's people might find.

* * * *

She might be a tired old woman, she thought indignantly, but she wasn't stupid. Irina Lukenov tartly disconnected the telephone and returned to her kitchen, where she automatically, without giving it thought, began to prepare to boil up the fruit she had just picked for jelly. She had tried to reach Sergey and Pavel in the offices of their new company in Lucerne, but she had been told they were in meetings all day.

"Meetings, my eye," she gestured menacingly at her kitchen window with a red-fruit-dipped wooden spoon. "I didn't survive as a Hizballah fighter for fifteen years without being able to develop my own intelligence network."

Ever since Irina and her son, Uri, had been spirited out of Cyprus three years previously with the help of Uri's friend, Andre Piccard, and Uri had been set up with a job in the Piccard shipping company's Zurich operation, Irina had thought that she and her family were safe at last. Once the wife of the Russian Intelligence chief in Cyprus, Irina had been kidnapped nearly twenty years before and had ended up, first as a befuddled, disillusioned hostage in the Hizballah terrorist organization-controlled Al-Baqa' Valley in Lebanon, and later as a willing Hizballah fighter and agent.

Her family had thought she had been killed by a bomb during a raid on a Beirut shop where she reportedly was being held captive. But she had not died then, or even had been in Beirut at the time. She had wanted her family to think she had died, however, and permitted them to believe that she had. Shortly before her kidnapping, she had suffered the shock of the death of her parents in a Chechnyan rebellion against Mother Russia, deaths for which she blamed her husband, who had known the attacks were to take place but who, under his Russian Intelligence operation orders, had not been permitted to tell his wife. She had also just been rejected by her childhood lover. She therefore had grasped the chance for a new life.

Three years ago she had tried to change her life again. She had been assigned to run counterfeit money on behalf of an Iranian general, the Hizballah being sponsored by Iran, to Cyprus, where it would be inserted into the economies of Europe to undermine the American and European economic systems. Although she had gone to Cyprus, as ordered, she had tried to disappear once she had reached the island. She had had enough of terrorism and only wanted to grow old and die in peace. Luckily her son, Uri, who had been searching for her for years, had found her before her Iranian employer had and had enlisted his friend Andre Piccard to help them escape and start a new life.

Piccard had gone to the length of reuniting Irina with her other son, Pavel, who had been trained as an Intelligence officer in Russia and had been inserted into an American company. At the same time, her former lover—and the real father of Pavel, Sergey Stepanov—had also escaped Cyprus, having become deeply embroiled in international crime there.

Uri and Irina had stuck with the new life the Piccards had made for them, but Sergey and Pavel had become close and had struck out on business interests of their own in Switzerland.

And now Irina had found out just what sort of business they had entered into. Their firm, Hartzel-Wegner, was a weapons and communications systems brokerage house. Irina knew too much about that business herself and about the past activities of Sergey, who had been trained as an operative of the then-Soviet Intelligence service, the KGB, not to know that Sergey was back in the thick of international crime again—and that now he had dragged her youngest son, Pavel, along with him.

They had both told her their involvement was restricted to the communications systems part of the operation and that they were careful to stay within the confines of Switzerland, where the Piccards had constructed protections for the family. But Irina now knew otherwise. She knew that Pavel had just departed on a trip to Russia, the Russians themselves not knowing that Sergey was still alive. She knew that Pavel's trip to Russia concerned the procuring of nuclear material from the Russian mafia sources. And she knew that Sergey was now gone from Switzerland also. He had supposedly gone to Germany. But Irina washed Sergey's laundry, and she had seen his collection of documents that he was too sloppy to remove from his pockets. She knew that, instead of being in Germany, he was, at this very moment, in London's Heathrow Airport, ticketed through to New York City.

This nonsense must stop, Irina exhorted herself, as she turned off the heat under the cooking fruit, dried her hands, and returned to the front hallway of her comfortable country cottage in the shadow of the Piccards' Alpine castle. She and Sergey had never really become comfortable with each other after they had, by the greatest of coincidences, been reunited on the Piccard hydrofoil passenger ship, the *Daphne*, while both were separately fleeing Cyprus. Therefore, she normally would not do anything to stop him. But he had embroiled their son in illegal operations as well—Irina had not previously fully learned that Pavel had, in fact, followed in the footsteps of both his father by name and his father by fact and was not the innocent toddler she always saw in him. Beyond that, Irina had had enough of terrorism and international crime in her life. She would not be party to any more, even by passively sitting and watching it happen.

When she had reached the foyer, Irina jerked the telephone receiver from its cradle and dialed the number of the Piccard Company in Zurich. She would tell Uri what was going on, and if he wouldn't do anything, she herself would do something. She had been steeled by years of both an unhappy marriage and love affair with Russian spies, weeks of wandering the streets of Grozny under bombardment by the order of Moscow, almost immediately followed by kidnapping at the hands of Hizballah guerrilla fighters, and a decade and a half as a Hizballah fighter and drug runner herself. She would show Sergey and Pavel that she couldn't just be ignored.

However, Irina did reach Uri, and Uri did promise to deal with the matter himself. The first action he took in trying to nullify the effect of the new business Sergey and Pavel had taken up was to contact his good friend, Andre Piccard, in Cyprus. The most disturbing piece of information his mother had passed on to him was that Sergey and Pavel's activities somehow involved Cyprus, although she had not been able to find out what form this involvement had taken. Because of everything Andre had done for them, he deserved to hear about this problem first—and Uri knew that Andre's fiancée was in a position to start tracking down this rogue weapons broker quickly, find out what the firm was up to, and counter its operations. He only hoped that Pavel, if not Sergey, could be saved in the process.

After Irina had spoken to Uri, she started to return to the kitchen. But then, on second thought, she began trudging up the stairs to the room she and Sergey shared. Entering the closet, she pressed on a slightly discolored section of the paneling at the shadowed side of Sergey's side of the closet, and a small section of the wall turned to reveal a slight recess between the panels. Once again Sergey had underrated her abilities and her interest in his activities. She had known about this hiding place for some time, but she had carefully never looked through the papers that she had found there, not knowing whether or not he had done something to them so that he would know if they had been disturbed.

But she was no longer worried about detection.

Her acquiescence to Sergey's new activities, especially now that he had embroiled Pavel in those activities, was at an end one way or the other. Perhaps these papers would tell a bit more about what she needed to know about Hartzel-Wegner and about what her family was doing for them. The papers did just that, but rather than relieve her fears, what she read made her blood run cold. It was worse than she thought. This had to stop right now. She had to get to Beirut.

Chapter Six

The sustained pounding on the slatted, metal door reverberated throughout the shop. Nabil Jallud had lowered it over his Damascus copper souk shop entry to keep the curious out while he repeated his attempt to reach his police official nephew in Cyprus on the powerful satellite phone scrambler in his back office.

"All right, all right, Ali," Jallud called out to the keeper of the adjacent shop who, he was sure, was pounding on the door because he was concerned that Jallud had closed shop for a second time in the middle of the working day.

"Everything's fine. I'll open up in a moment. I just had to run an errand. I don't know what your concern is though, my friend. My closing just means that my quality goods are not on display and that perhaps you can unload some of your own shoddy trash on unsuspecting American tourists."

Nabil and Ali had been best of friends for years and had maintained a steady stream of insulting, but playful banter for that entire time.

The banging continued, but Jallud finished what he was doing before he moved to the front of the shop and cranked up his shutter door. Not wanting to trust the information to his nephew's wife, Leila, Jallud had placed the business card that woman who had called herself Hartzel had given him into a stamped envelope, addressed to Ahmad Jallud at his Cypriot police headquarters address, and had dropped the envelope into his outgoing mail slot.

He could clearly see, through the slowly separating metal slats of the door, and well before the door had been raised that there was more than one insistent visitor and that neither of the burly men standing outside, scarves draped over their lower faces, was his neighbor Ali. Ali was there, certainly, in the street beyond. The pounding had gathered quite a crowd, in fact.

"The satellite telephone scrambler," Jallud thought in panic. The authorities had traced his transmission to Cyprus. They would find out about his emerald smuggling activities.

It was for times such as this that Jallud had maintained contingency plans. He had left more than one country in which he was well established a mere three paces ahead of the authorities. He was already thinking about making a grab for the bundle of clothes and valuables he kept near the small door to the back alley for just such occasions as he released the cord for the door to let it fall into place again.

However, the two men at the door were too quick for him. They both already had gotten a firm grip on the bottom of the lowest metal slat as the door had started to rise, and both gave a mighty heave and rolled under the door and into the darkened shop as the door once more crashed down with a loud bang, separating Jallud and the two men from the curious crowd in the street.

Jallud never got anywhere close to his escape door, although, after their knives had flashed, the two assassins themselves made quick use of his well-laid escape route.

* * * *

The sky was a clear blue and the sun glinted off the stately palm trees waving in front of the Piccard family mansion adjacent to the town park on the Limassol seafront, as Ellen Larkin rose from the sea and slowly walked out of the surf and across the hardscrabble beach toward the waterfront road between the beach and the town. Although already in her early forties, Ellen Larkin, the former Canadian Intelligence officer and now the director of the Cyprus computer data bank nerve center of the United Nations International Crime Investigation Service—UNICIS—was still the beautiful, petite, deceptively delicate blonde who so often had people staring in disbelief when they learned of her profession and her accomplishments.

Ellen was on vacation from UNICIS now. The world had seemed quiet, marred—or, rather, improved—only by yesterday's coup in Iran that turned out the ayatollahs and, it was to be hoped, their policy of exporting terrorism and Islamic fanaticism. And Ellen had come down from her own Kyrenia harbor apartment on the island's northern coast to Andre's stately mansion in Limassol on the southern coast to answer the question he had been pressing her about for months: Yes, she would marry him.

However, once here, she had not been able to come out with the actual words. First, there was her own important job with the UN. And her office was in Morphou, across the Troodos Mountains from Limassol, on the central plain. And she didn't intend on giving her job up. But the second impediment was, of course, the key one. She was considerably older than he was. The difference in age did not seem apparent to others when they were together, but she knew it. Andre, despite being a senior figure in an ancient and far-flung family business empire, was not yet thirty, and she herself was already over forty.

Why couldn't they just continue as they were, she thought, as she found an opening in the traffic—traffic which had slowed down to a crawl at the sight of a perfectly shaped little blonde emerging from the sea and crossing the road in her red bikini—and crossed to the large, ochre-stone Piccard mansion that had dominated the Limassol promenade for a century and a half.

Andre seemed preoccupied and slightly disturbed when Ellen entered the study after having showered and changed. She hoped he had not anticipated that she had planned to give him his answer during this visit and was assuming the worst because she had not said anything as yet. Andre could be so moody. Somewhat slight of stature as she herself was, he was slender of build and had the dark, handsome features of the people of the French Mediterranean port of Marseilles, the center of his family's shipping empire. He also tended to be quite serious and a little sensitive, which Ellen accepted and proficiently handled, as she was fully aware of his troubled childhood and, as a French Canadian, she was able to identify and appreciate some of the French traits that he reflected that sometimes seemed a bit out of place on the exuberant Mediterranean island of Cyprus.

She quietly entered the study and drew up behind him, encasing his shoulders in her arms and kissing the top of his dark, curly hair.

"Is something the matter, darling?" she asked in fear of what that "something" might be. "You seem a bit pensive." In answer, Andre smiled broadly and gently guided Ellen around and onto his lap, where they exchanged a few deepening kisses and a bit of exploration with their hands.

"Sorry. I didn't mean to seem upset. But I suppose I am. I just received a telephone call from Uri Lukenov in Zurich. His mother contacted him, saying that she thinks Stepanov and Pavel are involved in something illegal and dangerous, something that involves Cyprus."

"That's too bad," Ellen responded. "I never could accept that Sergey Stepanov would behave himself or live quietly in Switzerland, I'm afraid. And I've always regretted that you wouldn't let me tell Takis Koniotis or Ahmad Jallud that he was alive. It is very awkward, you know, for me to keep such things from my superior at the UN and from the chief of the Cypriot police. Stepanov is still wanted here for questioning in that international counterfeiting case three years ago."

Ellen could feel Andre's muscles tense up and she rose and took him by both hands.

"Come. It's inevitable. We'll have to contact either Takis or Ahmad now."

"Yes, I know," Andre sighed in resignation as he too rose from the chair and the two walked toward the study door. "But would you do something first? Would you yourself run the name of this company Stepanov and Pavel are supposedly working for now, Hartzel-Wegner, through the UNICIS computers? And, for now, tell just me what you have found? I'd like to know if something really serious is going on before we talk to Takis. I know you don't want Uri and his mother harmed; I don't think they have any part in this. And I'd like a chance to get them out of harm's way before the world's police get into it. We haven't exactly told Takis everything there is to know about where Uri and Irina are either, you know, and there are also arrest orders out for them here in Cyprus."

It was the least she could do. She had been keeping these secrets from Takis and Ahmad a long time now, and not just out of love for Andre. She genuinely had wanted to see Irina Lukenov have another chance at life. Life had not been generous to her up to the point of her arranged disappearance into Switzerland. In the end it wasn't all that difficult to accede to Andre's request. It neatly changed the subject from an answer to his proposal of marriage, and he could not say that it was her fault for having concentrated on something else just now. However, she would maintain certain priorities.

"Certainly I'll have the checks run through the data banks before we tell Takis and Ahmad. But even before that, don't you think we should make another visit to the upstairs."

Andre's eyes regained their sparkle, but he was forced to demur. "Sorry, but have you forgotten that I have to help Ginger dedicate the water recycling project in Galata this afternoon?"

"Oh, that. Yes, I had tried to forget. That's too close to Morphou and too close to the UNICIS Headquarters for me to want to remember."

"Well, I'll have to get on my way soon if I want to make the ceremony. Are you sure you won't go with me? Ginger said it promised to be a big 'bang up,' whatever that means. There were such strange expressions in the older generation, weren't there?"

But Ellen didn't respond. Andre had hit a very raw nerve without knowing it, and Ellen had swept up the staircase and out of sight before he could see the tears welling up in her eyes. The "older generation." That was precisely the wrong thing to remind her of while she was trying to convince herself to marry a man fifteen years her junior.

* * * *

It had been Stan Hodges's luck to have been stationed near the VIP room at Damascus Airport by Joseph MacAlister. He recognized her instantly. But she was moving along like the Queen Mary, stately and with an imperial air, so it was going to be very difficult to get close to her. All eyes were on her as she passed. She obviously was an important woman. She cut her way through the crowd like visiting royalty—a path naturally opened for her and no one came within a couple of feet of her. Hodges knew it was going to be difficult to do the job and to get away again. He could not approach her unobtrusively and he could not get close enough to her to kill and then retreat without being noticed. He also didn't have time to stake out any surveillance, as she was on the move and didn't have far to go before reaching the departure gate.

But Hodges was a professional. There was a job to be done. That was of first importance. Getting away clean was also important, but it was definitely of secondary importance. MacAlister had believingly explained to them all how important it was for the Hartzel woman to be taken down and to be taken down now, before she reached the safety of Beirut.

Well, it was now or never. Hodges took a deep breath, palmed the plastic switchblade that had been specially designed to bypass airport security detection devices, and shoved off of the pillar he had been leaning against and directly into the blade that was being supported at a nasty, upward angle by the muscular Syrian secret service bodyguard who had been assigned to Inga Hartzel. Hodges was making soft, terminal gurgling noises, as the bodyguard pushed him back into the waiting arms of another agent who came from behind the pillar and returned to that position with Hodges's stiffening body while the crowd that had gathered for the departure of the Beirut transporter was clearing.

Hodges had been identified as a possible assailant well before Inga Hartzel left the VIP room. He had been pointed out to the selected bodyguard when the latter had returned from making the arrangements Inga had "requested" and the bodyguard had been in the best position to act when Hodges started to make a move. The guard had been sure Hodges was an attacker because he had seen the mercenary palm the switchblade, but he probably would have killed anyone whose movements in relation to Hartzel at that moment had seemed suspicious. He had been told in no uncertain terms that she was to be delivered to Beirut alive, well, and satisfied.

He had already taken care of the alive and well, he thought smugly to himself as he walked toward the departure gate Hartzel had just safely cleared. The kill had been exhilarating and had started his juices flowing. It had been for just such opportunities that he had joined the secret police. He had been slightly bothered about the part of keeping the old woman satisfied, especially when he had been told beforehand in no uncertain terms what that might entail. But now that he had seen her and the presence she displayed and how she could take command, and in the excitement of the kill, he knew it wouldn't be so tough seeing that she would be satisfied as well.

"Damnation," Joseph MacAlister admonished himself as he saw Inga Hartzel sail through the departure gate at an impossible distance for him to prevent her escape. He was angry at himself for having become distracted. He had thought that he had seen Hodges over by the VIP lounge door and had assumed that Hodges had that approach under control. Hodges was one of his best agents. But then, there she was, moving out of the lounge and causing a flurry of interest that would satisfy a movie star. And MacAlister's eyes had also seen a small commotion of some sort over near the door to the VIP lounge. But he hadn't seen Hodges again, and when his attention was returned to Hartzel she was still on her feet and past danger. Well, he only hoped the people he had trying to get at the airplane itself had managed to get into position. He'd have to go track Hodges down and try to plan his next move. One thing he knew for sure. It was time to tell the Israelis and the Western Intelligence services about the Homewrecker threat.

* * * *

It seemed like everyone in the Solea Valley was descending on the town square of Galata, where the now-famous Ginger Patterson was to dedicate the opening of a new water recycling project. The benefits of Mrs. Patterson's work were on view all around them. The slopes of the valley were greener than they had ever been at this time of the summer, the fruit crop in the valley had been double that of the previous year, no one was even suggesting that the village would suffer water rationing this year as it had done so often in the past, and, for the first time in anyone's memory, the river that streamed down from Mount Olympus, through Kakopetria, Galata, and Kaliana, and then down onto the central Mesaoria Plain and to the sea at Morphou Bay, was still filled with swiftly running water.

The town school, adjacent to the park on the square, with its obelisk honoring the Greek freedom fighters of the anti-British period, was already filled to capacity when the explosion sounded and the center of the town disappeared. As the dust began to settle, it could be seen that the town's obelisk had been obliterated and, in its place, rose a baby blue-colored sports car convertible, its shattered nose buried in the ground and the lid on its trunk flapping like a flag.

As the survivors—those perpetual many in Cypriot society who would not arrive for the ceremony until it was half completed—stumbled out of their homes, different words were on their shocked lips. But all of these words pointed to a central, ominous accusation. In the initial quiet after the explosion, a wail of "Assassins," "Turks," "Gunyeli," "Revenge," and "To Arms" rose above the long-quiet village of Galata.

Galata, and other separately Greek and Turkish villages of the island, had not always enjoyed peace and quiet. Although few Cypriots alive remember the ethnic pogroms that had previously torn the island apart, set resident against resident, and caused whole villages to be wiped out in a single night, all

Cypriots had had stories of these events passed down to them. And all realized just how quickly they might be called upon to defend themselves and their neighbors from ethnic violence.

The peace and unity that the current Cypriot administration of President Chrystalla Ioannou had so painstakingly—and, largely, successfully—started to forge was crumbling before her very eyes.

* * * *

The two handsome naked bodies, exquisite in the stark contrast in their skin tones, were exotically entwined on the disarrayed sheets under the gently revolving ceiling fan. It was that brief period after lovemaking when time was suspended and all was right with the world. It was an interesting commentary on ethnic diversity that both the Cypriot police chief, Ahmad Jallud, and his wife, Leila, were Turks, in view of the considerable difference in their coloring. Ahmad, tall, wiry, and tightly muscled, was quite dark, whereas Leila, nicely rounded and of shorter stature, was almost translucently fair of skin.

Of course neither one of the two were really of Turkish descent.

Although Ahmad had been brought to the then-isolated Turkish Cypriot zone at a very early age by his uncle, the merchant Nabil Jallud, he really was of Lebanese descent. And even that might be brought into question in view of his very dark complexion, since the Lebanese are generally light-skinned as well. In upbringing, of course, Ahmad had very much become melded into the Turkish Cypriot culture.

It had, in fact, been Ahmad's mixed ancestry that had landed him the job as the national police chief following the island's political reunification. As part of the peace settlement, the police chief was to be from the Turkish zone. Ahmad, who by that time had risen to the senior ranks in the Turkish Cypriot police, had been fully acceptable to the Turkish side as a candidate for the police chief post because of his long affiliation with the Turkish Cypriots and yet had also been the most acceptable candidate in the Greek side's perspectives because he wasn't really a Turk.

Leila, on the other hand, who really did claim to be of Turkish origin, was really an Iranian, although this was a closely held secret that she had not revealed to Ahmad or to any other Cypriot.

As the moment of spent passion that often ensued as soon as Ahmad had returned home and espied his wife, whose voluptuous beauty and sexuality never failed to stir him, faded, the two, still entwined and being cooled by the overhead fan, began to move into their customary sharing of the domestic events of the day. Ahmad rarely talked about the work at the police office, although Leila claimed that she wasn't at all bored about what the police were up to and even tried to ask probing questions to show her wifely interest and concern in Ahmad's demanding job.

"Has anyone of interest called?" asked Ahmad as he began to tire of Leila's prattling of minor events in the house between her own searching, but usually unsatisfied, questions about Ahmad's work concerns. Today she had been especially interested in what was being discovered concerning the explosion in Gunyeli, but Ahmad claimed that nothing much had been learned as yet.

"Oh, yes. I almost forgot," Leila responded. "Your uncle, Nabil, called from Damascus."

"Oh?" Ahmad asked in genuine interest, as he began to disengage from the knot the two lovers had formed with their bodies. "Did he have anything important to say? He doesn't call very often anymore."

"Oh, no. He just said he wasn't feeling too well. But he thought he would call to find out how we were doing. He said it was nothing to worry about and that he would contact you sometime over the next couple of days again. He specifically asked that you not call him. Something about it not being wise to emphasize to the Syrian authorities his connection to the Cypriot police chief."

Leila nestled closer to her husband and began to let her hands wander over his body as Ahmad cogitated on his uncle's call. After a few moments, his mind drifted to other thoughts, and he stiffened a bit and drew away from Leila.

Leila sensed the change in her husband but only spoke again when it was obvious that her playfulness was not going to arouse his ardor. With a sigh, she finally pressed him to tell her what he was thinking. After a long silence, Ahmad blurted out: "You haven't been out today? You haven't gone anywhere?"

"Well, I went shopping, of course," Leila murmured.

"You didn't say earlier that you went out."

"I hardly considered going to Charlambides to get a chop for your dinner as noteworthy," Leila snorted.

"Someone told me today they thought they had seen you get into a car with a man outside the *Semerini* newspaper building this morning."

"They were mistaken."

And after a moment's silence, a switching of gears: "And you weren't in Larnaca over the noon hour last Friday?"

"No, of course not, silly. What would I be doing in Larnaca?"

"One of my friends said he saw you getting on Andre Piccard's yacht in the Larnaca Marina."

"That's such silliness," Leila cooed. "We've been over this many times before. Your friends just know how jealous you are and they play jokes on you to make you think I am not faithful. I think they are just jealous of you themselves. I just think all of your randy friends would like to have what you have at home. If I was seeing someone else, would I always be so ready for you?"

Ahmad didn't answer. He was working her words over in his mind. Intellectually he accepted that he basically couldn't understand how such a luscious woman could have chosen him to love. Emotionally, however, he was fully aware of the sexuality she exuded and the close attention she received from every man with a roving eye she encountered—which pretty much covered every man on Cyprus with breath. He knew that if he himself didn't have her, he would want her, even if she were married to his best friend. His fortune was just too good to fully enjoy.

Somewhat alarmed now, Leila moved her diversionary tactics into upper gear. Taking him by surprise, she pushed him onto his back and mounted him. Digging her hands into the silky dark hair that covered his chest, she began massaging his nipples with her thumbs and put her hips and knees and other talented muscles to work.

"If I were seeing someone else, would I have the energy to do this? And this? And . . ."

Leila ultimately was successful, as always, in drawing Ahmad's attention away from brooding on his jealousies.

Chapter Seven

The Iranian agent was in a panic. On less than two hours notice he had been instructed to fly from Tehran to London and within a forty-five-minute window to intercept Sergey Stepanov at Terminal Five at Heathrow Airport and pass on some highly secret information before the Russian caught his flight to New York. Not only was the content of the message secret but the very fact of the connection between Stepanov and Iranian interests, and, above all else, the identity of the one sending the message were so secret and explosive that they could only be communicated to Stepanov by word of mouth and by someone from Iran whom he would know and believe.

The agent's own plane had arrived at Terminal Twelve of the world's busiest, and, arguably, its most confusing airport. Heathrow had so many terminals now that it was a wonder that anyone made a same-day transfer connection through that airport.

The Iranian agent had had to purchase an ongoing ticket on the very same plane Stepanov was taking to New York just to be able to get into the departure lounge to pass his message. He had no intention of actually going to New York with Stepanov and had been strictly warned to have as little contact with the Russian as possible beyond conveying his information.

The message to be passed concerned what Joseph MacAlister and his mercenaries had found on the Homewrecker project in the subterranean vaults of Tehran's Ghasr Prison. Stepanov was to be warned that the operation had been compromised and that either it was launched within the next week and succeeded instantly in tilting the balance in the Middle East in favor of the interests in Iran that had supported the Homewrecker effort, or those same Iranian interests would have to start closing out all connections to and vestiges of the Homewrecker project.

Although the Iranian agent knew the content of the message, not even he knew who was sending it. He only knew it was someone who still wielded significant power in Iran, even after the overthrow and disappearance of the ayatollahs. He suspected that Stepanov would who sent the message. But the Iranian agent didn't want to know, and he strongly suspected that it was not particularly healthy for Stepanov if the Russian knew.

The Iranian's plane arrived at Heathrow five minutes late. An index to the power of his employer was revealed when everyone else was held on the plane until he had exited. A motorized cart was waiting to take him to the terminal connection station, where he would take a passenger tram to Terminal Five. Thus far, everything was working well. But only thus far. At the terminal connection station after a seven-minute ride on the cart, a large queue had formed of passengers waiting for terminal trams. Apparently, several jumbo transporters had arrived at Terminal Twelve simultaneously. A further six minutes were wasted as the agent's cart driver negotiated the agent toward the front of the queue, all of whose "waiters" were tired, cranky, and trying desperately themselves to make tight connections.

At last a tram arrived and the cart driver elbowed the agent into it and cheerily waved good-bye, as the door snapped shut and the agent realized that this capsule was headed for Terminal Six, not Five. Another eight minutes were wasted, as the capsule steamed along to the Terminal Six connection station, which, thankfully, was nearly deserted. However, here the agent learned that one could not get directly to Terminal Five from the Terminal Six connection station, but, rather, had to go to the Terminal Ten connection station and take another tram back. A five-minute ride to the Terminal Ten connection revealed that several jumbo jets full of tired, crabby, and tight-scheduled passengers had apparently just arrived at Terminal Ten. By this time, the Iranian agent had a very serious "don't mess with me" expression on his face, and, thus, it was only twelve-minutes later that he arrived at the Terminal Five connector station—to be faced with the back of a long queue of tired, crabby, and tight-scheduled passengers at the security station. There were four X-ray security booths open and operating at the entrance into Terminal Five. However, there was only one person checking the passports of everyone before they went to the security booths.

The agent had three minutes to get into the terminal and to find Stepanov. Fifteen minutes later, he cleared through the security booth. He was tired and crabby and ready to kill. He raced into the lounge area and looked up at the flight schedule screen. The screens were showing commercials. To increase revenues, the airport had started showing commercials on its flight schedule screens some years earlier. Four minutes later, the flight screen came back on and the flight to New York was still blinking. The departure time had been amended for twenty minutes from now.

Praising Allah to the highest, the agent sprinted down the corridor to the gate area. The flight to New York naturally was at the last gate down the corridor. Ten minutes later, the agent huffed up to a completely deserted departure gate. No plane was in sight. However, there was a perky young lady at the

117

podium who was informing one and all—if they asked—that the flight screen had been in error and the New York flight was leaving from a gate located half way back to the terminal.

Seven minutes later (the Iranian agent was definitely beginning to slow down), the agent reached the correct gate. Sure enough, more than a hundred already tired and crabby passengers were milling around the six chairs that had been provided for the departure gate, all occupied by a group of teenage mountain climbers, already wearing their gear. A passenger jet was, indeed, hooked up to the departure ramp, and the words "New York/JFK" were blinking above the podium.

Not stopping to catch his breath, the Iranian agent began to search for Sergey Stepanov, first unobtrusively and then in panic, among the milling passengers. Why couldn't these people stand still for a single minute, the agent thought angrily to himself. All of this movement was confusing him. Stepanov didn't appear to be at the gate. He didn't appear to be in the nearby men's room. He didn't appear to be in the bar either. But everywhere the agent turned, he seemed to see the same two serious-looking men in the green uniforms.

It turned out that the men in the green uniforms were looking for the Iranian agent. Thanks to the UNICIS computer assistance to international airport security, the agent's false passport had set off alarms. By the time the security agents had apprehended him, however, he was in no condition to resist, object, or, unfortunately, provide any information to the security officers.

At the same moment, entirely oblivious to the Iranian's search for him, Sergey Stepanov, traveling with a very expensive false passport that had been obtained from the very recent on-order disappearance of a Danish business executive who closely resembled Stepanov, was boarding a plane in Frankfurt Airport. The flight was bound for Philadelphia. Stepanov had always changed his international travel plans at the last moment, and on this day he had performed a double change, having booked an earlier flight to New York from Frankfurt as well as this flight and the one from London. That was one way he had remained alive for so long. He was smug in the smoothness of his changed plans this time, but, truth be known, he probably really would rather have received the message the Iranian agent had been trying to get to him at London's Heathrow Airport.

* * * *

The news of the explosion in Galata had taken Demetris Mattas out of bed. Buzzers had gone off on his *Semerini* computer at a very delicate moment and he had roared off to call his home office to see what the hell was going on. What the hell that was going on had then prompted him to send a kill notice on tomorrow's "At Your Service" column and to sit down at the computer and prepare to pound out a substitute essay.

While he sat there contemplating his first acidic sentence, the computer's e-mail system started going wild. The screen started blinking "contact editor" at him in angry capital letters.

"Screw the editor," he muttered, as he blotted out the screen and started punching away at his new column. Demetris could substitute his column at this late time and he could ignore his editor, because, in addition to being the principal political columnist for the Greek-language Cypriot daily *Semerini*, Demetris Mattas was also its publisher.

Probably eight people out of ten would have been able to guess he was a newspaperman if they could see him now. One of the others would likely guess he was a street person and the other would have located him in an insane asylum. He was sitting in front of his computer screen, his slat-backed chair reversed, and his open bathrobe—the only stitch of clothes he had on him—flowing out behind him. A cigarette was hanging out of the corner of his month and a half-empty bottle of Johnnie Walker Red was in easy reach.

Demetris Mattas, the brilliant man with words, had come a long way since his divorce two years previously from the Cypriot interior minister, Maria Solonos. And the entire trip had been downhill. Still a handsome man—but just barely—with fine features and just a bit of graying at the temples, Mattas was quickly going to pot. His muscle was in the process of turning to flab; always a nasty drunk, he was now drunk more often than sober; everything he touched smelled of rancid smoke; his face rarely saw a razor, but he refused to let it go to a beard; and the laugh lines around his striking blue eyes that had once been his best feature had not had a reason to appear in months.

His political observer *Semerini* column formerly entitled "Under the Grape Vine" had once been a masterpiece of understated, but precisely targeted satire on both Cypriot and foreign society and political life. The "At Your Service" column that replaced it in the wake of his bitter divorce from his long-suffering politician wife was also a masterpiece of writing, but, where the previous column was witty and forgiving, the new column was biting and combative.

The explosion in the Greek-dominated village of Galata, following as it did on the heels of the explosion in the Turkish-dominated village of Gunyeli, was made to order for Demetris Mattas in his present mood. For months he had been tearing at the Ioannou administration for its conciliatory stance toward the Turkish minority and its calls for closer unity between the two ethnic communities. Twice, to his great pleasure, the office of his former wife had complained to *Semerini* that his columns constituted an incitement to riot and warned him that he was on the edge of being charged with treason.

"Well, good on them," Mattas chortled as he reached the bottom of the column and took time out to take a swig from the scotch bottle. "*This* one will put me over the edge then," he continued, as he flipped back up to the lead on the column and keyed in the title "ENOSIS! A CALL TO EOKA ARMS." The word "Enosis," the integration of Cyprus with Greece, and the acronym "EOKA," the revolutionary force that sought Enosis through violence, were sure to catch Maria's attention. And if she didn't react to this, he would write a column on all of the little love tricks that had driven the interior minister wild with desire, and he quite possibly would conclude with a tribute to the high government official's wife who he was screwing now and whose attentions, unknown to Maria, had caused the breakup of their marriage.

As Demetris punched the spellcheck key, the woman in question appeared at the bedroom door, also only in her bed jacket, which also was hanging open. But there was no question that she had brought off the fashion statement much better than Demetris had. She was a beauty. Raven haired, tiny, but perfectly proportioned, and a face that belonged in the cinema. Her skin was milky white, and her hazel eyes were finely framed with thick, dark lashes.

Seeing them together, one would immediately have wondered what the woman saw in Demetris, who admittedly was once the embodiment of a Greek god, but who now could more closely be described as a shipwreck. But then, such a person could not have known the woman very well. In the first place, she had a strong attraction to danger and an aversion to sleeping alone or to lack of variety. In the second place, no matter what Demetris was becoming, he still was a powerful voice in the Cypriot community, through his newspaper, and this woman was compelled to seek out power and to bend it to her own needs.

Demetris found it quite difficult to tear his eyes from the woman posed in the doorway and to return to his newspaper column. She had not found such a provocative stance since the night she had perched in the nude on the bar stool on the yacht Andre Piccard had lent them for a cruise. Now *that* had been one wild evening.

The woman revealed her major interest in Demetris now, if not to him, as she slipped up behind him and started reading the new column over his shoulder as it rolled through the spell check program.

"Yes," she thought to herself in triumph, "this would do quite nicely. This just may be his last column, but it's absolutely perfect."

But then it hit her that he may have cooled down since writing it and may make alterations after the spellcheck was concluded. She could not have this. But there was a way to keep him from changing the column. She would distract him. Moving slowly and sensuously between Demetris and the computer, she buried his face between her breasts. She made quiet meowing noises as his lips found and alternated between her nipples. She could hear behind her the slight beep that indicated that the spellcheck program had been completed. With one hand, she pulled Demetris's bathrobe over his head, and purposely got it tangled in front of his face, while she half turned so she could see the computer screen and, with her other hand, pressed the send button. The editors wouldn't dare question the publisher's column, but, in case they might, she also pushed the mute button. Then she twisted down beside Demetris and to the thick carpet.

Demetris moaned in ecstasy, and the woman answered, her eyes on the computer screen, the computer screen that Demetris couldn't see. The computer screen that screened "contact editor" briefly in large, angry letters before dying out in resignation. Demetris's lack of response always meant the editors were being overridden by the publisher.

As the last "contact editor" died out, the woman's attention returned to the job, a job she would have to sustain for a while longer to ensure the presses at *Semerini* had begun to roll on tomorrow's edition. An enslaved Demetris was moaning her name: "Leila, Leila, Leila."

* * * *

This was beginning to look to Caitlyn like some sort of conspiracy. But why would anyone want to keep the Department of Archaeology out of the Morphou area?

Caitlyn Koniotis's old friend and former employer, Andriko Visiliou, who still held sway in Nicosia as chief of the now island-wide Department of Archaeology, had just left her office at Eastern Mediterranean University outside of Famagusta after reporting to her that the site the archaeological institute had been preparing to excavate on Morphou Bay on the island's northwestern coast had been blown up. Anything that might be there now had most likely been obliterated.

There were many archaeological sites all over Cyprus, the development of a large number of them having been started more than a century previously. But there were other areas, like the Morphou area, which had not been explored at all until after the island was formally reunified fifteen years ago. In Morphou's case, it had been under Turkish occupation and had largely been designated a denied military area for much of the time modern era excavations were being planned for Cyprus because of its proximity to the green line separating the north from the south. Thus, the Morphou area, although it did have excavations that were suspended many decades ago, was largely unknown ground in modern archaeological exploration terms. The region was the most undeveloped part of the island in economic terms, as well.

Both Caitlyn and Andriko had wanted to open up some representative digs there to ensure that nothing was being missed in the exploration of the island's past by overlooking the area. But it seemed almost as if someone didn't want the Morphou area opened up. Morphou was a neutral canton under the 1999 agreement, which meant it was neither Greek nor Turk dominated in its administrative setup. The Archaeological Department, however, had found the predominately Turkish residents of the area unenthusiastic, on the whole, about archaeological digging in the area. The police had similarly dragged their feet in issuing permits, and, like the most recent excavation effort near the Greek ruins at Soli, their efforts were being sabotaged. It had even privately been suggested to Caitlyn that the Turkish Cypriot vice president, Lala Hatan, who had been buying up land around Morphou for years, might be responsible for impeding any other efforts that would bring attention and activity to the Morphou area. If he was involved with this, both Andriko and Caitlyn wondered what his motives possibly could be.

"If I could call Takis, I bet he would know how to sort this out," Caitlyn said out loud without thinking. And then the thought hit her in the solar plexus and she found she could hardly breath. If, if. When would she ever get past leaning on Takis, she wondered bitterly. Probably never, she admitted to herself. And when she was truthful with herself she realized she didn't really want to stop leaning on him ever. She wanted him back, and she was bewildered at how they could have gotten themselves into the mess of this separation.

As she was trying to clear her mind to plan the next move on the Morphou exploration, the telephone rang and she suddenly had a far more serious bombing to think about. The first thought that hit her when her friend, Maria Solonos, the interior minister, informed her about the Galata bombing was the realization that both Ginger Patterson and Andre Piccard most certainly would have been there, at the center of the event. To her unspoken question, Maria quickly answered.

"No, I haven't heard about any specific people having been among the victims. And I didn't want to alarm you by calling, but we're trying to find Takis, and we've tried everywhere else. He isn't there with you by any chance, is he?"

Caitlyn answered with a stiff "No," hoping that the regret she felt in her heart did not show in her voice. She didn't want to talk with Maria about her marital problems. Maria had had serious problems of her own along that line, which had ended in a messy divorce, and Caitlyn didn't want even to think about the possibility that her relationship with Takis might be headed in the same direction. A separation was one thing; divorce was unthinkable.

When she had rung off, her thoughts and prayers returned to Ginger and Andre, but then an even worse thought surfaced. Her son, Eric, had contacted her from Platres, which was not far from Galata. Hopefully he had not chosen to go down to Galata for the water recycling project ceremony. She found herself in the almost ridiculous position of trying to remember what her son's position was on the environment. Was he interested enough in that to have attended the ceremony?

She couldn't remember and gave up on that line of thought, although not without castigating herself. What kind of a mother was she? She couldn't even remember what her own son's interests were. When they had been living in New York she had known. It was only after Takis had dragged her back here to Cyprus, away from her sons, that they had started becoming hazy to her as people. Why couldn't Takis have waited until the boys graduated from college and started their own lives? Weren't Eric's problems all wrapped around having been abandoned by his parents?

Caitlyn realized that this line of thought wasn't getting her anywhere either, but she couldn't avoid one last dig before she started to figure out how to find Eric on her own. Fine. Nobody can find Takis.

When a whole village has exploded and we don't know whether our own son was there, Takis, the world's leading policeman can't be found. But then she stopped again and sat down at her desk and buried her face in her hands. This was NOT the direction she wanted life to take her.

* * * *

Andre Piccard was very thankful that Ellen Larkin was asleep in the big pine four-poster bed when he finally returned to Limassol. Obviously she had not heard about Galata yet. Tomorrow he knew she would have to leave and go back to UNICIS headquarters in Morphou to help start the search for those who were trying to tear the country apart again. But he would not deny them this last night together for a while. He wished she would give him a favorable answer on his marriage proposal, but, if she could not do that yet, he didn't want to press her. He would much rather have the issue remain in suspension than for her to say "no." He knew he could not live without her, and he himself could go on as they were if Ellen turned his proposal down, but he knew that, if she did not accept him, she would leave him.

He did not quite know how to tell her about the miracle that had saved his life in the Galata explosion. Similar things had happened to him in the past, and he didn't quite know how to tell Ellen that his grandmother, Eleni, now long dead, was still watching over him and protecting him. He had arrived in the town square of Galata shortly after Ginger had arrived, and both had been due to speak in the school within a half hour. But both, without speaking, had started walking up the hill, toward

Kakopetria, rather than to the school. Again, without discussing what they were doing, both had instinctively headed for the new church of Kakopetria and to the grave of Eleni Piccard. Ginger had never even been to Eleni's grave before and, as she remarked later, she loathed the mere thought of graves and of death. But both Andre and Ginger had found themselves at Eleni's graveside when the explosion obliterated the center of Galata.

Andre, of course, knew instantly that Eleni had reached out from the grave once more to protect his life. That had happened before, so this had not surprised him. What had surprised him was that Ginger seemed to fully understand that Eleni had done the same for her. And, as they were returning to the southern side of the Troodos in a police sedan after having done what they could for the survivors in Galata, Andre found Ginger quizzing him closely about Eleni's philanthropic interests while she was still alive and whether the Piccards had been keeping the Ledra Foundation she had founded to help with the discovery of the Cypriots' history and heritage fully endowed. Andre knew he would have to start finding the answers to Ginger's questions in the morning or she would hound him relentlessly. But in the meantime, he didn't want to spoil this one, last peaceful night with Ellen for some time to come. She turned to him and nestled in his arms as he climbed into the family's sturdy old four-poster.

Chapter Eight

Takis Koniotis stood, opened his fist, and let the disturbed soil in his hand scatter in the breeze floating in from Morphou Bay. No matter how long he worked in law enforcement, he thought, there was always yet another baffling crime. And there was no question in his mind that this had been a crime.

While his estranged wife, Caitlyn, was wondering why he wasn't investigating the new round of peculiar happenings in Cyprus and his former assistant, the Cypriot interior minister Maria Solonos, was frantically trying to find him to consult on the explosion in Galata, Takis was, in fact, on the job—perhaps even more than he realized.

Koniotis had come to what was to be the archaeological institute's new dig at Elea, due west of the capital of Nicosia and on a gentle slope above the wide Morphou Bay. Here Caitlyn and Andriko Visiliou had hoped to revive the search into the heritage of the northwest sector of the island, which probably was as rich as that of the rest of the island but which had not been explored in recent decades because of the region's political isolation.

This did not mean, however, that the region didn't have as full a cultural history as the rest of the region, of course. Not far to the east of this site was Philia, where archaeologists had found a type of red polished pottery that was indexed to the period of 2300 BC, on the western Anatolian plateau in what is now Turkey and, it was speculated, found its way to the western area of Cyprus' central plain in the possession of refugees from the political upheavals of that time in Anatolia.

To the northwest, beyond the town of Morphou, where Koniotis's Cyprus UNICIS headquarters was located and which he could clearly see from the now-cratered Elea hillside, toward the Cape Kormaktiki northwestern point of the island, lay the excavations of Ayia Irini, which had been inhabited from the Iron Age (1050–725 BC) to the Hellenistic Period (325–58 BC).

Looking across the southeastern edge of the bay, Koniotis could first see the now-sleepy fishing village of Karavostasi—the "mooring place for ships," that had been the harbor for the Hellenic city state of Soli since the fifth-century BC and that, for the following twenty-five centuries, ending not more than a century ago, had been the port for the shipment of the copper that was mined in the Troodos Mountains, looming to the southeast. This was the same copper that had given

"Cyprus" its name. Soli itself, which reached its height in the Roman Era (58 BC–AD 395), was located on the hillside above and to the southeast of Karavostasi. And just to the southwest of that, high on a seaside cliff and clearly within Takis's vision from Elea, were the ruins of the fortress of Vouni, built in the fifth-century BC by the Phoenicians with the cooperation of the Persians to watch over the expanding influence of the Greeks in Soli.

This planned excavation at Elea, now ruined by a large detonation that had churned up the earth to a depth of several meters, would not have been the first exploration of the region's cultural history by any means, but it would have been unique in its own right. The site had first been selected by Caitlyn Koniotis's uncanny, but often demonstrated, ability to stand on a barren hillside and to sense the life that had pulsated there in ancient times. Her isolation of the Elea area as a possible archaeological site was backed up by the institute's modern and very sensitive seismographic instruments, which had confirmed that habitation here had gone back to at least the early Neolithic Period (about 6000 BC). This was much earlier than any other excavated site in this sector of the island.

And now the institute's plans had been dashed.

Not wanting to believe the destruction was intentional, Takis had come out to investigate the situation himself. But, there was no doubt about it; he had found evidence of plastic bomb elements among the debris. In addition, some of the residents of the area had said that several four-wheel-drive vans had driven into the area the previous evening and they had seen torches bobbing around. The residents had just assumed it was a team of the archaeologists, starting to prepare the site. After talking with them directly, Takis had believed those in the area who claimed they were disappointed the dig had been sabotaged and had wanted it to go ahead. This was the most economically depressed region of the island, and the area residents had been looking forward to the local jobs the project would create—plus the tourists that might follow if this was found to be a major archeological site.

This was all very disturbing and confusing to Takis. Andriko Visiliou had told Takis that he thought someone was trying to keep the institute out of the Morphou region, but Takis had scoffed at the idea. He wasn't scoffing any more, but he still found it inconceivable that anyone would object to archaeological excavations on isolated, unused land that the government had already purchased. And he couldn't imagine any Cypriot destroying such a site with explosives. With the recent explosion to the east in the Turkish village of Gunyeli, a menacing unease had settled over the island. The Cypriot police, with the help of Koniotis's UNICIS, needed to stop these bombings before they became a way of life.

As Takis returned to car, however, his mobile phone was ringing, bringing him a call that would add yet another unexplained bombing—in the Greek village of Galata up the Soli valley in the Troodos Mountains—to his list of menacing and confusing events.

* * * *

The young Holst Meinhart wasn't looking at the spectacular twilight view of the Shenandoah Valley and Massanuttan Mountain from the Skyline Drive lookout parking area just to the north of the Beaverbrook Lodge complex. Instead, he was whiling away his time by paging through the travel brochure one more time. Sand, sea, women, pubs, sailing, skiing, women, pubs. There was more than enough excitement for the young Austrian in the prospects of his next destination to engage his attention. The old Blue Ridge Mountains of Virginia, just south of the U.S. capital of Washington, D.C., were uninteresting foothills as compared with the sight of the Alps from Lucerne.

One of the men in the back of the van muttered something obscene in the darkness and a match flickered and then died. The view in the crowded interior of the van was nonexistent—the five men back there were used to action, not waiting, especially in the darkened interior of a small vehicle on a warm evening.

Holst could hear the other car approaching before he could see it, and he had time to drop the brochure on the floorboard, hiss a warning to his mates in back, and duck down into the seat before the convertible, its radio blaring, swept past him and rolled to a stop near the edge of the overlook's cliff some ninety feet across the parking area. Raising his eyes above the level of the passenger-side window and motioning his comrades to creep toward the front of the van where they also could get a good view, Holst and company had something far more interesting to watch for the next half hour than the Shenandoah Valley, a travel brochure, or the tips of burning cigarettes in the darkness.

Meanwhile, a hundred yards underfoot, General Sarah Bristow was preparing to make her final rounds of the subterranean Army Research Lab for the evening. Only two more days and this would all just be an entry on her professional résumé. It had been a good assignment, however, and she was already being courted by several defense industry contractors. She just hadn't made up her mind, however, whether she wanted to keep working at all or retire for good to her condominium in Naples, Florida. She had noticed over the past few months that she was tiring more easily, that her reflexes were off, and that there was an insistent little pain in her side. She was sure it was just nerves, but perhaps she would check into a clinic and have a full physical before she decided on her next move.

However, her *first* move was to wrap this assignment up in style and to leave the post with as many laurels as possible—all deserved, of course. None had been manufactured just because she was a woman, and there still were so few women of general rank in the U.S. services.

And in order to gather as many honors as was possible, Bristow needed to have that large photo-optics night-vision device contract on file before the end of the month. She turned to her desk and leafed through her papers. No, Hartzel-Wegner hadn't faxed in their copy of the contract yet. They had indicated it would be here before tomorrow morning, but perhaps she should call them to make sure everything was in order. She picked up the telephone and punched in the number of Hartzel-Wegner's number in Lucerne. Just as the recording on the other end began its soothing explanation, Sarah herself realized that it was now well past business hours in Switzerland and she disconnected the call in embarrassment before the recording gave her the opportunity to identify herself. General Bristow did not like to be caught in any forgetful behavior.

She would call first thing in the morning. In the meantime she would make her evening rounds of the lab. Turning to the clothes tree near the door, the general—who very much wanted to make the point that she was a general—donned her much beribboned army jacket and her gun belt. The jacket was actually functional, as the labs were kept at a very cool temperature, helped considerably by the surrounding walls of the cavern located deep within the mountain.

The gun belt was primarily a reminder that she had actually served in combat—in the successful defense nearly a decade earlier, while on temporary reassignment from the lab, of the Taiwan islands from mainland China. But it too was functional, as Bristow had maintained her championship marksmanship status over the years. In fact, it was the vanity of her reputation in this skill that had kept her from fighting her retirement at the end of the month. The trials for the new marksmanship rankings would start next month, and Sarah had noticed that her aim had been off considerably over the last several months. She knew this was a clear sign she was getting too old for this work, and she had decided to exit a winner.

The time had come and the couple in the convertible were still at it. Holst signaled to the men in the back of the van to leave the vehicle as quietly as possible. If the couple in the other car noticed them, the two would have to be taken care of before Holst and his comrades met up with the others. The door at the back of the van opened with a click, and five dark-clad mercenaries quietly exited and vanished into the wooded area the van had parked beside.

When he heard the click of the rear door, Holst peeked out of his window at the rocking convertible. Good. No sign the others had been noticed. Leaving the keys in the ignition, Holst gently opened his own door and rolled out onto the ground. The closing of the door sounded like a gunshot to him in the tension-filled air, but a quick check of the convertible indicated that the couple were still totally engrossed in their own activities.

The six men moved with stealth through the woods, toward the Beaverbrook Lodge. The others were already at the small, fenced shed behind the lodge building when the six reached it, two other groups of men having converged on the area from three different directions. Upon seeing that all eighteen had arrived, a masked Gerhard Mueller gave a silent hand signal, and two of the men crept up to the fence, where the shed blocked their activities from the view of the lodge. Inside the lodge lights blazed in a large, fully windowed porch-style room where young men and women, dressed as waiters, were bustling around and setting tables for the lodge's evening meal. None peered out of the windows with curiosity, but within the hour the room would be filled with diners, the grounds would be fully lit, and the single door into the shed would be in view, albeit purposely in the shadows to deaden the visual effect from the lodge of the chain-link fencing.

Gerhard Mueller turned to the heavily masked man beside him and explained that they needed to be back on the surface and clear of the site within a half hour to avoid detection by the diners at the lodge. Otherwise, they would have to create a larger mess in this operation than they had hoped to do. For a truly successful operation, they needed to avoid leaving any sign they had been here. Better that the U.S. authorities thought that some army research project in the lab had just gone very wrong.

One of the two men who had gone to the fence had finished tying insulated electrical cords to joints in the fencing and lifted and tied these together in a bundle attached to the fence at about a two-yard height. The other man then started clipping the fence between these connections from the ground line up to about one and a half yards. As he clipped, the other man bent the fencing back from the cut.

Now, after an almost one-yard-high and one-yard-wide opening had been made in the fence, had come the most dangerous aspect of the operation. One of the men went through the fence and turned, while a third man approached with a bowl-shaped device and handed this to the first man. The first man took a deep breath, wiped the sweat out of his eyes, and dried his hands on his trousers. Meanwhile the second man had moved to an edge of the fencing, where he could see into the lodge's dining room. At an all-clear signal from the second man, the first man took another deep breath, set something on the bowl-sized device, and then quickly crab-legged around to the side of the shed facing the lodge and rammed the circular device around the knob in the shed's door. There had been razor-sharp points in the rim of the device, which easily entered the soft wood of the door and held the device in place around the knob and the lock. The man disappeared back around the side of the shed as soon as he was sure he had driven the device home, and all eighteen men hugged the ground in anticipation of the next event.

Within a minute, there was a popping noise, as the device hit the ground, the mechanism having neatly eaten through the wood and melted the locking mechanism on the door. Upon individual all-clear signals from the man watching the activity in the dining room, the mercenaries, one by one, slithered around the side of the shed and into the escape shaft that connected the lab area of the subterranean Army Research Lab with the surface.

Some one hundred feet below, General Bristow had already passed the entrance to the escape shaft and was inspecting the photo-optics lab. All of the labs had been cleared for the evening, and the last of the workers would be leaving via the administrative section near the facility's entrance on the valley floor. She entered the main lab, with its windows out onto the corridor, and looked around for security violations. The night guards would be along in a half hour, and they were the ones responsible for detecting security breaches, but there had been no violations for three months—because Bristow herself

141

had been personally checking first. And she wanted to maintain that record up to her retirement. She flicked off the light in the main lab as she finished and moved to one of the back offices. She always turned off the light as she left an area as a marker that she had completed that area. There was enough light coming in from the corridor to enable her to return to the hallway through the darkened labs, and the guards could turn the lights back on themselves while they were checking.

As Bristow turned off the light in the last of the back offices in the photo-optics lab and turned to leave, she heard an unfamiliar sound in the hallway and moved closer to the windows. Her heart almost stopped and the pain in her side gave a noticeable tug as her incredulous eyes saw many black-garbed figures, most with Uzis in their hands, streaming out of the escape shaft door and into the corridor. Some were moving toward the administrative sector, some were moving toward the lab area where controlled land-mine detonators and the low-altitude rocker triggering devices were being tested prior to being turned over to the factory, and a few of the figures were melting into the lab areas at the back of the complex, obviously checking to see if the labs were deserted.

Turning on her heels, General Bristow began feeling her way back to the project coordinator's office so that she could sound the alarm. Unfortunately, it was harder to see in the darkness at the back of the lab than near the windows, and Sarah turned over a chair before reaching the project coordinator's office.

While Gerhard Mueller was supervising the stripping of the rocket-launcher triggering device lab of prototypes, formulas, and designs, the other leader of the expedition and a hand-full of men had gone into the administrative complex. This was a most delicate part of the mission, as they wanted to avoid detection in this area so that there would be a good chance the operation would be written off as a lab accident. Luckily, most of those who remained in the lab were now concentrated near the entrance, where the evening guards were busy checking them out. Also luckily, as Mueller had noted, Bristow's office suite was nearer the lab section than the entrance. The leader and his small band found only one secretary in Bristow's office, and she was dispatched quietly and clinically. The first of the explosion devices were set here. The leader wanted to be sure that all evidence of the dealings of Hartzel-Wegner were obliterated. Working their way back toward the lab area, the squad laid further explosive devices in the corridors between the administrative area and the labs and then went to wait by the escape shaft door.

All of this was done without detection except for the appearance of one young man, who, having heard a commotion in General Bristow's office, had left the computer center to investigate. He didn't show surprise when he saw what the invaders were doing, but walked directly up to their apparent leader and spoke in a stage whisper.

"I'm Nat. You know, the man who destroyed the computer files for Mr. Mueller. Is he here? I have to talk to him about what he said I would be getting."

Nat then received both silencer barrels of what Mueller had intended to give him.

"Good," the squad leader thought as he and his compatriots backed toward the lab area. "That saves time. I didn't have to go looking for him."

Holst Meinhart, Uzi in hand, heard the sound of the chair falling, as he reached the open outer door to the photo-optics lab. Crouching low, he rolled into the room just as the first of the explosions went off in the tunnels linking the administrative areas and the labs. Now the intruders were protected from detection and counterattack from the facility's entrance area, but they also were fully dependent on the slender stairwell leading to the back of the Beaverbrook Lodge for their escape.

Taking a chance on the location of the light switch, Holst popped up and reached for a switch at the side of the entrance door. General Bristow saw his profile against the light in the corridor and reached for her service revolver. The lights flashed on, and it took Holst's eyes a precious two seconds to latch onto Bristow's figure and an extra one to recover from seeing a woman in full military dress. However, Sarah's reflexes had been slowed by the sound of the explosion and by the sudden searing pain in her side that radiated down her arm. Thus, both fired at the same instant.

Hearing the gunfire, Sergey Stepanov and his squad darted into the photo-optics lab only to determine that their help was not needed. The shots of both Holst Meinhart and Sarah Bristow had homed accurately, and both were dead. No one would ever know that Bristow would have been dead moments later from a massive heart attack even if she had not remained a champion marksman to the end.

Ever practical, Stepanov immediately picked up the body of the young Austrian mercenary and moved it close to that of the general. He was fully aware of who Bristow was. He had known her ever since they had been on opposite sides in the NATO spy scandal in Belgium three decades earlier. He felt no emotion over her death, however. He never had liked her anyway. His primary thoughts at the moment were to ensure that no sign of what had happened would ever be detected by the Americans. He thus took the last two explosive devices the squad had and placed them near the bodies of Bristow and Meinhart.

Devices had been placed in the other labs as well, and, when it had been signaled that Mueller and his team and their precious cargo had cleared the shed at the top of the stairs, the devices were set and Stepanov and his own squad raced to the top of the shaft.

Doreen and Chance Hooker from Luray, Virginia, which stretched out in the valley near the entrance into the Army Research Lab, were enjoying an early anniversary dinner at the Beaverbrook Lodge. They had had to rush the event, because two of their five children, their twin boys, were playing in a late-night Little League Baseball game in Front Royale that evening. With two jobs and five children, the couple rarely had time to celebrate alone, and, although Chance had insisted that this year they *would* have an anniversary dinner, they found they only had time to go up to the lodge on the drive for an early dinner while they were en route to the game in Front Royale.

Doreen had wanted to sit by the window but she also wanted a corner seat, so they were somewhat unobtrusively located in the dining room, although both could clearly see into the still-darkened back garden. Of the two, Doreen had the better view of the length of the back lawn. When the back-garden lights flashed on precisely at 7:00 PM, Doreen and Chance both saw the movement, but they never were to agree what exactly they had seen and for several hours the ensuing events knocked the whole issue from the consciousness of both of them.

Doreen said she distinctly saw several dark-clad men running into the woods. Chance was to insist that he had just seen a group of deer that had been spooked by having the garden lights come on. In the end, the authorities, however, had carefully checked out the possibility of Doreen's story, and it became pretty much accepted that she was right. And the fact that she had contributed to the investigation had kept her in good graces with her sons when she and her husband failed to attend the Little League game and missed seeing their sons each hit a home run.

What both temporarily knocked the observation out of Doreen and Chance's minds but what also sharpened the memory for Doreen when the police had arrived, was the rumbling underfoot that had started right after the garden lights had gone on and that continued for some seconds after the shed behind the Beaverbrook Lodge and its surrounding chain-link fencing lifted off the ground in a column of fire and disintegrated over the Skyline Drive. Sarah Bristow's prized subterranean Army Research Lab had died with her and had become her tomb.

Chapter Nine

Caitlyn Koniotis was both disappointed and angry, and the only thing that kept her from throwing the pottery bowl far out into the Mediterranean was the look on Andriko Visiliou's face. Visiliou's face had turned ashen, and he sat down on the low stone wall in the early morning light of a new day so abruptly that Caitlyn lost all concern for the condition of the excavation and knelt beside him. But he was all right. The shock of the discovery had just knocked the wind out of his sails. This was really too much, having come on the heels of the sabotage of the site at Elea on the western coast.

Caitlyn had had a premonition that something was wrong at this site near Rizokarpaso, almost to the tip of the Karpas Peninsula that probed toward the underbelly of the Turkish mainland at the northeastern point of Cyprus. Visiliou had had to authorize a major excavation here because the archaeological institute had been informed by the vice president, Lala Hatan, that the ruins of a very early-settlement site could be found here. Hatan had said that his office had been hearing of many stories in which ancient pottery was found in this area and was making its way into the black market.

There was nothing about the site itself that Caitlyn had found off-putting. It was in a good location to have had a long history of settlement. However, the site had never "spoken" to her. And, although only her closest associates, those who had actually seen her premonitions work out precisely as described, would put credence in her divining of the past, her instincts had never previously failed her.

Not that Caitlyn was vain or fully convinced herself about her powers to locate ancient sites. She was sincerely prepared to be wrong and for more scientific methods to be correct in locating sites for the archaeological institute to sink its resources and efforts into. After hearing about the site from several sources, however—from others as well as the vice president—Visiliou had had the usual, quite expensive seismology tests done. The results had been mixed, but there clearly were evidences of habitation at levels that would make settlement of the site quite old.

The institute had not had sufficient resources to concentrate on both the Elea site and the one at Rizokarpaso. Lala Hatan and others had pressed them to concentrate on Rizokarpaso. For her part, Caitlyn had been unable in good faith to endorse the Rizokarpaso site over the one at Elea, which had insistently spoken to Caitlyn as an unusually rich archaeological site. But she had not become insistent in backing up her instincts. In the end Visiliou had decided to excavate at both sites at a somewhat slower than desirable level of effort.

And now, with Caitlyn and Andriko standing together out on an isolated and barren hillside on the Karpas Peninsula, the two realized that all of the institute's efforts and resources over the past six months had gone for naught. The site at Elea had been demolished beyond scientific usefulness, and now they had discovered that the Rizokarpaso site was false. It had been carefully salted with cheap replicas of pottery. They had been duped and misled. But why?

Both Andriko and Caitlyn had been called late during the previous evening and told that they needed to come to Rizokarpaso as soon as possible. The team on the site had encountered several confusing and suspicious things in their preliminary working of the site in which they cut a single, deep "plug" into the site to determine just how many layers of ancient habitation were involved. This was a new process being tried at sites where they were considering developing a special exhibition site, such as the one that had been pioneered at the nearby Bogaz site, where the different eras of history represented at a site were lifted and recreated on different floors of an exhibition hall adjacent to the actual excavation site. They said they were suspicious enough about what they had found that they needed the special skills of Caitlyn Koniotis as a carbon dater and they needed her expertise soon.

When Caitlyn and Andriko arrived in the early morning light, it toke little time for Caitlyn to discover that all of the items that had been unearthed were recently fashioned fakes. The site had been salted with fake artifacts.

As the sun rose in the sky and Andriko went off to tell his archaeologists to close down the project, Caitlyn's thoughts turned yet again to her estranged husband. Something very sinister was going on here. Caitlyn could not make herself believe that this was all being done just to put the archaeological institute out of business. It was much too expensive and intricate for that. But what was happening? It was almost as if someone had purposely diverted their attention to the Karpas Peninsula and discouraged their interest in the Morphou area just to keep them out of that region.

And what part was the Cypriot vice president playing in this? Everyone knew Lala Hatan was buying up land around Morphou and had been doing so for a decade. But why, then, would he be interested in keeping the archaeologists out of that canton? The area was economically depressed. It could only make sense for Lala Hatan to encourage any development possible for that region.

This was Takis's line of investigation. And where was he? Caitlyn asked herself. And was he avoiding taking an interest in the cases of archaeological sabotage just to spite her?

* * * *

Ann Wynette, the head of the U.S. Secret Service office of the American embassy in Nicosia, had also been disturbed very early that morning and was trying to get her body and mind in working order so that she could start taking care of the call she had just received from the States. The diminutive red head with the frizzy hair and purple fingernails sat on a stool in her orange robe and hung over—and onto—the breakfast bar, a cup of strong coffee in one hand and a cigarette in the other, as the cobwebs of her previous evening at the Navarino Wine Lodge were being brushed away so that she could think. The early morning market sounds coming from beyond the thick stone walls of her eighteenth-century old-town restored row house within the Venetian walls of Old Nicosia did not help her thought processes or her disposition one bit.

Where did they expect her to start looking on the flimsy evidence they had given her—and just what, exactly, was she looking for? She may have had too much wine to drink during the previous evening in celebration of her triumph on the local stage as Regina Giddens in Lillian Hellman's *The Little Foxes* with the Anglo-Cypriot Theatre, but her reasoning powers weren't impaired.

She cursed the high-level official in Washington, D.C., who had called her and had breathlessly described the attack on the Army Research Lab in Virginia's Shenandoah Valley at some length before Ann had managed to point out that this seemingly had very little to do with her job in Cyprus as coordinator for the Aegean and Middle East for the concerns of the U.S. Secret Service. She had awakened a bit, however, when the bureaucrat had told her that one of the weapons systems the army had been experimenting on might be headed toward her area.

"How close to my area?" Ann had asked.

"To Cyprus itself," had been the answer.

"And what is the evidence of that?" Ann asked with developing interest.

"A Cyprus Airline travel brochure on the island," had been the response.

"And you found this travel brochure in the hand of a dead terrorist at the site?" Ann queried sweetly.

"No, in a parking area on the mountain above the bombed subterranean facility."

And Ann had immediately lost interest again.

But the bureaucrat had persisted in his story and had very carefully told her that the attack had obviously been trumped up to look like some sort of lab accident but that the attackers had been seen escaping from the emergency exit shaft that opened onto the Skyline Drive above the facility. When the authorities had subsequently scoured the area around the Beaverbrook Lodge, they had found evidence from the light rain that had fallen on the mountain during the late afternoon that heavy vans had been parked in three different locations nearby. A young man from Front Royale had called in to report that he and his girlfriend had been sitting at one of these locations in the early evening, an overlook, and had seen a van parked almost in the trees. They had seen glimmers of lights from inside the vehicle when they first pulled in but the vehicle appeared to be empty when they left the lot.

The travel brochure had been found beside the van's tire tracks at this overlook. It had arrested the investigating authorities' attention not only because it was an unlikely place for such a brochure to be found—none of the police at the scene had ever even heard of Cyprus—but also because the brochure was in German.

Wynette had not been particularly impressed, but the next piece of apparently unrelated information had at least gotten her out of bed and headed in the direction of the coffee pot. The facility's commander, General Sarah Bristow, who was missing and presumed to be among the few persons who had died in the explosion, had, according to the records on recent telephone calls from the facility, tried to reach a firm in Switzerland just before the explosion.

Bristow had also had dinner with some high administration officials in Washington a couple of days previous to the attack in which she had wondered out loud about the identity of one of her new clients—a certain Sergey Stepanov, whose past had set off alarms in several security data banks and who had been connected with international crime and terrorism in Cyprus before. The computers seemed particularly upset because they had identified him as "presumed dead."

"The firm connected to both the telephone call and Sergey Stepanov was the Hartzel-Wegner armaments merchant," the Washington bureaucrat said smugly. "You have heard of that firm, have you not, Ms. Wynette? You have, I am sure, been reading the worldwide cables we've been sending."

Yes, Ann certainly had read the cables querying the activities of the Switzerland-based Hartzel-Wegner firm—its recent collection of interesting weapons materiel, including reports of queries for nuclear material, and the trips of its officials—with the identities of its top officials being very hazy—to Syria, Lebanon, Iraq, and Iran, all considered until just a few days ago, when there was a coup in Iran, to be supporters of international crime and terrorism.

What was the U.S. Army Research Lab doing dealing with the Hartzel-Wegner firm? Ann wondered. Wouldn't we ever learn not to be fighting international crime on the one hand while doing business with it on the other?

Her Washington superior's primary concern of the moment, however, was for the budding Middle East peace effort. He told her that the favorable coup in Iran had broken the log jam on the Middle East peace talks once again and that the U.S. administration was already heavily involved in bringing the Arab states of the region together once more with Israel in what promised this time to be successful talks that would bring peace to the region and at last put paid to the activities of the international terrorists in that area of the world.

The bottom line was that he wanted Wynette to watch for any evidence of one of the weapons systems on record as being developed at the Army Research Lab appearing in her region. Washington wanted to know what such a system was being procured for, who was doing the procuring, for what purpose, and what was the involvement, if any, of Hartzel-Wegner. And, oh yes, Washington wanted the whole effort stopped in its tracks and stopped quietly so that no fallout was felt in the developing Middle East peace process.

She had to admit to herself as she drank her second cup of coffee that, if there was any possibility that the Hartzel-Wegner firm was involved in the attack on the Army Research Lab, it must be involved in something very big and very serious that could only bring harm to her region of responsibility. But where to start?

That was the easiest answer. She would call the UN under secretary general for security affairs, Takis Koniotis. He could get the ball rolling for her, and she had blanket permission from Washington to work directly with UNICIS folks on such issues. She tried calling Takis at home but received no response.

Well, the UNICIS chief, Ellen Larkin, would be just as good. She tried calling Larkin's penthouse apartment overlooking Kyrenia harbor. No answer there either, so Wynette left a short voice mail explanation and a request for a continual UNICIS computer trace on Hartzel-Wegner, after which she got dressed and headed for the door en route to the American embassy. She would get hold of Koniotis or Larkin from work later in the morning.

As she reached the door, her secure telephone buzzed gently again. It was the bureaucrat once more, who, surprisingly, had called back to specifically direct her not to include the UNICIS organization in the search for the moment. The whole episode was much too sensitive to start bringing in foreign powers, he advised. Wynette couldn't understand why she was being encumbered this way from her best source of information, but she left the house glad that she hadn't been able to reach either Koniotis or Larkin after all.

* * * *

It was dark, damp, and gloomy in Switzerland, one time zone away from Cyprus, when Sergey Stepanov returned to Irina Lukenov's cottage outside of Lucerne. Still, Sergey had expected her to be awake already and for lights to be on in the house. Irina had always been an early riser.

But now the house was completely dark when he drove up to it, and her car wasn't in the drive. He was slightly disturbed at seeing a vehicle—a rental car, he had noted—at the side of the road a short distance from the house. One did not often see unfamiliar vehicles in this section of the country. Thus, Sergey was already at full attention when he approached the front door of the house. It was off the latch and was slightly open. He turned and returned to his own vehicle, which had been parked at the airport while he had been attending to business in the United States. He wanted to make it appear as if he had forgotten something in the trunk of his vehicle, but he really wanted to decide what to do. This didn't look good.

When Sergey burst through the French doors between the patio and the drawing room, he came very close to wiping out the Iranian agent who had been sent to warn him that documents on the Homewrecker system and the connection with Hartzel-Wegner had been lost into unfriendly hands during the recent coup in Tehran. The agent had been specifically instructed to deliver this information to Sergey and Sergey only and by word of mouth. The agent didn't tell Stepanov an earlier attempt to reach him at Heathrow Airport had failed, because the agent himself didn't know that. If he had known it, he might also have been curious about what had happened to the earlier agent after he had been seized at Heathrow, but the details of the agent's death probably would have dampened the second agent's enthusiasm for the assignment.

This disturbing information would change matters significantly, Stepanov mused after he had disposed of the body of the agent by stuffing him in the trunk of the rental vehicle. Someone from the office would be by to pick up the vehicle and ensure that neither it nor the body surfaced again.

There was no time now to transport the trigger device materiel by a safer route. It had gone to the French city of Marseilles, where it was to have been loaded onto a yacht that would sail seemingly aimlessly around the Mediterranean until it reached the Cypriot harbor of Kyrenia. Now the materiel would have to go direct.

Sergey sent the necessary signal to Marseilles and placed a telephone call to Beirut so that the information he had received from Tehran could be passed on to the Hartzel-Wegner office there. This accomplished, Sergey realized he was hungry. It was only then that he remembered that Irina had not been in evidence when he arrived. When he reached the kitchen, he was surprised to see congealed fruit jelly in the sink and rotting in a large pan.

For a few moments Stepanov considered the mildly interesting possibility that the Iranian had killed Irina. But she was not to be found in a search of the house, and Sergey lost faith that she would be found as soon as he saw that her suitcase and many of her clothes were gone as well.

Then he remembered that she had been upset with him when he had left. She had criticized him for involving her son Pavel in his business schemes. What exactly did she know about his activities? Sergey had come to think of Irina as just the cook and housekeeper. Could he have let her learn more than she should about the Hartzel-Wegner operation? He had to try harder in the future to remember that she herself had once been an active Hizballah fighter. Perhaps it had been unwise to leave her here when he had left for America. When she came back maybe he needed to take care of that little loose thread. But then he would have to find another cook and housekeeper and maybe Pavel wouldn't be too happy.

"Well, first things first," Sergey muttered to no one in particular as he walked back to the phone. When he had gotten through to Irina's other son, Uri, in Zurich, Stepanov was told that Uri had not heard from his mother recently either. The man was obviously telling the truth, because he seemed quite disturbed that the woman had taken her suitcase and left the house in the middle of a cooking project.

"Stay right there, Sergey," Uri said down the line, "I will drive over and we can decide how to proceed on finding her. Is Pavel there, or do you know where he's gone?"

"Yes, sure, I will be here when you arrive," Stepanov responded cheerily, "and, no, Pavel isn't here. Perhaps he and Irina are together."

"Yes, perhaps. Just remain there. I'm coming right over."

But, of course, when Uri and the police arrived, Stepanov was long gone. And he knew that Pavel was not with Irina. Pavel had gone to Moscow to close the deal on the nuclear materiel for the Homewrecker warhead. Irina would never be enough of a fool to try to return to Moscow. Most everyone she had known in Moscow thought that she was already dead, and those that knew she was alive would be quite willing to change that status if she ever again showed up in Moscow.

* * * *

Takis Koniotis's telephone was still ringing when he got out of the shower, but it was silent once more before he could get to it. The caller had not left a message. This was just as well because Takis had promised Andriko Visiliou that he would helicopter out to the Karpas Peninsula this morning to sift

161

through the salted Rizokarpaso research site for clues into the strange happenings at the archaeological digs on the island. He was just as convinced as Caitlyn had become that the preparation of the Rizokarpaso site and the destruction of the Elea site were more significant than mere vindictiveness toward the archaeological institute. His keen investigative mind was, as a matter of fact, already trying to weave these happenings in with the explosions at the Turkish village of Gunyeli and the Greek village of Galata.

Immediately after sitting down to his breakfast to read the morning's edition of *Semerini*, Takis was back on his feet and headed for the police department's helipad. Demetris Mattas's provocative column had poured fire on the already explosive charges and threats that were being exchanged between the Greek and Turkish communities over the explosions. Takis could already see that the law enforcement forces had no time to solve these explosion cases. It was either finding a neutral explanation for the explosions quickly or silencing people like Mattas until they could find the solution—or both. And, there continued to be a little voice at the back of Takis's brain telling him that the troubles with the archaeological digs were the key to this particular puzzle.

Chapter Ten

Ann Wynette was sitting in her American embassy office in the Engomi suburb of Nicosia and staring at a peculiar little square window on the wall behind her desk, but not really seeing the window. Rather she was consumed by contemplating a dilemma of the first dimension. What to do with the information she had just surfaced.

Ann Wynette had left her small village house in the center of the old walled city that morning with a determination to find out more about this Hartzel-Wegner arms merchant company and about its activities in Cyprus and the Middle East region. But the directive she had received from Washington had posed a formidable obstacle to her.

Her first instinct had been to call Ellen Larkin for research help from the UN international security database, but it had been a good thing that her call had not gone through, since a follow-up signal had put her on her own and proscribed her from contacting UNICIS. She had received this restriction in spite of the fact that the computers of the world's reputably most complete and research-responsive data banks on world affairs, international crime, terrorism, and intelligence were located right here in Cyprus, at the Morphou headquarters of the UN's international security directorate. The UNICIS system was considered so good because it was the only central data bank into which the classified police and security ministry computers of the UN states fed.

It was Ann herself who limited the uniqueness and superiority of the UNICIS computer systems to the "reputedly" level, however, and her government's curb on her use of UNICIS had only served to whet her appetite to take the UNICIS computer system on in a contest of research skills.

Ann Wynette, with her diminutive stature, her frizzy red hair, her somewhat unfortunate—to some—choice in clothing color combination and style, and her nervous habit with chewing gum at a demented cow rate, didn't look all that brilliant. But she *was* brilliant. She was, firstly, a first-rate actress—as those who had tickets to the previous night's performance of the Anglo-Cypriot Theatre production could attest. Her acting ability had, in fact, helped her to worm her way into the Cypriot archaeological scene some three years earlier as a visiting archaeologist, a subject she had known next to nothing about, and it had helped her to participate in the uncovering of major plots to flood Europe with counterfeit euro notes and U.S.

dollars and to help foil a murder plot against the Cypriot president.

She also was one of the U.S. Secret Service's best field agents.

But more germane to the current situation, she had been a brilliant mathematician at the University of Michigan and she now was a genius at computer search techniques. Because of this, she had often wanted to have the chance to spar with the UNICIS computer system. Her theory was that the ever-expanding GlobeNet worldwide computer networks with their sophisticated search engines could uncover information from publicly available sources that rivaled that of the closed-data banks UNICIS system.

Today Ann had spent all morning and past the lunch hour proving that she was right. But now she was almost sorry she had taken the time to challenge the UNICIS system. She really should verify what she had found with the UNICIS system, because this was just too explosive for her to be proven to be wrong. But her superiors had specified that UNICIS should not be brought into this yet, and, under the circumstances, she felt she could hardly take this information to Takis Koniotis and Ellen Larkin anyway—at least not without substantive proof that went beyond the circumstantial evidence she had before her.

She was saved from her dilemma by the buzzer.

The embassy switchboard operator put through an urgent telephone call for her from the company that managed her house during those long spells that she was away from the island on business. A pipe had burst in her kitchen. This had been reported to the management company by one of her neighbors, and the repairmen were on their way to her house. Perhaps she wanted to be there when they arrived to let them in and to survey the extent of the danger.

Damn right, she thought. She was almost grateful to be released from her dilemma concerning what she should do about what she had put together on the Hartzel-Wegner company. However, she was somewhat perplexed as she skipped down the embassy stairs—the elevators once again being out of order—as she had just recently had all the piping in her old, restored house replaced.

It was too bad that Wynette hadn't given more thought to the logic of her pipes having burst as she roared toward home in her Mazda Miata convertible. Her mind was still possessed with the dilemma of who to tell concerning her discoveries about Hartzel-Wegner and when to tell them as she whipped between the Cyprus Museum and the Municipal Theatre and rounded the "Billy the Bomber" circle—which, with its statue of a youth hurling a grenade, had gained its informal name in honor of the Cypriot lad who wiped out a nest of British soldiers in the fight for independence—in front of the Paphos Gate into the city, and started around the outer perimeter of the dry moat around the old city of Nicosia.

After clearing past the convergence of the city's main shopping streets at Eleftheria Square, she started her cruise toward the street breaching the wall at the old Famagusta Gate. This historical gate, one of three original entrances to the walled city, still connected the inner city with the base of the dry moat in the shadow of the Caraffa Bastion, which now, like the Famagusta Gate itself, provided the base of the municipal cultural center.

As Ann rounded on the Caraffa Bastion, her eyes focused on the outdoor theater located in the moat at the outer entrance to the Famagusta Gate. She had long wanted to play that theater.

And then she got a closer look at the amphitheatre and got, at last, to have her dramatic scene at the Famagusta outdoor stage, as a black Mercedes overtook her to the right and bumped her Miata across the road, over the wall separating the walk way and the dry moat, and to the rocky moat bed below. However, her exit wasn't quite as dramatic as she might have wished. Since her vehicle was one of the new ones operating on solar power, she didn't go out in the blaze of glory that she had always envisioned for herself. She simply exited the vehicle before it hit the ground on the top of her and broke her lovely neck in the process.

The Mercedes stopped. Two men got out and ran over to the wall overlooking the moat. It was with a real sense of accomplishment that they returned to their vehicle, provided a detailed report of the scene below to the amused woman hidden in the interior of the vehicle's rear seat, and sped off into the suburbs outside the walls.

Ann Wynette wasn't missing much at home. Her pipes were just fine, and no neighbor would have subsequently owned up to having reported otherwise even if asked.

* * * *

Everything was just lovely in the afternoon sun in the spot of England known as the Episkopi Sovereign Base Area on the south central coast of Cyprus just to the west of the port city of Limassol. The very British-style housing areas of Kensington and Gibraltar on the ridges of cliffs projecting into the Mediterranean were quiet during the afternoon siesta. White stucco, Tudor-style houses of uniform design, with red tiled roofs and blue window trim were nestled in lush stands of oleander and bougainvillea. No one, however, was on the avenues winding through these officers' quarters housing, and the last of the gardeners had long since escaped into the dim interiors of the buildings to laze under slowly turning ceiling fans, swig on their gin and tonics, and escape into the romantic and steamy world of their Barbara Cartland–vintage Romance novels.

All of the outdoor activity of the base area, one of three on the island for which Britain had retained sovereignty in the 1960 granting of independence but which, like the other bases, was being slowly whittled away by reclaiming of territory by the Cyprus Federated State, was concentrated in Happy Valley. This verdant, green-lawned patch at the base of a gorge leading into the Mediterranean was the sports center for the base. Located at the very hub of the base operations and housing areas, Happy Valley contained polo, rugby, cricket, and football fields and a small golf course—all of the amenities to help keep bored British soldiers in the base and away from the pubs of Limassol, where they tended to earn Britain a bad reputation with their pugilistic and generally boyish behavior.

The only sound heard over the base area this afternoon was the sound of a polo ball being struck in the valley below, a sound that reverberated off the surrounding cliff walls and into the quiet officers' quarters on the ridges of the surrounding cliffs.

Fiona Burton-Richardson, wife of the headmaster at the base's St. John's school and long-time resident of Cyprus, where her father had once served as the colonial deputy military governor, rose from her chair in a house overlooking both Happy Valley and the Mediterranean on Isle of Wight Drive in the Gibraltar housing compound. Above the sound of the polo ball, Fiona had heard another sound, the sound of a vehicle approaching up the drive and slowing as it approached her house.

It must be Ginger Patterson. She was a bit early, but Ginger was unpredictable. However, to Fiona's delight, Ginger also was thoroughly entertaining and not prone to taking on airs.

Fiona and Ginger had first met each other in Brussels some thirty years earlier, when both had been married to British military officers assigned to NATO headquarters. Fiona had not liked Ginger in those days. She had found the woman to be deeply opinionated, scathing in her comments on her acquaintances to their faces as well as to their backs, and, on the whole, very disagreeable. Ginger, however, had also been terribly sophisticated and had always managed to be the center of attention with her beauty and her wit.

Fiona, then much the younger woman and highly impressionable, had always found herself to be unwillingly drawn to the other woman. In later years, after both woman had moved to new husbands—Fiona to the St. John's administrator and Ginger to a newspaper political columnist—and to Cyprus, they had resumed their acquaintance. However, it wasn't until Ginger had changed and had become more human and caring that they had become deep friends.

And they had forged a friendship that had survived Ginger's widowhood from the newspaper columnist, followed by her marriage to and widowhood from the UNICIS scientist John Patterson. The close, easy relationship had even weathered Ginger's enrichment and worldwide acclaim by her inheritance of the solar power storage technology that had enabled the development of the entire world to forge ahead.

Ginger had remained a true friend in spite of her new position in the international business arena, and she often drove down from her Bermuda-style pink stucco mountain-top Limassol home to the nearby Episkopi sovereign base for a quiet, innocently chatty afternoon with her old friend.

It was, thus, with genuine pleasure, that Fiona moved to the entry door of her cliff-top officers' quarters to welcome her guest to relieve the boredom of the lazy afternoon—only to be knocked back and pulverized in the blaze of the explosion that obliterated both the Gibraltar housing section of the Episkopi Sovereign Base Area and the polo game in Happy Valley, as the cliff collapsed onto the manicured green lawns below.

* * * *

Ismail flashed a smile of triumph as he ordered the long gun barrel lowered and the roof closed of the corrugated tin building. Hidden from view from the town of Morphou, located just to the west, by a rock outcropping, the maneuver was sure to go unnoticed by the local residents.

The telephone call from the town of Kolossi, located between Limassol and Episkopi and famous for its Knights of St. John's castle keep and for being the first wine-growing area on the island, had just reported that they had almost reached the sea this time. When the new triggering device arrived, Ismail was sure that the Homewrecker test weapon being developed at this hidden location would be able to manage not only the distance but also the precision targeting required to reach Tel Aviv from the Golan Heights. Also, the nuclear device they planned to use from the Golan Heights would enable it to far surpass the destruction zone they had managed to cause here with the tests in Cyprus.

Although Ismail was mildly sorry that one of the test firings had obliterated the Turkish village of Gunyeli and that one had fizzled so badly that it landed not far from the launch zone, he was delighted that subsequent tests had hit on the Greek mountain village of Galata and the base area of the British devils. All four bombings had served to meet the secondary objectives of the sponsors of this project here in Cyprus, the fomenting of ethnic differences within Cyprus so that it could return to its usefulness as a cradle for the service of Islamic fundamentalist terrorism.

His work here was almost finished. And none too soon, from what he gathered. They were all being pressed to have the Golan Heights weapon operational within a matter of days. All he needed now was one successful test firing with the triggering device Stepanov was supposed to provide. He knew the nuclear warhead had not arrived in Syria yet, but that was someone else's problem. That could not be tested; they would just have to go on faith that it would work when fired.

He heard the vehicle approach almost as soon as he received word that she had arrived in her shiny black Mercedes. This was good timing. She would be very pleased with their progress. Ismail found himself patting down his hair and checking the presentability of his clothing even though he knew he did not stand a chance with her.

* * * *

Uri Lukenov changed his mind for the hundredth time as he flicked his cigarette off the shallow balcony opening off Frieda's bedroom, arcing it so that it seemed to be swan diving toward the dark waters of the Limmat River at the base of the hill. The countess stirred in the mammoth bed in the room's shadows and took in a sharp breath as she caught sight of her lover illuminated by the early morning sunshine in the French window of her yellow-stuccoed miniature Baroque hill-side palace. The young, blond Russian giant with the massive, muscled chest and slim waist was standing with his back to her. He had started to dress before the pensive mood had taken him to the window high above the wakening city of Zurich below, but he had gotten no further than pulling on his bikini briefs.

He had been moody and noncommunicative, although, as ever, polite and almost sufficiently attentive to her needs for the past few days. Frieda Piccard von Meisse, the manager of the Zurich office of the Piccard shipping conglomerate, could tell that her relationship with the assistant that her cousin, Andre, had sent her was at a crossroads. She could feel him withdrawing from her, but she didn't know why. He had known she was married, but he had also known that hers was a marriage of convenience, more a friendship and business arrangement than anything else. He had never seemed to be interested in any more of a permanent relationship than she herself had been. But ever since Uri had gone to Lucerne for the day, he had been remote and a bit on edge with her.

She had the urge now to rise and join him at the window and to bring his moodiness to a head—forcing him either to lash out at her or to make love her there, on the balcony high on the hill just below the Kunsthaus, the art gallery, and just above the spires of the Grossmunster cathedral. But she was afraid. She didn't really want to lose him. He was such a fine man. And, more important, he was a fantastic lover. She was both mesmerized and paralyzed. She couldn't make a move. All she could do was lay there, drinking him in and making love to him with her eyes.

As he watched the bustle of Zurich's main commercial street, the Bahnhof Strasse, across the Limmat, Uri was once more organizing in his mind what he had learned at the offices of Hartzel-Wegner in Lucerne. Making the most of both his relationship to the firm's manager, Sergey Stepanov, and its executive administrator, his own brother, Pavel, and of their absence from Switzerland, Uri had done enough sleuthing at the arms firm, along with what he had already known, to piece together the rudiments of the Homewrecker project and its testing site activities in Cyprus. He had to assume that his mother, Irina, had also pieced the story together and was even now in or headed for Cyprus. If so, she was headed for danger, as she was wanted there for her earlier involvement with terrorists. Of course, he himself was also wanted in Cyprus on similar charges, but he wasn't giving a moment's thought to any danger to himself.

Uri couldn't decide whether to stay here and just keep Andre Piccard, who was already headquartered in Cyprus, apprised of the developments or to go to Cyprus himself to try to save his mother and brother from further harm. He looked out, across the Quai-Brucke bridge at the mouth of the Limmat and toward the western edge of the Zurich See. What he saw there seemed to cause him to make up his mind. A large ferry was sailing out onto the lake from the pier at the foot of the Bahnhof Strasse. He would dress and telephone Andre—he didn't want to chance the paper trail of an e-mail—but he also would be on the noon flight to Cyprus.

Sensing that he was being watched from within the room, Uri sighed and took one more look out over the comfortably stuffy banking capital of Europe. Then he slowly returned to the bed. He knew he had been neglecting the countess these past few days as he was struggling with his thoughts. He had a good two hours to make it up to her before he had to set off for the airport.

Just before he left for his flight, Uri telephoned the Piccard offices in Limassol, Cyprus. He couldn't reach Andre directly, but one of the French businessman's secretaries assured Uri that he would be met at Nicosia Airport upon his arrival. Uri was met, as promised, but it wasn't by Andre or anyone else representing the Piccard holdings. As he approached the green line through customs, he was pulled aside by a pair of burly policemen, his hands were cuffed behind his back, and he was whisked quickly and professionally through a side door. His fellow passengers on the flight didn't even notice his unexpected departure.

Chapter Eleven

At Pavel Lukenov's command, the Russian mafia prince's small jet, the services of which had been thrown in on the nuclear warhead deal, banked gently to the left above the western coastline running into the foothills of Cyprus's Troodos Mountains. Was that a flash of light he had seen near Morphou on the island's central plain? He had been trying to discern what could be seen of the secret weapons testing site, hidden in an old warehouse, from the air. He had not intended to land in Cyprus on his way from Moscow to Damascus, but he had been asked to make this flyover and check out the effectiveness of the site's camouflaging.

No, they were too high and too far away for him to discern much of anything. He asked the jet's pilot to dip further north and further down in altitude. He still couldn't make the site out, but what had that flash been? It had come from where he would have expected to see the warehouse area.

Pavel twitched hard against the seat harness in surprise as the jet's radio began to crackle. The pilot talked into his head microphone and then turned to Pavel and shrugged, muttering that maybe it was just the Cypriot authorities asking why the jet had left its travel path. He couldn't understand what they were saying, however. It must be Greek, although he didn't understand Greek—and it didn't sound Greek to him. The pilot murmured in irritation that he thought English was used for in-flight communications in this region. He *did* speak English, and this wasn't English.

Pavel grabbed for the headset in controlled panic. The pilot didn't know what he knew—that the two large crates in the hold that the pilot thought merely concealed arms and counterfeit U.S. banknotes actually contained barely concealed nuclear warheads. They simply could not land for inspection anywhere this side of Damascus. As Pavel set the communication systems earphones over his head, his breath deflated in relief. It was Arabic. Someone was talking in Arabic, and the excited voice was apparently addressing itself to Pavel's jet. It was repeating their false Greek fuselage numbers and asking them to respond—in Arabic. Luckily Pavel spoke Arabic, as the best customers of Hartzel-Wegner were in the Middle East.

Lukenov was further relieved when he realized that it was the Homewrecker test site that was trying to connect with

178

them. He assured them that he was unable to pick the warehouse compound out from the air, but they seemed more excited to tell him something else. By now the jet was above the monorail line that ran from the southern commercial port city of Limassol up the center of the island to the capital city of Nicosia on the island's central plain. It was chancy, but Pavel knew they had to check it out. He leaned over and instructed the pilot to circle the jet to the south over the eastern end of the Troodos and to fly back along the southern coast of the island toward the southwest. The Cypriot authorities be damned. He knew that they had no aircraft that could match this small jet in speed. Most countries in the area didn't. That's why the jet hadn't been seized before now. And, if it came to a dogfight situation, this supposedly innocuous personal jet had a few surprises of its own.

There it was. To the west of the sprawling city of Limassol. A whole area of the southern coast, where the British sovereign base of Episkopi was located, was afire. From the air, it seemed to cover almost a perfect circle of land centering on a long and wide gully and stopping almost exactly at the water's edge. The brush fires that had been set off in the high stands of withered grasses and trees, now already dried out in the wake of the end of the short rainy season, were steadily expanding the circle.

As they flew closer, Pavel could see that the explosion had engulfed the center of the base area, its epicenter being the once-green and manicured Happy Valley sports complex.

This was quite satisfactory. More than satisfactory even. The test was supposed to put the payload in the sea off the southern coast, but it had reached far enough for the testing purposes, and it had wiped out a nest of British colonialists. How very fitting. From the air, the devastation was very impressive. And this had been a payload of just conventional explosives. How much more and wider the destruction would be using these nuclear devices under his feet!

Pavel reported his find back to the eagerly attentive launch site across the Troodos range to the north and then gave the pilot instructions to head on back to the south, toward the Syrian coast.

As he handed the earphones back to the pilot, the radio came alive again. This time even he could tell that the communication was in Greek. Angry Greek. *Very* angry Greek, which switched to more reasonable English when the pilot finally answered. The pilot smoothly explained to ground control that they had seen the explosion in Episkopi and had just been flying by to observe what was happening and would now be on their way. Ground control would have none of that. All aircraft were to come down at Larnaca immediately. There had been a massive explosion on the southern coast, one of several of late, and all aircraft had to come down until the authorities were comfortable that they were not involved in the incident.

The pilot shrugged to Pavel and started a descent toward Larnaca, located to the east of Limassol on the southern coast. Pavel gripped the pilot's arm, however, and whispered the true nature of the cargo in the hold in his ear, including its relationship to the destruction they had just seen below.

Pavel had to admire the other Russian's nerves of steel. Although the sweat started to pour off his brow, he didn't permit the panic to affect his speech. Speaking very slowly in English, he began to spin out his description of the damage they had seen at Episkopi to an enthralled Cypriot ground crew. At the same time, he edged the jet out over the water and off the straight path onto the Larnaca runway. He continued to spin his yarn right through the first voiced objection to the deviation in his flight path and, at the second sharp command, he cut his mike and turned the jet directly out over the Mediterranean to the southeast, toward the Syrian coast.

The Cypriots didn't even bother to try to scramble their aircraft. They knew the jet would be in someone else's territorial airspace before their aircraft could even get airborne. But whose airspace? The Cypriot authorities quickly contacted the Israeli authorities to warn them that there had been a bombing in Cyprus and an aircraft that possibly was involved was headed in their direction.

The Israelis probably would have caught the Russian mafia jet, and thus ended a serious threat to their existence that they didn't even yet know as a mortal threat, if Pavel's associates hadn't planned the jet's flight very carefully and if the Israelis were not as susceptible to the element of surprise as is anyone else. Coordinating their flight with their comrades in Lebanon, the Hizballah, Pavel and the pilot were under only limited threat from the Israeli air force, which, just then, was busy countering a now-rare but very strong Hizballah mortar attack on Israeli settlements in the Lebanese border area.

The Israelis were, however, able to scramble a few fighters to find the Russian jet. And they *did* find the aircraft, but not until it was in Syrian airspace and starting its descent into Damascus. That didn't stop the Israelis from pursuing, however. But the sun got in their way—a purposeful move on the part of the Russian aircraft's talented pilot—and they lost sight of their quarry. But their quarry did not lose sight of them and used that opportunity to deliver the ultimate surprise. Suddenly, the civilian aircraft with Greek markings launched an air-to-air missile from one of its disguised weapons pods and an Israeli fighter was hit. By the time the Israeli planes had recovered, the Syrian air force had scrambled, and the two Israeli fighters were streaking for home and a third was limping toward the Mediterranean, where it could ditch over neutral territory.

Pavel's aircraft had been expected in Damascus and the festivities commenced as soon as he had touched down and the jet's cargo had been gently unloaded and wheeled away.

* * * *

Trevor Hawkins had just been standing there, paralyzed in shock, his paint brush suspended between palette and canvas. He made a more interesting picture in this pose than the abstract designs he had been slapping on canvas that in his eyes—and, admittedly, in the eyes of a legion of admirers—would pass for the spirit and soul of the town of Morphou, set in the sweep of the Mediterranean in the distance.

Trevor Hawkins, the flamboyant British illustrator and wine and fine dining writer for both the in-flight glossy magazine of Cyprus Airways and the in-room glossy magazine for the island's Sunotel resort hotel chain, was a legend in his own right. Having settled in Cyprus following a successful journalistic career on London's Fleet Street in pursuit of sand, sea, sun, and handsome young Greek men in the last half of his life's century, the short, rotund, rosy-cheeked Hawkins had taken to painting late in life. To his surprise he had been an instantaneous success in the art world in Cyprus, and this success had given him entree into the island's upper crust and a blind tolerance for his sexual proclivities. He simply had been too urbane, witty, and deliciously catty to be resisted in the salons of Nicosia, Limassol, and Paphos.

Truth be known, however, painting was his third career and Hawkins had never given up his first career, which was with British Military Intelligence. His new life had proven to be a perfect cover for his real activities. His intent was never questioned. Few doors were closed to him. He could leave Cyprus at will and on whatever short notice his Intelligence duties required on the pretense of attending or being featured in an art exhibit or collecting material for a magazine article. And he could, just as he had done today, spend hours in unnoticed surveillance accompanied only by canvas, paints, and brushes.

He had come to Morphou for two purposes. One was to check out for the British the destruction at the Elea archaeological site, beside which he now stood transfixed. And the other was to try to piece together bits of information that had come in to the British Military Intelligence contingent at the Episkopi Base concerning the two bombings that had occurred in the country. Rumors had spread that these were connected either with international terrorism or with a resurgence of domestic ethnic fighting. Neither of these possibilities was pleasing to the British, who had heretofore depended on their three sovereign base areas on the island to support their military interests and activities throughout the eastern Mediterranean and the Levant and whose presence in Cyprus had come under new attack in both Cyprus and at home in Britain.

But the rumors of the bombing activity had mentioned the Morphou area too often to be ignored. So Hawkins and his paint box had been dispatched to take a look.

Hawkins had not found anything of interest at the Elea archaeological site and, following a five-hour stint of painting and observing, he had not seen much of anything that could be connected to bombing activity either. That is until his gaze was pulled away from the vista of Morphou and the sea to the northwest as he was replenishing the magenta on his brush to capture the ever-present bougainvillea. His attention was drawn in this direction just as the roof of a dusty, supposedly derelict warehouse a bit to the northwest was rolled back, a huge gun barrel was raised, and a big boom sounded, accompanied by a flashing light.

Hawkins wasn't frozen for long. The sound of a low-flying jet overhead brought him out of his trance. He reached for his mobile phone and punched in the numbers for the private office of Brigadier James Tymes-Smyth, the commander of both the Episkopi Sovereign Base and the British Military Intelligence contingent on the island. The call was answered at once in a brisk voice by the brigadier. But, as Hawkins was starting to tell the commander about what he had just found, there was a loud commotion on the other end, Hawkins heard a strangled "My God!" and the connection was broken.

While starting to dial again, Hawkins looked back at the warehouse compound and noticed that there was a sleek Mercedes sedan parked near the building that he had not seen. But, to his consternation, he also noticed something else. There were men leaving the compound. Armed men. And they appeared to be fanning out toward the surrounding countryside. Hawkins had had just enough time to gather his painting supplies and hide in the collapsed ruins of the bombed crater at the Elea site before one of the men reached the rim of the crater and settled in for a stay. Luckily, he didn't seem interested in what was in the Elea ruins but was watching the roadway below. Also luckily Hawkins had parked his car in a village several miles to the west.

It was several hours before the watcher had returned to the warehouse compound and Hawkins felt safe enough to try to connect with Episkopi again. He could not reach Tymes-Smyth, who was out helping with an emergency on the base, and was only able to keep the brigadier's aide on the line long enough to give him a sketchy idea of, what he had seen near Morphou. Unfortunately, the aide had been under a security ban to tell anyone about the nature of the Episkopi emergency and he had also been too rattled to see the possible connection of what

Hawkins was telling him—or even to get all that Hawkins was telling him on paper clearly.

By the time Tymes-Smyth had received Hawkins's message, Military Intelligence was unable to raise their agent on his mobile telephone.

* * * *

Ginger Hamilton had been just as paralyzed as Trevor Hawkins had been by the testing of the Homewrecker gun. As she had driven past the Greco-Roman ruins at Curium on the southern coast road and had reached the signpost for the Episkopi garrison near the site of the ancient Temple of Apollo, the world exploded in front of her, and her new convertible plowed off the road and into the brush. Luckily, she had veered off toward the right, on the landward side, however, as the road passed by a nasty cliff down to the sea on the other side at that point.

Ginger had been nearing her journey's end to visit her friend Fiona Burton-Richardson in her cliff-side house above Happy Valley. One moment Ginger was humming pleasantly to herself and devising juicy gossip to try to scandalize the wife of the school headmaster and the next moment she was hemmed in front and sides by foam bags and feeling the searing heat reach out to her from where the Episkopi officers' quarters had serenely stood only moments before.

For some reason Ginger knew in an instant what had happened. And this was the second massive bombing she had missed by seconds and circumstance. It was almost as if someone was targeting her purposely. It also was like some unforeseen force was protecting her.

But if someone was targeting her, what had she done? Recently, that is. All of her past sins started to race through her mind. She started to tremble and to giggle and cry at the same time. On top of everything else, she had lost her hat and there was a gripping pain in her chest. She was still trembling, giggling, and crying softly to herself a half an hour later when emergency crews found her and bundled her off toward the Limassol General Hospital.

* * * *

Uri was lucky—indeed, all of the "good guys" were lucky—that the United Nations security affairs official, Takis Koniotis, was paying a visit to the police authorities at the Nicosia International Airport at the time of the explosion at the Episkopi Sovereign Base that had taken place almost simultaneously with the seizure of Uri Lukenov as his flight arrived from Zurich. In the middle of their discussions with

Takis, the officials had heard of the bombing and the UN official had politely withdrawn to the Customs Police section of the airport while the higher-level authorities took stock of the situation. There apparently was also a concern with a nonresponding aircraft in the Larnaca Airport airspace that was adding drama to the occasion.

Koniotis himself was deep in thought, contemplating the bombing of the British base, as he walked into the Customs office, only to be jolted back into the present by a visage from the past. And a very weary face it was as well.

A few years previously Uri Lukenov and his mother had been implicated in an international counterfeiting scheme in Cyprus in which Koniotis had become embroiled while ostensibly on vacation in Cyprus from his UN Headquarters job that had then been centered in New York City. Uri and his mother had been whisked away from the island by the shipping magnate Andre Piccard while under an arrest order. It had subsequently been discovered that Irina Lukenov had principally been trying to escape the counterfeiters after having betrayed them and that Uri had only been trying to find and protect his mother. But the arrest order had never been dropped.

Someone had warned the authorities that the wanted man was arriving on the flight from Zurich, and when Uri had finally convinced the authorities to call the Piccard shipping offices in Limassol to verify that he was an employee of that firm, the Limassol office had declined to do so. Uri had not been all that surprised. He had not been able to get through to his old friend Andre Piccard and, for his own protection, Uri could understand that his employment in the Zurich office would not have been general knowledge in Cyprus, which he had escaped as a fugitive on a Piccard ship. The Customs Police had pushed Uri off to a corner to cool his heels until they had time to decide what to do with him next.

Not long thereafter Takis Koniotis showed up and solved their problem. He recognized Uri, and Uri was disconcerted enough concerning his situation to unload all of the concerns about Stepanov's activities, the Hartzel-Wegner firm, a long-range gun possibly being tested in Cyprus for use somewhere else, and the disappearance of his mother onto the willing and now very much enlightened international police chief.

Koniotis could see many pieces of the puzzle fitting into place now, and what he heard gave him, as the UN security chief, at least shared jurisdiction in the investigation. Quickly and smoothly taking charge in the airport Customs Police office, aided by the fact that he had once been the very popular chief of the Cypriot national police forces, Koniotis placed calls to the offices of both Interior Minister Maria Solonos and current Police Chief Ahmad Jallud, both of whom quickly patched him to the mobile telephones of their respective chiefs, who were already headed by separate vehicles to the southern coast bombing site.

Both of his old friends immediately saw the importance of what Koniotis was piecing together and its relevance to the recent bombings in the country, and the three agreed to meet privately and quietly at Koniotis's residence in Nicosia the next morning to take stock of the situation and to merge their investigations. After talking with Solonos and Jallud, Koniotis also tried to call Ellen Larkin, the chief of UNICIS, in Morphou, but he was told that she had left the country on short notice and wouldn't be back for a few days. Having reached the chief of the UNICIS computer lab, Stuart Claymore, instead, Koniotis directed the brilliant computer researcher to take Larkin's place at his home the next morning.

While he had been on the telephone with Maria Solonos, Koniotis had also arranged to have the charges against Uri Lukenov dropped, and he now invited the young Russian to stay with him at his Nicosia residence and to help with the investigation. Lukenov seemed excited at the prospect, but he also seemed to be holding back on accepting the offer.

"It's no trouble, Uri, really," Koniotis pressed. "I am living alone now and could use the company. And you've uncovered so much about what is happening with this Hartzel-Wegner monster that I would like to have you nearby. You may actually know more about the issue than you or we realize."

"Yes, I'd very much like to help with the investigation, but . . ."

"But you feel you must concentrate on finding your mother and taking her out of harm's way," Koniotis completed Lukenov's thought for him. "That's your concern, isn't it?"

"Well, yes, of course. Well, at least a big part of it."

"I think we can provide the best help possible in trying to locate your mother," Koniotis declared.

And then he promptly set in motion an Immigration Service search of the files to see if Irina Lukenov had entered the country on any of the names she was known to have used in the past when she was connected with the Hizballah terrorists. The next day, he would direct a more extensive and deeper search in the comprehensive UNICIS computer banks.

"There," he said after clicking off the telephone. "That's your mother taken care of—at least the best we can do for now. I presume your other concern is for Sergey Stepanov?"

"Oh, God no!" Uri exclaimed. "I have no concerns about that scum other than to see his activities stopped in their tracks. No, my other concern is for my brother, Pavel. I'm afraid he's involved in Hartzel-Wegner up to his neck, and I want him stopped as well. But, he *is* my brother. I can't not worry about him."

"I understand," Koniotis responded gently. "We can't make any promises about your brother, of course, if he is directly involved in constructing and delivering this weapon. But wouldn't it be better if we found him rather than letting this spin out to however the terrorists will deal with him? Either way, whether the weapon is delivered or found and destroyed, it is unlikely that your brother will live a day beyond his usefulness to the terrorists. You know that that's how they work. Don't you want to help us find him?"

"Yes, I suppose you are right," Uri responded quietly following a moment's thought. "That being the case, I would be happy to stay with you and join in the investigation. But could we try contacting Andre Piccard again before we leave? He should know I am in Cyprus and be given some sort of idea why I'm here. I had told him something of my worry a few days ago."

Koniotis tried, both at Andre's office and at his various residences in Cyprus, but he was no more successful in connecting with the business executive than the Customs Police had been. He mused briefly on whether the absences of both Ellen Larkin and Andre Piccard could be related. They had been a real "item" for some time, but he had noticed a certain tension in their relationship of late. He certainly hoped they would clear up whatever problems they had. They obviously were in love with each other.

Chapter Twelve

Ellen Larkin awoke to the morning light streaming off the Mediterranean Sea and into the windows of the large suite of the Saladin Intercontinental Hotel on the seafront corniche of the revitalized Beirut city center. She stretched luxuriously in the silken sheets of the massive four poster and once again pinched herself for assurance that this wasn't all just a delicious dream. She felt relaxed and at peace for the first time since Andre had asked her to marry him. Mrs. Andre Piccard. It now had a happy, lilting ring to it that it had never had before, although she had already decided to keep her own name for professional purposes.

In the end the decision to accept Andre's proposal had been simple and relatively painless. At first she had thought that when she hit him with the results of her medical exam two days previously, this would finally make him back off and would cause him to break their relationship, something that she herself could never build up the courage to do. But when he had heard that she was unexpectedly pregnant, his response had been immediate and exuberant, and she had not been able to resist the marriage proposal that he had once again pressed on her.

What had followed had been equally quick and had convinced Ellen that the marriage proposal had always been genuine. For when she had accepted his proposal in the heat of the moment and had started talking about plans, he had revealed that he had had standing reservations for both ceremony and honeymoon in Beirut since his first proposal. And, under the circumstances, he suggested, the sooner they got married the better. They could always have a proper ceremony later in Cyprus, Canada, or France, depending upon her inclination.

Ellen, always the realist, was readily able to see the wisdom of tying the knot as soon as possible, and so here she was. They had taken one of the Piccard hydrofoils from Limassol to Beirut on practically no notice, had been married in the Lebanese presidential palace on even shorter notice, and here they were in the best suite of one of the best hotels in what was once again becoming the Paris of the Middle East. But then, as she turned in the bed, she realized that, at least for the moment, "they" weren't here. Andre was not lying beside her, as she had expected him to be. She rose from the bed, gathering the negligee about her that had miraculously appeared on the bed the previous night, and padded quietly about the suite and then out onto the sweeping balcony overlooking the seafront and the yacht basin below. No Andre.

As Ellen returned to the bed, she saw the note on the nightstand. Andre had risen early and had gone to the coffee shop. The note, which suggested that she call for room service and await his return, concluded with the wistful phrase "No escaping business, I'm afraid."

"Wait for his return. Nonsense," Ellen snorted as she picked out a particularly colorful sundress and reached for her hairbrush. Fifteen minutes later she was dressed, and, frankly, looking radiant, and was approaching the door to the terrace where, she had been told at the desk, her husband was breakfasting with his party. As Ellen approached the door, however, another woman, an older woman, entered the lounge from the terrace. Ellen murmured an apology and stepped to the side as the woman majestically bore down upon her. But then Ellen looked into the other woman's eyes, turned ashen, and neatly collapsed onto an overstuffed sofa and toppled over onto the floor.

* * * *

Within hours, the Koniotis home at the foot of the acropolis hill in Nicosia had been transformed into an annex of the UNICIS facility in Morphou, complete with watch office, computer banks, and multiple computer and communications lines. In many ways, moving the facility to the relatively remote area of Morphou following the terrorist attack on its predecessor nerve center on the then-UN base near the Nicosia Airport had been a mistake. True, the Morphou office was less than a twenty-minute monorail trip from Nicosia, but many of the people who Koniotis had gathered at his transformed Nicosia house this morning to start piecing together the Homewrecker threat, such as Maria Solonos and Ahmad Jallud, were simply too busy with their own jobs in the capital to be able to rail out to Morphou for daily meetings. And since secrecy and their undivided attention were of the utmost importance, this annex in one of the older, established residential suburbs of the city was ideal.

Koniotis, Jallud, and the shadowy representatives from the Intelligence arms of the British high commission and American embassy had spent the initial precious moments of their first summit meeting of security chiefs trying to calm the interior minister down.

The morning *Semerini* page-one headline had read "Good Riddance to the British; May They Be Bombed Into Oblivion," and the caustic boxed description of the explosion at the Episkopi Base the previous day had referred the reader to Demetris Mattas's "At Your Service" column, which had dredged up all of the stories of misconduct by British soldiers from the sovereign bases over the past several decades; had provided an exaggerated, one-sided argument on the illegality of the sovereignty claim over the bases; and had specifically called on Mattas's former wife, Maria Solonos, as interior minister, to join with the EOKA forces to drive both the British and Turks off of the island for once and for all.

"This time he has gone too far," Maria was sputtering. "I will take out a writ and close his paper down."

"And that's just exactly what he wants you to do, Maria," Takis said soothingly. "He's just doing this to get your goat and to get you to fight with him in public. You know he owns the license on several other newspaper mastheads. He'll just publish under a different masthead each time you shut one down. Then he will accuse you in print of having taken Gestapo tactics just because of your personal relations."

"I agree we should concentrate on the investigation at hand," Ahmad interjected. "We've amassed quite a bit of information on this threat now. I think the way to silence Demetris is to solve the case and end the threat."

And then all present, the three police authorities, the two diplomatic agents, and the UNICIS computer lab chief in the continued absence of UNICIS chief Ellen Larkin, began to review what was known about Homewrecker, starting with a briefing on what Uri Lukenov had found out through his contacts in Switzerland, home of the Hartzel-Wegner arms merchants.

Uri told those present that the Hartzel-Wegner firm of Lucerne, the Swiss office of which was managed by Sergey Stepanov, had been assembling the parts of a long-range gun for a terrorist organization based in Lebanon. The gun apparently was to be mounted somewhere where it would be a threat to Western interests in the Middle East. He added that his own brother, Pavel, had gone to Moscow to obtain from Russian mafia interests nuclear material for the warhead of the shells to be fired from this weapon and had not returned to Switzerland. In addition, his mother, who had once worked with the Hizballah in Lebanon but who had broken with them, had gone missing. He had come to Cyprus looking for her, because both she and the information he had ferreted out in the Hartzel-Wegner offices had indicated that Cyprus was somehow connected with the operation.

The British and American intelligence chiefs and the UNICIS computer lab chief had added several more significant facts. The Americans revealed the operation by Joseph MacAlister's commandos in Tehran that had surfaced the Homewrecker program and had connected it with the former regime in Iran as bankroller, Syria as host for the weapon, Israel as the target, and Hartzel-Wegner, the Hizballah terrorist organization, and a mystery woman operating out of Beirut as

199

the enablers. The Americans also added the probable theft of one of the gun components from the subterranean Army Research Lab southwest of Washington, D.C., and the recent suspicious death of U.S. Secret Service agent Ann Wynette, who had been assigned to investigate the issue shortly before her death.

The British had been in contact with the Israelis, who had been made aware of the threat to their territory of the gun from Joseph MacAlister's sponsor and who were openly preparing to preempt the effort as soon as they could locate the weapon's site.

Both the British and the American diplomats stressed the vital need to resolve the issue before the Israelis took action against Syria, Lebanon, and/or Iran, because, in the wake of the recent "democratic revolution" in Iran, the Western powers were planning another serious effort to open a Middle East peace conference and to push settlement of the region's problems to a conclusion. Jallud was able to add that the Israeli authorities had reported that the suspicious aircraft that had flown over the Episkopi bombing site the previous day had been armed and had obviously been expected and aided by Damascus, where it had landed. The Greek fuselage numbers had been put on trace but had not turned up anything. The computerized profile of the aircraft that was registered in the UNICIS data banks, however, identified it as belonging either to a Belgian diamond merchant or a nationalistic Russian member of parliament, who was running for president and who was strongly suspected of having Russian mafia connections.

Jallud's people and the UNICIS computer researchers had also been working together overnight on the Cypriot immigration records for recent months, and they had isolated several individuals who had arrived but who had not been known to have left and could not be located and who had backgrounds and connections that would be compatible with both Middle East terrorism and advanced weapons testing.

"So, we can agree that there is enough evidence that a nuclear weapon to attack Israel exists and that the testing of the delivery system for the weapon is being done here in Cyprus that we can reasonably go ahead with a detailed search for a weapons testing site," Takis concluded for the group.

"It certainly looks that way," agreed Maria. "And for Cyprus, at least, that is somewhat of a relief. It may mean that the explosions in Gunyeli, Galata, and Episkopi are not related to Cypriot political problems."

"Or won't develop into being related and initiating further ethnic violence if we can find that test site and shut it down," added Ahmad grimly as he folded the copy of *Semerini* and dropped it into a nearby trash bin.

Maria stood. "That seems to be our cue, Ahmad, to get our people out on the roads and into the countryside on a hunt for the testing site."

"Thanks, Maria," said Takis. "In the meantime, our diplomatic friends, the UNICIS computers, and I will try to keep the components from reaching the operational site, wherever that is. Uri, I would like you to stay here and help run our watch operation. Every single thread of information needs to be collected, recorded, and woven, if possible, into the cloth. It's good we had this meeting. We know far more than I realized. Now it's a race with the clock."

"I just wish Ellen Larkin were here," Takis continued. "We need all the brain power we can get on this one. And it would be good to have someone we could send to Beirut. I think that's where much of our problem is. Same time tomorrow?"

All assented in their own way as they rose and started to shuffle out of the building. All except Maria, who had already risen, but who was standing by the table and looking very pensive.

"What's wrong, Maria?" Takis asked. "Did we miss something?"

"No. No, I don't think so. I was just thinking where to start. Ahmad will get the police teams out into the countryside. I think . . . I think that a visit to our exalted Vice President Hatan just might be in order."

"Well, I can see you are still a couple of steps ahead of me," Takis smiled grimly. "While we were talking about the explosions in Gunyeli, Galata, and Episkopi, I couldn't help but think of the problems Visiliou and Caitlyn were having with their archaeological digs. And those problems always seemed to trace their way back to Lala Hatan. Yes, I agree that he might be a good lead on this issue. But, you don't have to go see him now. We'll both be seeing him tonight."

Maria stared blankly at her former boss.

"The president's reception for the departing Episkopi commander, Brigadier Tymes-Smyth, is this evening. I see that Hatan is on the guest list for that. I couldn't miss his name. Everyone knows about the tiff he had with President Ioannou. This will mark his first foray since then out of his lair in the Turkish sector of Nicosia and back into the Greek sector. Don't look so startled. I know it is in bad taste to party after the Episkopi bombing. But protocol is protocol. Tymes-Smyth is still leaving, and I confirmed by e-mail earlier this morning that the reception is still on."

Maria wrinkled her nose. So be it. She would try to corral Hatan later in the day. So, what should she do now? Maybe she should go back to her office and stick pins in an effigy of her former husband, Demetris. As she passed the trash bin, she extracted the copy of *Semerini*, tore off the front page and the page on which Mattas's column was printed, and wadded them up in a very small ball. Someday Demetris would get his just desserts, and she wanted to be there to serve them.

* * * *

Ellen awoke to a collage of faces shoving at her and a magazine assaulting her right ear as it was being flapped back and forth. One of the faces seemed to be that of Andre. And he was looking extremely concerned. The faces were replaced by a glass of water and someone was pushing the back of her head, putting her face on a collision course with the rim of the glass. She swallowed and sputtered and started to push at those who had crowded in on her.

"Oh, good, she has come to," said one helpful voice.

"Give her more air," said a much more helpful voice.

She sat up onto the sofa under her own volition and latched her eyes on those of her new husband's.

"She's alive. I saw her," she managed breathlessly as she avoided another encounter with the water glass.

"Who's alive, Dear?" Andre asked solicitously. "Are you all right? It's not the bab—?"

"Yes, I'm just fine," Ellen responded with irritation. "I didn't faint because of the baby. I've seen a ghost."

The woman having come to and become vocal if not particularly coherent, the concerned hotel guests began to drift away, and Andre sat down on the sofa next to his wife.

"I don't understand. What do you mean?"

"I saw her. I saw Ingrid. She was coming off of the terrace. Surely you saw her. You were on the terrace."

"Ingrid? Ingrid who?" Andre answered in a low, reasonable-sounding voice that he hoped would serve as a model for calm. "I'm afraid I was so involved with my business discussions that I didn't notice anyone else on the terrace."

"Ingrid. Ingrid Bittmann Isaksen. The Ingrid who was supposed to have died in an earthquake in Famagusta three years ago. The former UN official Ingrid Bittmann who ruined the last Mideast peace conference. The Ingrid who stole John Patterson's solar energy designs. The Ingrid who was involved with an international counterfeiting operation when the earthquake struck."

Andre didn't answer. He just sat there, speechless.

"The Ingrid Isaksen who was *your lover*," Ellen punctuated the air with the water glass that had somehow found its way into her hand.

Andre still sat, incredulous, spilled water dribbling down his elegant shirt front. At last he spoke. "I suppose you may have seen someone who looked like Ingrid, but—"

"I know who I saw, Andre." Ellen stood in total exasperation. "I *was* a *spy*, you know," she declared to the entire lounge in a voice that caused all heads to snap up in attention. And then, more calmly. "And what's more, she obviously recognized me as well."

Andre also stood. He was eyeing the now-very-interested guests strung out through the lounge. "I think we should go back to the room to discuss this."

"And I think we should go back to Cyprus. Believe me, this has been a terrific honeymoon, Andre. One I certainly never will forget. But I must get back to Cyprus now."

And she was gone, leaving a very distressed new husband standing in the center of the hotel lounge, trying his best to look nonchalant and avoiding eye contact with the other guests.

* * * *

Sergey Stepanov was a master at changing plans, but he didn't much appreciate it when he was forced to change his plans. And he was particularly displeased when those changes in plans put his life into jeopardy. It was thus one sour Russian who rode the large launch into Karavostasi's Xeros jetty at the southern end of the nearly deserted sweep of Morphou Bay on Cyprus's west coast.

The first irritating change had been in the forced decision to deliver the triggering device stolen from the Americans directly to Syria through Beirut in a ship out of Marseilles harbor in France rather than the original plan of sending it to the Cyprus testing site by yacht through Kyrenia harbor. He had now been informed that they didn't want the triggering device in Cyprus at all. The whole operational schedule for Homewrecker had been moved up dramatically, and now they wanted the triggering device to bypass the Cyprus trials. And they also wanted him to stop in Cyprus and pull out all of the other components that were being tested for delivery to the operational site as well.

Sergey was very irritated. Others were supposed to handle these dangerous deliveries. Others were much more expendable than he was. And he was too well-known in this region to be seen moving weapons components around.

"They'd better know what they are doing and what is at stake," Stepanov thought grimly to himself as he jumped from the launch to the jetty. "And they better be prepared to sweeten the pot considerably, as well. If they think I'm going to go to all of this extra trouble for what we've already agreed to, they are sadly mistaken."

He cleared his mind for the job at hand. This would be chancy at best. The warehouse was a good twenty-minute drive from the jetty. It would take an estimated three separate launch trips to get all of the component parts out to the *Daphne*, which waited off the shore, just beyond Cypriot territorial waters. And it wouldn't all be completed until after dark. Considering its historical connection with smuggling activities, the Xeros jetty was no place to be caught transferring illegal cargo after dark.

The parts. They had only told him to transport the parts. They hadn't told him to bring any of the people out as well. And if any of them wanted to come out with him, it was going to cost them.

No, Sergey Stepanov didn't like changes in plans that were forced on him one little bit.

* * * *

With a single significant exception the reception that evening at the Presidential Palace to mark the long-scheduled departure of Episkopi Sovereign Base Commander Brigadier James Tymes-Smyth was every bit the bust that Takis and Maria had projected that it would be. The fact that a good third of those who had been invited, most of the contingent from the base, were missing because they still lay under the rubble of the bombed-out Happy Valley was the primary reason why the reception didn't have a chance. Another reason was that Demetris Mattas, with recorder, and a *Semerini* photographer had stationed themselves, along with anti-British posters, outside the palace gates on Dhimostheni Severi Avenue and were harassing those who entered.

Those were the overriding reasons the evening didn't jell. But there were a lot of little reasons as well.

Maria Solonos had leaned out of the window of her limousine at the gate and had slapped her former husband hard across the mouth in answer to his gibe on whether she still preferred a specific and very kinky sex position. The photographer naturally got a very good shot of an angry interior minister backswinging into a laughing journalist.

The brigadier himself was being a pill at the party. He made several caustic remarks to all present concerning continued British sovereignty over much of the country's real estate and the civilizing influence British colonialism had had on the island. He ended his insensitive diatribe with a statement that he himself was about to wrap up the mystery of the explosions around the island. And he rejected the pleas of Takis Koniotis, Maria Solonos, Ahmad Jallud, and even his own high commission representative to share whatever information he had in this regard.

Soon after Tymes-Smyth's swan song performance, Vice President Lala Hatan hit the road in indignation after Maria Solonos had tried to engage him in conversation over what he might know about the bombings.

Ginger Hamilton had come, straight from the hospital and in tribute to the victims of the Episkopi bombing. But she wandered around with a glazed expression and looked more than her age this evening. More than one of the other guests remarked that Ginger was the best reflection of the condition of the reception itself.

The reception also brought Takis a personal setback. Caitlyn and the Visilious were there as well, and the estranged pair seemed to be making mutually desirable eye contact that promised to bring them face-to-face for a reasonable, and possibly healing conversation before the evening was over. However, just as it looked like Caitlyn might walk over and speak to him, Leila Jallud minced up to Takis in a tight evening gown with a neckline and skirt side slit that met at her waist, playfully mussed his hair, and planted a sweet kiss directly on his lips. When he was allowed up for air, Caitlyn was gone, and he didn't see her the rest of the evening.

The one bright spot involved the presence of Ellen and Andre Piccard, who had returned from Beirut by hydrofoil just that afternoon. The news of their quickie wedding was the talk of the party, and, as happy as Takis was for the couple upon their marriage, he was even more affected by the news that Ellen had whispered to him—that she had been sure that she had seen a living Ingrid Isaksen in Beirut that morning. They promised to talk further on this development when Ellen reported to work the next morning. While telling her that they were meeting at his Nicosia residence for the time being, he suggested that she might take a few days off to spend with her new husband. He was delighted and relieved, however, when Ellen declared she intended to return to work the next day. And, as the other guests were leaving—considerably earlier than the invitations had indicated, Takis filled Ellen in on some of what they had uncovered concerning the Homewrecker operation, including the presence and role of Uri Lukenov at the temporary UNICIS facility.

There was another slight, pleasant surprise for those who had attended and survived the reception. Demetris Mattas and his photographer were gone when most of the guests were departing the palace.

Unfortunately, Brigadier James Tymes-Smyth, having survived the explosion at Episkopi, was not one of those who survived his farewell reception at the Presidential Palace. As his vehicle approached the split in the superhighway from Nicosia that directed traffic toward either Larnaca or Limassol, a large, dark Mercedes sedan pulled up beside him and peppered his own Land Rover with machine gun fire. As the stricken Land Rover continued down the Limassol split, rammed into an overhead roadway abutment, and burst into flames, the Mercedes veered off on the Larnaca split, dumping pro-EOKA and anti-British and anti-Turk leaflets in its wake.

Chapter Thirteen

"Well, all right then, you old cow," Eric Koniotis retorted, as he pushed the clinging Anita away and moved further down the bench on the grapevine-covered terrace of the Platres taverna. "If you want to visit the Kykko Monastery, go right ahead. I'm tired of the arts scene and just want to go to the beach."

"Don't be unreasonable," Anita responded amiably. "We have plenty of time to do both and to get to Paphos for our hotel reservations there."

"That's another thing," Eric fired back. "You are being entirely to frigging 'nice.' I can't even have a good fight with you, and it's getting on my nerves."

Anita just laughed, drew closer, kissed him on the ear, and placed her hand on his thigh.

Eric pushed her hand away and jumped from the table. "That rips it, Anita. I feel stifled. I've got to get some space of my own for awhile. I'm going for a smoke." And, as he moved to leave the table, he turned and said: "And maybe you just won't see me again until Paphos."

"Whatever," Anita answered nonchalantly, as she lifted her wine cup again. Anita was about as laid back as they came, and she figured that she was treating the young Eric so good in bed that he wouldn't stray far. If he *did* skip the monastery and go to the beach, he'd probably just be all that more anxious to see her in Paphos. She was so intent on trying to read the label on the last bottle of Cypriot wine that had been delivered to their table that she did not see a woman rise from the shadows of the terrace and follow Eric into the afternoon sun.

Eric had stopped not far away and was sitting on the rim of an ancient stone watering trough that was almost smothered in bougainvillea. He pulled out a cigarette, lit it, and took a heavy drag as he shuffled his feet in the dirt at the side of the mountain road and muttered obscenities under his breath about life in general. Two young Cypriot girls gave him the eye and giggled to each other as they passed by. To them he looked just like a sophisticated mainland Greek movie star, with his sullen but handsome features, the black curls falling over his eyes, and a muscle shirt and cut-off jeans shorts that set off his sensuous body in a way that was natural for him but would have been embarrassing for most Cypriot youths.

He was so engrossed in his own thoughts and with the tough decision what to do next that he didn't notice the woman come up and sit at the other end of the trough until she spoke.

"Girl trouble?" she asked. "I couldn't help but see your little scene back there in the taverna."

"It's OK. Nothing I can't handle," Eric muttered without looking up. Something about the voice, its richness and smoothness, however, kept him from telling the woman to butt out.

"Your name wouldn't be Koniotis, would it?" the mesmerizing voice continued.

Eric looked up in shock and was immediately stunned—and smitten. She was one of the most beautiful women he had ever seen. Small, with raven-dark hair offsetting a porcelain-white complexion. Perfect eyes and lips that made him want to come closer to her. And he found he *was* involuntarily leaning closer to her. He never had felt this way before. She was older than he was, but he had always been attracted to older woman. However, he had always been the pursued. He had always had to be courted and wooed by the woman. Never before had he been hit by an instantaneous desire to have a woman. But he felt that now. As he leaned slightly toward her, she shifted a hand on the edge of the trough and also leaned imperceptibly toward him, causing the scooped neckline of her buttoned shift to show more cleavage. Eric gulped as his eyes plunged down the front of her dress and involuntarily spread his legs apart to relieve the heightened answering tension he could feel growing in his own body.

"Y-e-s. Yes, I'm Eric Koniotis. But how did you know that?"

"I thought so," the woman answered with a lilting laugh that almost melted the youngster. "I know your father, and you are the spitting image of him."

This didn't please Eric in the least and he sat up straighter. "You know my father? Then perhaps you are in police enforcement as well?" He hadn't made it sound like a respectable profession.

"Oh, no indeed. My name is Leila. And I guess you could say that I'm sort of on the other side of your father's business. Oh, no. I don't think your father would be pleased with some of my friends."

There would have been nothing more intriguing she could have said to him. He slid closer to the woman as he responded. "That sounds very interesting. Tell me more. I promise not to tell. My father isn't very pleased with me either."

The two were close now. The woman had a clean smell with a gentle hint of freesia. Eric's eyes were locked onto her full, red lips. The woman's hand was raised to brush Eric's lips and then moved languidly around his neck, her fingers buried in his long, curly hair.

215

"I could tell you quite a few interesting things if you like and also show you something your father can't find but would very much like to find. But first, wouldn't you like to see what's behind this bougainvillea here?" With that she rose, took Eric's hand, and led him around the edge of the foliage. Behind the bougainvillea, hidden from the street, was a narrow passageway between two buildings. There were no windows on the passageway and about half way along the space the ground abruptly began to fall off, opening to a narrow view of the valley below.

Leila let loose of Eric's hands, skipped some distance away, and turned back toward him. She was leaning against the wall with her palms flat against the stucco surface. She gave him a sensual, inviting look with her eyes and slowly unbuttoned her dress and dropped it to the ground. She had been wearing nothing else but the wrap-around shift.

Eric was on her in an instant, his hot-blooded youth out of control. He kissed her all over her face, as she reached down and pulled his shirt over his head. She guided his hands and lips to her breasts, as she worked on the buttons on his cut-offs. Eric broke hold to slip off his shorts, and Leila turned him around so that he was between her and the wall. And when he was free, she jumped up, straddled him, and started to control the action by leveraging her knees on the wall at his back.

When the two were spent, Leila whispered in her young lover's ear: "Now, if you really want to be a bad boy, I'll show you what I've been keeping secret from your father. My vehicle and driver are just around the corner."

As they gathered up and donned their clothing, Eric was thinking that now he didn't have to decide whether to go to the Kykko Monastery with Anita or to the beach by himself. Leila Jallud had darker thoughts. She was thinking of how much simpler—and more enjoyable—this method of kidnapping was than drugging and mugging would have been. She had been prepared to go either way, however.

* * * *

The watcher sat on the patio of the deserted row house and watched the front door of the Koniotis residence in Nicosia. He had been told that it was being used as some sort of temporary office. He couldn't stay here too long, though. There was too much activity on the street and who knew when one of the neighbors would get nosy and start asking questions about a man sitting on the patio of an empty house? He couldn't move too far away from his own vehicle, though, and he had to keep the door of the Koniotis house in sight.

He had been given the picture of the Russian early this morning and had been told to follow him and kill him the first time he left the house. His employer wanted it to look like an accident or he wanted the Russian to disappear without a trace. He didn't want to arouse suspicion that a hit had been ordered, and, under no circumstances should the hit man permit his own activity to be detected.

"Easier said than done," mumbled the watcher as he tried to blend in with the shadows by the house.

No one had told him that the house would have more people coming and going than a supermarket.

* * * *

Trevor Hawkins ducked his head down to the level of the Elea crater rim as the Mercedes sedan appeared on the road and returned to the suspect warehouse near Morphou. Hawkins cursed his mobile phone for having broken down before he could talk personally with Tymes-Smyth. Any time now he would have to try to break cover and get to a telephone. But every time he had tried to steal away, there had been activity at the warehouse as patrols of guards had been sent out to check over the surrounding countryside again. He was very lucky he hadn't been detected yet. But he knew that what he had found out would be totally useless unless he could get it reported to the proper authorities.

The evening was starting to come on when the Mercedes appeared. It was the same vehicle that had visited the warehouse when the gun had been fired. Hawkins decided he would check out this latest development with his binoculars and, when dark had fallen, he would simply have to try to retreat to the village where his own vehicle was parked.

The Mercedes had parked near the warehouse. There appeared to be four people in the vehicle. One of them was a woman. Hawkins increased the magnification on his binoculars.

"Oh my God," he whistled softly to himself. The woman unmistakably was Leila Jallud, the wife of the Cypriot police chief. She appeared to have been kidnapped. One of the men had her in a strong grip, and she seemed to be grimacing. She might even have been drugged, as she was leaning heavily on the man and her head was on his shoulder.

This changed the whole complexion of the issue.

Now Hawkins had to try to see if he could rescue Jallud's wife. There was no telling what might happen to her if help was late in coming. He would make an effort to get to her within the next couple of hours and, if he couldn't, then he would go off and raise the alarm.

As he made these plans, he spied another vehicle, a covered truck, cautiously approaching the warehouse compound from the Morphou Bay direction. The truck was waved into the compound and pulled up very close to the large doors at the end of the warehouse. Hawkins tried to change positions to get a better look at what was happening in the compound, but the arrival of the truck had signaled another foray into the hills by the armed guards, and the artist was forced to retreat deeper into the cratered Elea ruins.

"Tonight," Hawkins resolved. "I'll try to get into the compound tonight. But, one way or another, I am reporting back." The truck was worrying him. It hadn't looked like it was loaded. He was afraid that meant they would be clearing the warehouse out. That gun had to be seized here. Its reign of terror had to come to an end.

* * * *

"This man is no equal of his father," Inga Hartzel smirked behind her fingers, as the Syrian president swung around his audience room, trying out his impression of an American gangster of almost a century earlier.

"Now his father . . . ," Inga's smirk had turned to a shudder, "there was a man who could cause shivers to run down your spine with a mere gaze of disapproval."

The current Syrian president had inherited his post following nearly fifty years spent as a playboy and mediocre race car driver, and he had never developed the ruthlessness and, alas, did not even have the intelligence to run his country as efficiently and as menacingly as his father had. Inga didn't give him good odds to last out the decade in his position, and she was quite happy just now to be facing him rather than his father.

"We can give you the gun, in place, in two week's time," she informed the president in a business-like tone when he had stopped his posturing and returned to where she was sitting. "Of course, the contract is for delivery in four weeks, so I'm afraid we will need more money in the contract to get it accelerated."

"Well, I don't know . . ." The Syrian president's voice trailed off as he sat down and bit at a hangnail. "He said we are running out of time. He said that news of Homewrecker has reached the Israelis and they've started to plan a pre-emptive strike. And he said if Homewrecker isn't operational before the UN secretary general announces the plans to open a new Middle East peace settlement conference, we will have lost the initiative."

"And just who is 'he'?" snorted Hartzel derisively.

"I am 'he,'" informed a new interlocutor pointedly, as the double doors at the end of the room swung open and a tall man in a gray suit swept into the room.

Inga's head snapped around and she suddenly realized that the rules of this particular little game had changed dramatically. Here was the match for the current Syrian president's father. His eyes were cold and cruel and bore right through her, pushing aside all of the bravado and authority that she herself had built up over the past four decades. She felt a shiver of both fear and sexual interest slicing through her.

"Permit me to introduce myself, Madam," the man said smoothly as he stood in a dominant position before the Syrian and the Austrian. "I am the Iranian prime minister, Assadollah Egbal, and it has been me, not the ayatollahs, who commissioned the building of this weapons system."

"I was just telling Ms. Hartzel," the Syrian president stammered meekly, "that we would like to have the system operational in two weeks and she was about to tell me the additional financial requirements for early delivery."

"This is not business. This is war. And Hartzel-Wegner is now engaged in this war no less than Islamic fundamentalism. The system will be up and running and the first launch will be in three day's time. Any time less and the Israelis will have made mincemeat of your operational site and the entire Golan Heights. And there will be no more money. We have provided more than enough money already. I presume I have made myself clear."

The Syrian president was busy gagging on his drink and was unable to respond at all. Inga Hartzel voiced a simple assent. She could tell that negotiation would be counterproductive, and she so liked a masterful figure. She already was contemplating the extracurricular possibilities.

* * * *

Eric Koniotis started to get a little scared as Leila Jallud proudly showed him around the test site that had been set up for the long-range gun in the center of the old warehouse building. He tried not to show his concern, however. He had given the woman the impression that he rejected all of his father's values and he was afraid that the situation would get a little unpleasant if he acknowledged how shocking all of this was. He was no Zionist, certainly, but he wasn't particularly political either. He saw nothing noble in people killing each other for political, religious, or even ethnic reasons.

He had grown up knowing about the ethnic and religious differences that had set the Greeks and Turks at each others' throats in his father's native Cyprus, but he had been raised on the comforts of America. He could understand random violence and violence in conjunction with one person trying to wrest physical property from another, but violence in the service of some personally held ideal was beyond him.

And, when Leila happily told him that the weapon had been responsible for the destruction in Gunyeli, Galata, and Episkopi, he was simply appalled. He had been close enough to the Galata explosion to have felt the attack personally. He and Anita had gone down to that town to view the resulting carnage and both had been viscerally affected. They had planned on

223

leaving Platres sooner than they did, but what they had seen in Galata had shocked them in place and had suspended their travel plans.

Eric was fairly numbed from the tour when Leila led him into a room at the back of the warehouse. The light from the small, dirty-paned window placed high on the wall was dim, but he could make out a table and chair and a mattress on the floor. Leila's hands were wandering as they entered the room and there was little doubt why she had brought him here.

They went straight to the mattress, stripped each other, and made love. Eric welcomed the activity as dulling the shock of what he had seen. It had occurred to him as Leila had been fondling the barrel of the large gun out in the warehouse that, if this was the sort of thing his father had dedicated his life to stop, then perhaps Eric had been a prick. Perhaps his parents and their values had been right after all. And perhaps it *had* been important for his father to be off fighting international crime so much of the time that there had been little time left for the family.

Leila left Eric so exhausted that he didn't hear the arrival of the truck or particularly notice when she slipped off the mattress, dressed, and left the room. He also was taken completely by surprise and was too weak to respond effectively when Leila's two "drivers" rushed into the room, trussed him up in all his naked glory like a prize roasting chicken, and locked the door as they left.

* * * *

Uri Lukenov had volunteered for the late shift at the temporary UNICIS watch office. Most of the others had families or established activities on Cyprus and he was sleeping here in Takis's house anyway, so he reasoned that it didn't matter much if he was one of those answering the phones and e-mails and keying new information into the computers while most of the investigators enjoyed their normal sleep periods.

Thus, it was he who received the telephone call from the Swiss authorities that reported that his brother, Pavel, had returned to Lucerne. They had traced his recent movements back to Damascus, although they also had had reports of his presence in Moscow the previous week. He had shown up on the appointment calendar of the nationalist Russian political leader who was suspected of having traded away some of the former Soviet Union's stockpiled nuclear material. The Swiss themselves didn't necessarily want to talk with Pavel—they were still insistently neutral, but they had received "inform" notices from several different countries as well as Interpol, and the Swiss authorities were querying UNICIS about what they should tell the others. Israel's Mossad Intelligence organization appeared particularly insistent on knowing where Pavel Lukenov was. Without revealing that he was Pavel's brother, Uri thanked the caller and said that UNICIS would develop the information from there. He said that none of the others needed to be informed, because UNICIS would issue a general bulletin to all.

For more than an hour after he had taken the telephone call, Uri sat in the semidark of the makeshift watch center, smoking a cigarette and weighing the situation. Eventually he made up his mind.

Turning the communications center over to another watch officer, Eric said that he needed to take a walk and clear his mind. He returned to the guest room Takis had assigned to him and telephoned a Russian friend he had met the last time he had lived in Cyprus and who had retired to take up deep-sea fishing from Kyrenia harbor. He now owned three good-sized trawlers, each more than capable of quickly reaching the Turkish coast some forty nautical miles to the east of Kyrenia.

After disconnecting, Eric retrieved his passport and his money clip from his suitcase and, bypassing the room where the watch center had been established, slipped out the kitchen door and into the dark night.

* * * *

It was profoundly dark in the small warehouse room when the shifting of heavy objects out on the main floor stopped and all became quiet. Tears of frustration were making wet trails down Eric Koniotis's cheeks as he lay trussed up on the mattress. He knew that the weapons system equipment was being moved out and delivered to the operational site somewhere in Syria and that the terrorists were moving one more step ahead down the path of entering the nuclear age in their age-old war with Israel. And he knew that his own chances of survival in this situation were meager.

He had been such a fool. He could now easily see the evil and folly of what was happening. Leila had tantalized him by openly bragging about all they were planning to do with their weapon, and now he was completely powerless to do anything about it. What had her purpose been in bringing him here? Had she hoped to recruit him? To protect himself, he had tried to make that appear to be a possibility in her eyes. But she hadn't even given him time to pretend to join up before he had been bound and left here in this room. How had he betrayed his growing misgivings?

He struggled with his bonds, but it was useless. They were beginning to cut into his wrists and ankles, and the tape across his mouth was driving him mad.

The door to the room opened, and Leila came in and turned on the overhead light. She didn't say a word. She just looked at his bound, naked body with the same carnal expression that Eric had seen before. Leila came to the mattress and lowered herself beside him. She kissed the tears of frustration on the youth's face as her cool hands explored his defenseless body. Eric's frustration and anger only increased as he felt himself involuntarily responding to her intimate caresses.

At length, she withdrew and Eric was alone in the darkness with his fear and his frustration.

Chapter Fourteen

"There's a good reason why he hasn't shown up for his morning coffee. He's not here. I've looked everywhere around the house, and he's gone."

Takis Koniotis plunked down a basket of burned toast, poured himself another cup of strong coffee from the carafe, and sank into an engulfing bamboo-framed chair. To escape the bustle of the temporary UNICIS watch office in the living areas of the house and to gather their thoughts for the morning meeting of principals, Takis and Ellen Larkin had retreated outside. They had found refuge in the open-sided ground-floor space underneath the bedroom wing. Caitlyn had turned the area into a garden, albeit more of an overflowing depository of archaeological stone tidbits. It had been from this covered area that the excavation of a royal tomb at the base of the adjacent acropolis hill had taken place several years previously. Some of the lesser finds of stonework in the tomb had not yet been cleared from the examination site.

"Gone? How do you know he's gone?" responded Ellen as she warily fingered through the blackened bits of toast and decided she didn't really need a second breakfast. Takis was never much for cooking, and she didn't know how he was managing to survive this separation from Caitlyn. In fact, she wished they would both snap out of their long-suffering attitudes and stop this nonsense. Everyone could see that they still were very much in love and would be together now if they had not had such a problem with one of the children.

Children. A pang of apprehension and responsibility gripped her, and her hand involuntarily went to her abdomen. She looked sharply up at Takis, but he was busy lacing his coffee with sugar and attempting to respond to her question.

"When I couldn't find him anywhere in the house, I looked through his things. His passport was gone and he hadn't left any money here. My surmise then is that he must have decided we weren't moving fast enough on finding his mother and brother and he would go it alone. The bed hadn't been slept in, and he was still here, on duty, when I went to bed at about 1:00 AM, so he must have slipped out near the end of his shift. Otherwise, the others on duty would have noticed his absence and reported it in the log. I've put out a 'to be notified' notice for him at the ports of entry. That's about all we can do for now. I'd had all charges on him dropped, so we can't just have him apprehended."

"But is it wise to just let him roam free?" queried Ellen. "Didn't we need him for the information he had, and are you sure he's not one of them and that he didn't come in just to find out what we knew?"

"Good questions, of course. But I think we already managed to capture all of the pieces of the puzzle he could contribute, and I think he's genuine. He told us far more of importance to the investigation than he had to to win our confidence, and it was too much of a coincidence on how he connected with me. He had no way of knowing that I'd fortuitously be at the airport or that I would bring him into the watch center. No, my gut reaction is that he is genuine but just prefers to work alone and at his own pace."

Takis held his cup suspended in air long enough for Ellen to notice and to ask him what had arrested his thoughts.

"His detention at the airport has bothered me," Takis said. "He had been gone from Cyprus long enough that the system would have not detected his entry immediately, and the Customs police said they had received a tip-off that he would try to enter the country—and through the Nicosia Airport. That must mean that someone here knew he was coming and wanted him stopped. That was probably the people at the test site. But then that means he must have told someone in Switzerland of his intentions—someone he trusted—and they betrayed him.

Hmm, I guess we didn't get all of the information out of him that would have been useful."

At that point Koniotis was called back into the house to take a telephone call from New York. When he returned to Ellen's side, he looked a bit harried.

"More trouble?" the UNICIS chief queried.

"I guess you could say that, Ellen. That was the secretary general. He wanted to warn me that the major powers had managed to convince most of the key Middle East countries that, with the change of power in Iran, the time was ripe to open another Middle East settlement conference. They hope this will be the final one."

"And I suppose they need you to go elsewhere to set up for that." Ellen's worry was obvious in her voice. "You can't be in two places at once, of course, but if we can't wrap up this investigation quickly and stop this weapons system from going operational, there probably can't be a peace conference now. Either the forces of terrorism will regain the position they lost with the demise of the ayatollahs in Iran or the Israelis will preempt the weapons system in an act of violence and solidify the region in opposition to them once more."

"I won't have to leave Cyprus. And, knowing the importance of wrapping up this investigation first, I won't leave it either. The UN wants to hold the peace conference here, in Paphos."

Ellen registered surprise, and Takis explained: "As you know, it was here, in Cyprus, on the Amathus coast, that we tried to hold our last peace settlement conference, the one that had so much promise and might have worked if the terrorists hadn't suborned Ingrid Bittmann, the conference chair. So, for symbolic purposes, they want to come back to Cyprus to pick up where they left off."

"Sounds like you will be stretched pretty thin," Ellen commented skeptically.

"Me? don't you mean we?" Takis said, with a smile on his face. "It's not something I can do without your help. But all the more reason to get this investigation concluded quickly. Damn, I wish I had thought of trying to find out who Uri Lukenov told in Switzerland of his plans to travel here to track down the Homewrecker test site and to find his family. We're doing pretty well on this investigation, but we need all of the separate leads into those controlling this operation that are possible. I wish I had assigned someone to keep an eye on Uri."

With a sigh, Ellen rose and started collecting the cups and plates. There was too much work to do at the watch center for them to sit out enjoying the garden any longer.

Although Takis hadn't thought to do so, someone else had assigned a watcher for Uri, but that watcher didn't seem to be in evidence on the roadway outside the entrance to the Koniotis residence this morning. That probably meant one of two things. Either the watcher had grown weary of the surveillance from his exposed position, or the watcher had already found Uri, as assigned.

* * * *

Caitlyn's voice was trembling as she rang off from the disturbing call she had just received in her university office outside Famagusta. She admitted to herself that she had had a feeling of foreboding in the back of her mind about her son, Eric, ever since his last call to her from Platres.

At first she had thought that it had been intuition about the bombing of the nearby mountain village of Galata, and she had been beside herself for two days following that bombing in which she had received no communications from her son. This in itself wasn't surprising. Eric was completely self-centered and would not even have thought of the relief he could have brought to his mother's mind by simply letting her know that he hadn't been in Galata at the time of the bombing. But then she had taken the effective expedient of putting some more money into his account. When that was promptly withdrawn, she was fairly certain that Eric hadn't been killed or wounded at Galata.

But the nagging fear at the back of her mind for her son's physical safety had not gone away, and now, with this most recent phone call, it was pounding away at her brain. The call had been from Eric's traveling companion, Anita. She had called Caitlyn to find out if Caitlyn had heard from Eric. Anita was worried because Eric had disappeared the afternoon before and she had all of his baggage. He had just walked out on her in a Platres taverna the previous day and hadn't gone back to the hotel for any of his things.

Anita admitted that the two had had a little tiff and that Eric had left saying he might go the beach rather than to the Kykko Monastery with her. But he hadn't taken any gear with him—not even his bathing suit. Caitlyn had tried to reassure Anita and convinced her to go ahead with her plans in anticipation of Eric catching up with her again in Paphos. But Caitlyn herself had the premonition that all was indeed not right with her wayward son.

There were only two things that Caitlyn could think of doing for the moment. The first thing she did was to wire some money into Eric's account again. If he was well and hadn't changed personalities in the last two days, he would withdraw the money and she could log into her account and find out when and where the withdrawal was made. The second thing Caitlyn did, but not without a good deal of thought and stalling, was to try to call Takis on his home phone. After all Eric was his son too, and it was time for Takis to show some parental interest even if he wasn't speaking to the boy.

But all she got was a busy tone. She waited ten minutes and tried again. Still a busy tone. With a huff and a snide comment on the dependability and usefulness of her estranged husband, Caitlyn turned back to the telephone and, in a snappish voice, began the process of cutting through the intervening layers of bureaucracy to contact her old friend, the interior minister, Maria Solonos. Maria assured Caitlyn that she would notify the police to try to find Eric. They were already scouring the countryside for evidence of a weapons test launch site. After disconnecting, Caitlyn took a variation of Maria's advice to go get some rest and drove up to the Salamis ruins to walk the beach and calm her nerves.

The first time Caitlyn tried to connect to Takis, he was otherwise engaged in receiving a shocking call of his own.

"We have your son," declared a muffled voice. "He's safe now, but he certainly won't be safe if you don't pull UNICIS out of the investigation of the explosions."

Takis had had the presence of mind to push the caller trace button as soon as he realized this was a threatening call.

"What son?" he responded, trying to buy time. "Neither of my sons . . ." He didn't bother to go on because the caller had disconnected. And the tracer had not had time to locate the call. He had tried to say that both of his sons were safely in the United States, but he knew this wasn't so. Andriko Vasiliou, worried about Caitlyn, had contacted him a few days previously to report that Eric was in the country and was causing Caitlyn concern.

Takis was now full of self-remorse for not having tried to contact either Caitlyn or Eric earlier. He always seemed to be losing golden opportunities. Well, he wouldn't lose this one. He picked up the receiver and dialed, trying to reach Caitlyn. There was no answer at her Famagusta home and her telephone at the university was busy. Well, he couldn't just sit around trying to find Caitlyn. She was probably off absorbed in one of her dusty digs anyway. Instead, he called the police chief Ahmad Jallud and asked him to set a search in motion. If the kidnappers thought that he could be scared away from this investigation, they didn't know him very well.

* * * *

The Countess Frieda Piccard von Meisse stood at the balcony window of her tiny Zurich hillside palace, observing without absorbing the pace of life along the Limmat River below on a particularly rainy and gloomy day. Zurich had its charm even in the rain, which was good, since it rained quite a lot in Zurich. The countess's mood fully matched the weather.

"I have betrayed him," she was chastising herself.

"I have betrayed them both."

Sometimes it was a real bother to have had such an interesting and intriguing past. Intriguing. Yes, that was just the word. Well, she wasn't all that sure he was really that fond of his brother, and when it came down to it, she wasn't all that sure which one she would pick if it was up to her to pick one to live and one to die. But, she sighed and turned back into the room as she heard the door chime in the front hall below, hadn't it really come to that? She was told otherwise, but, of course, she never believed what the American said. Still, the American had his own sort of charm as well.

She continued the mental game as the footsteps approached up the stairs. Uri Lukenov or his brother Pavel. Which was it to be? It probably was too late to choose, but she did so love these romantic games. Uri, blond and ruggedly handsome. Broad shoulders, muscular, straightforward, and masterful. Or Pavel, smaller, darker, more delicate of feature. But inventive and just a touch of danger and cruelty.

She smiled broadly at Pavel Lukenov as he entered the room, having been invited to attend to her earlier that day. He was almost trembling in anticipation as he strode to her, drew her to him, hands firmly encasing her buttocks, and began to unbutton her blouse, one button at a time, with his teeth. Within seconds he had her stripped in the most delightful way and had pushed her back onto the bed. Starting with her pendulous breasts, he suckled and nipped his way down her body until he found a more central point of interest.

All of this delighted the countess to no end, but even as she was mewing and moaning, she was playing her game in her mind. "All told, I would pick Uri. This is all very nice, but, yes, I think I would pick Uri."

Which was a good thing, for just as Pavel was becoming completely absorbed in his pleasurable work, Joseph MacAlister and a friend stepped out of the countess's bath and picked Pavel.

The struggle was brief and a bit brutal. When they had left, the countess sighed, a bit disappointed that MacAlister was so impatient and could not have waited longer. But then he always was the serious and impatient type, she thought, as she returned to the balcony window. But maybe this put paid to the favors he had done in separating her so effectively from the clutches of the Romanian secret service colleagues she had taken up with—and spied for—in her youth.

Did MacAlister and his master ever put paid to a favor, however?

She didn't know what MacAlister wanted with Pavel Lukenov. He had said something about the Israelis and the Mossad, their covert action arm. Frieda didn't really want to know more. She didn't want to know that much. The mere thought of the Israelis gave her a tummy ache.

As she gazed down into Zurich, she suddenly noticed that the sun had come out. She drew out onto the balcony to enjoy the sight of the sun glistening off the wet roofs, turrets, and spires of the small city.

"Ah, nothing like sunlight after the rain. I wish Uri would get back. It's so boring here without appropriate companionship."

* * * *

It would have been fairly easy to determine that they were husband and wife, for Caitlyn and Takis exhibited exactly the same range of expressions when they ran into each other outside Ahmad Jallud's office door. The initial looks of surprise and of pleasure and longing were replaced simultaneously with looks of hurt, merging into a flash of anger and irritation, displaced at last by guarded wariness.

What surprised them most was to discover that they had come on the same mission, to consult with Jallud on the hunt for their son, Eric. After Ahmad had settled the two at separate corners of the desk, Caitlyn attacked first.

"You mean, you've known Eric was missing, and you didn't contact me first? You just went directly to the police alone?" she snapped.

"I did try to call you first, but you still never seem to be there when I need you," Takis retorted. "Just as soon as the kidnappers called me, I tried calling you at home, and you didn't answer there. And then I tried calling you at the office, and the line was . . . God, Caitlyn, what's the matter?"

Caitlyn had turned ashen and nearly slumped onto the floor from her chair. "Kidnapped? Eric kidnapped?" she managed between gulps for air.

"You didn't know?" Takis asked incredulously. "I thought they had called you too?"

"All right, you two," Ahmad interjected in a commanding voice. "This isn't a war zone. Now, Caitlyn. How *did* you know Eric was missing?"

The initial shock over, Caitlyn was able to respond a bit more calmly: "His girlfriend, Anita. They had a fight in Platres yesterday. He walked out on her and didn't come back and didn't take his things from the hotel room. She was worried and called me."

"Eric brought one of his women to Cyprus?" Takis was hissing. "And they've been traveling around my country like vagabonds? And neither you nor he told me?"

"You had already said you had no interest in what your son did," Caitlyn answered acidly.

Takis was about to strike again when Ahmad exploded: "Will you two stop it and let me get this interview over so we can go back to work? You're not the only ones with this kind of worry."

Both Caitlyn and Takis backed off in surprise.

Ahmad never lost his temper with them. He was a volatile person in general, but never with them. And in that moment, both husband and wife realized what silly children they were being—although they were nowhere close to admitting it to each other or even to Ahmad. In mutual guilt, they turned their concern on Ahmad. "What do you mean, Ahmad?"

"What's wrong?"

"It's Leila." Jallud himself was close to breaking down at this point. "She hasn't been home for the last two nights. This isn't like her and we haven't been fighting. I'm afraid something has happened to her. And ever since you told me about the kidnap call, Takis, and about their demand that you drop the Homewrecker investigation, I've been sitting here waiting for the telephone to ring and deliver the same demand to me."

The three retreated to self-absorbed silence. They were all exhausted by their individual concerns and tensions, and now each had given the other more of a burden to bear. At what personal cost came a devotion to justice? Few not involved in police work had any concept of the heavy toll it took.

* * * *

The informer had given his report and was already outside of the office door and counting his money on the way to the elevator without having given any notice to the damage he had wreaked in the *Semerini* publisher's office. Demetris Mattas, in shock and at a rare loss for words, blindly sank toward his desktop and missed. On the way down, he turned over a half-full scotch bottle and brought his computer monitor clattering to the carpet. He was no longer at a loss for words and was cursing a proper blue streak when two assistants from the outer office poked their heads into the doorway to see what was the matter and then quickly withdrew. The high and mighty publisher was in one of his moods.

This "mood" was unlike any other Demetris Mattas had had. It was the mother of all moods. It was the Mata Hari of moods.

"She's been using me!" Mattas bellowed. "The bitch has just been using me!"

No response from the outer office. Mattas's assistants had been with him for some time. They knew a good deal about his love life since he had split with Maria Solonos. And the words "using" and "bitch" seemed to be entirely in character with the company their boss had been keeping for the past couple of years.

Mattas's generous-sized rump found his chair at last and he reached for the scotch bottle, only to have his mood darken even further, as he found the bottle empty and in more than one piece underfoot.

He took a look at the report the informer had given him. The sniveling little snitch hadn't even known that Mattas knew Leila Jallud. He only knew that the information that she was Iranian, not Turkish, and that she was an Intelligence agent for Iranians should be worth money to *Semerini*. Normally that would have been the case. This was just the sort of story Demetris liked to sink his claws into. But in this case, sinking his claws into Leila Jallud's activities would only make him bleed himself.

All of her interest in him. All of it had been to use him to foment unrest in Cyprus and to harry the British. Not that he wasn't fully in tune with doing that himself. But to be used! And to be used by a woman with the thought that she came to him because she enjoyed having sex with him. But then, he didn't think she objected to the sex with him. Leila may be beautiful, but she was also a nympho. She'd have sex with anyone and enjoy it. She'd have sex with Demetris's dog if he left them alone. She'd have sex with a vacuum cleaner. Probably wouldn't know anything else to do with a vacuum cleaner. She'd have sex with . . . Demetris now was laughing so hard that he couldn't go on with his list.

Good. He was beginning to recover already. Leila was nothing but a lying, betraying bitch. That was no surprise. All woman were lying, betraying bitches.

"All but Maria," a little voice interjected in the back of his mind.

"*All* women are lying, betraying bitches," Demetris declared forcefully over the little voice that was quibbling with him in his own mind.

He rose, strode to the door, announced for the benefit of the entire *Semerini* newsroom that all women were lying, betraying bitches, laughed heartily, slammed the door, and returned to his desk.

He picked the computer monitor up and placed it gently on his desk. He then went to the cupboards behind his desk and picked out another full scotch bottle. All of the time he was muttering to himself about the story he would write about Leila. He was wording it in his mind so that he could avoid being implicated in her activities. He would get the bitch without breaking step in his anti-Turks, anti-British, anti-Ioannou campaign.

But, not more than two words into his first sentence he stopped and stared into the computer screen. A broad grin formed on his face and he popped off the lid of the scotch bottle and took a deep swig.

There was another way to get the bitch. A better way. Yeah, that would take care of her. And it would take care of that other pain in the ass as well. Yes, he liked this idea. He liked it a lot.

Chapter Fifteen

The *Daphne* was riding the waves well and was making very good time to the Lebanese coast. Sergey Stepanov stood at the rail and reveled in how well the plan was going. He had already been informed that Pavel had reached Damascus with the nuclear warheads, and he had the rest of the components of the gun here with him on the *Daphne*. The tests in Cyprus had gone well, even without the advanced-systems triggering device they had taken from the Army Research Lab in the United States. With the addition of the trigger that had already been aboard the *Daphne* when he had taken on the other components off the Morphou coast the previous evening, they would be able to put the nuclear payload down the Israeli prime minister's throat.

This gave Stepanov a particularly gratified feeling. Many years ago he himself had been the chief of security for an Israeli prime minister. She had been a particularly feisty and tough little woman, and Stepanov had actually enjoyed working for her. It was probably the only legitimate job he had ever had, and he would have enjoyed continuing it. But that prime minister, who had gone out on a limb and endangered her own life to try to strike a genuine, even-handed settlement with the rest of the Middle East nations, had been hounded out of office when a significant peace conference, held on Cyprus's Amathus resort coast, had broken down. The woman had put all of her effort into the peace initiative and had even resisted the violent opposition of a husband who she had loved dearly to maintain her principles. When she had been defeated and turned out of office by the nationalistic party of the current prime minister, she was a crushed woman, and she had died from a series of strokes soon thereafter.

That prime minister, Rachel Gilat, was possibly the only person—quite certainly the only "good" person—Sergey had ever respected. If she had not been defeated and humiliated, he was sure that he himself would be an entirely different person now. But she *was* defeated and humiliated, and Sergey had always blamed Ingrid Bittmann, a UN official and chair of the peace conference who had been bought off by the Mideast terrorists, for the failure of that conference. That was why in the ensuing years Sergey had never been far from Bittmann's side. He had always meant someday to do to her what she had done to Rachel Gilat.

And now he would get his sweet revenge on the Israelis who had destroyed Rachel and had turned their backs on an equitable Mideast Peace—and he might at long last lay to rest his resentment at Bittmann as well. He wasn't involved with this Homewrecker project just because the arms firm he worked for had taken the contract.

And he was taking particular pride in how Hartzel-Wegner was fulfilling the contract at this moment. The Iranian backer had moved the delivery up to two days from now, and, at the rate the *Daphne* was moving toward the Lebanese coast, they would actually be able to make delivery and have the gun assembled and in operational mode by tomorrow evening.

Of course Stepanov didn't trust anyone else in this project in any way or form—not the Iranian backer, or the Hizballah intermediaries, or the Syrian implementers, or even the managing partner of his own firm, Inga Hartzel. For that reason he had taken out insurance to make sure that he would get his share of the profits on this one. The project was going very well, of course, but he was making sure that it wouldn't go at all without him.

As the Lebanese coast hove into sight, Stepanov was called to the bridge to take a call from Beirut. He had assumed that the call was yet another nervous query about when the *Daphne* would make landfall, and Sergey was prepared to dress the Hizballah agent down again for discussing such matters over open marine channels. However, although it was the Hizballah agent who was calling, he had called Stepanov to warn him that Irina Lukenov had shown up in Beirut and was looking for him.

This was an irritating wrinkle that Sergey certainly didn't need right now, and he asked the Hizballah agent if they couldn't do something to shut the woman up. He didn't seem all that concerned at the moment that they had been lovers as youths, or that she was the mother of his son, or that they had been living in a common law marriage near Lucerne for the past several years. She was a nuisance, and Stepanov didn't like having extraneous nuisances getting in his way while he was working on a delicate project.

He was even more steamed when the agent told him that, no, they would not take care of Irina Lukenov for him. She had been a particularly popular member of the Hizballah while she had been fighting at their side for many years in the past, and she was under the protection of the organization's leadership. The agent said huffily, as he broke the phone connection, that he considered it a special favor to Sergey just to have warned him that Irina was in Lebanon and looking for him.

As he growled at the dead phone connection, Sergey became aware of the noise of jet engines above the bridge. He raced out and to the railing in time to see three fighters with Israeli markings fly at very low altitude overhead.

Uri Lukenov had returned to Switzerland after his surreptitious journey from Cyprus through Turkey and was motoring from Lucerne to Zurich at about the same time Joseph MacAlister was passing both a report and the somewhat limp person of Pavel Lukenov on to a Mossad team that had been sent to Zurich specifically to take possession of both. The report was given more urgency than was accorded to what was left of Pavel, whom the Mossad would wring dry at their leisure.

The most important information that Pavel had revealed to MacAlister during the previous night had been the name of the vessel that was taking the tested parts of the Homewrecker weapons system from Cyprus to Lebanon for onward delivery somewhere in Syria. By Pavel's timing, the ship should have been loaded the previous night and should now be on its way to Beirut, where it would sit at anchor off the coast for a delivery under the cover of darkness.

The Mossad team concentrated on the shipment.

What MacAlister had found out from Pavel had pointed to two important facts. If the shipment was to be stopped before it got to the Levant, the Israelis had to strike now, for the brief time it was in international waters. The operational site was another matter. To ensure destruction of the threat and to provide a lesson to the enemies of the Zionist State, the operational site, which obviously was in Syria, had to be eliminated.

Pavel had identified a site in an oasis to the west of Damascus, well within Syrian territory. This had somewhat surprised the Israelis, as they had thought the site would be nearer to Israeli territory, possibly somewhere around the Golan Heights. But, upon reflection, it made sense that the Syrians would want the site to be well protected and as distant from the Israeli military reach as the distance specifications on the gun would permit.

Thus, the Mossad team dedicated their effort to calling in air strikes on the ship and the oasis, while notification of the location of the testing site in Cyprus was left up to MacAlister. MacAlister, in turn, decided to leave that decision up to his employer in Texas, who he would dutifully contact after he had completed all of his own reports on his activity. Overall, he was very pleased with the previous day's work. It had been a stroke of luck that he had connections from the murky past with, and a certain control over, the countess in Zurich. He had been delighted when his sources had informed him that she was the paramour of both Lukenov brothers and thus could serve as the bait to lure Pavel out of cover.

All of this activity surrounding his brother was unknown to Uri Lukenov as he drove up Zurich's Rami Strasse and turned onto Hirschen-Graben. He was both apprehensive and irritated at the thought of what he would find when he reached the small yellow Baroque villa that floated on the hillside across from the Kunsthaus on the tree-lined street. He had searched Pavel's haunts in Lucerne most of the previous evening and night before a worried office assistant at Hartzel-Wegner had admitted to him that Pavel had not been seen since he had departed early the previous day, having received a telephone call from the Countess Frieda Piccard von Meisse in Zurich. Pavel had had an appointment for an important business meeting in Lucerne the previous evening, but he had not shown up for that appointment.

Uri had long suspected that Frieda and Pavel were involved, but, although it angered him that Pavel couldn't find his own women, it didn't particularly bother him. He had considered his relationship with Frieda as part of his job, and having her bed available to him saved him from paying rent in the very pricey city of Zurich. It wasn't as if he were her husband or anything. She had a husband, or so she claimed. No one had actually seen her husband to Uri's knowledge. Still, this duplicity behind his back, if indeed Frieda and Pavel were having it off, irritated Uri. At least there was a chance that he would be able to run Pavel to ground here, and they could have a little family "chat" in the privacy of the small palace.

But Uri didn't find Pavel at the countess's. What he found when he reached the door was the countess herself, flying into his arms and sobbing into his shoulder.

"Oh, I'm so glad you've come back, Uri," the countess snuffled into his shirt collar. "The most dreadful thing happened last evening, and I've been beside myself concerning what to do about it. I almost summoned the police, but I couldn't decide if that would be wise or not."

"Come upstairs, Frieda, we'll discuss it there," Uri responded, his eyes taking in the curiosity of the two servants who had gravitated toward the commotion in the entrance foyer.

Frieda absentmindedly toyed with undoing Uri's shirt buttons as they mounted the stairs, and had completed that job by the time they reached her bedroom.

"Now, what is the problem?" Uri asked when they had reached the settee beside the fireplace. As they had approached the room, he had been looking warily around for signs of the presence of his brother.

"It's Pavel," the countess got directly to the point. "He called me yesterday to say he needed to talk to me about your safety. He said that you were in some sort of danger. So, I watched for him and was at the entry door when he entered the garden gate. But just then two big men appeared at the gate and dragged him off. I was so scared, I couldn't even scream. And since then I have been in such a state. I didn't know what to do or who to call. I thought of the police, but, I don't know, somehow . . ." Her monologue trailed off as she took increased interest in one of her favorite pastimes, kissing a particular mole on the side of Uri's neck and running her hands over his muscular chest. Frieda had trouble maintaining two activities at once.

"No, you did right," Uri sighed, as Frieda's ministrations prompted him to explore within the folds of her robe. Not surprisingly, the robe was all she was wearing. "I don't think we should get the police involved in this. Still, there are some people I will need to talk to. That's why I came back at this time. I needed to see Pavel. It's very important."

Uri started to rise, but Frieda picked that very moment to unzip his linen trousers and tug down and out on the waistband as she sank artfully back on the arm of the settee, the movement serving to cause her robe to open and slide away from her body.

Uri stood over her for a moment, indecisive about whether to depart and start once again to try to find his family or to stay momentarily. In that moment of indecision, Frieda's searching hands went to him and settled the decision.

* * * *

The Israeli air force struck quickly and decisively. As quickly as they had reacted to the information that had been wrung out of Lukenov and delivered to Tel Aviv by the Mossad team, however, they had nearly lost the interception of the ship. They had located it in Lebanese waters and steaming directly for Beirut. It was not anchoring off the coast to permit it to unload under the cover of darkness, as the report had indicated. The ship also was closer to the Levant coast than the Israelis had estimated it would be following an early morning departure from off Cyprus' Morphou Bay. But, all that mattered was that they had found it before it reached Beirut and had blasted it under the waves.

The Lebanese were furious, but that didn't matter. The Israelis never worried much what the Lebanese thought about justice and rights under international law.

The oasis near Damascus had been another matter altogether. It had been much harder to reach and then to withdraw from the Syrian interior, but then the oasis had been just where they expected it. Oases don't move around like ships do. But they can, like ships, completely disappear. And the one that Pavel Lukenov had betrayed and the Israeli air force had targeted had disappeared as effectively as the ship had.

The Syrians were even more furious than the Lebanese had been. But the Israelis cared even less for the Syrians' wounded pride than for that of the Lebanese. The important thing was that the threat to the Zionist State had been rooted out and destroyed.

Or so the Israelis thought at the time.

* * * *

From his hillside vantage point, Trevor Hawkins watched in shock as Leila Jallud walked out of the Morphou warehouse under her own steam and coyly folded herself into the Mercedes. She appeared to be in very good spirits and seemed more to be commanding the actions of those around her than suffering the deprivations of a prisoner. How could he have been so mistaken the previous day? It wasn't like him to jump to conclusions, but obviously he had. And in doing so, he had lost the opportunity to report the apparent transfer of the long-range gun parts from the warehouse the previous night. He had become more concerned for the well-being of the Cypriot police chief's wife, and it had cost him the chance to have the shipment seized before it got very far from Morphou. With the wisdom of hindsight, British Military Intelligence would probably roast him for the choice he had made.

He had actually become quite worried concerning the topic of British Military Intelligence's attitude toward him. He had now been out on the Elea hillside for several days and the British forces had made no attempt to reach him. Surely by now they had figured out that his mobile phone had gone on the blink. That happened often enough. Or at least Brigadier Tymes-Smyth would have figured it out and sent someone to the rescue. Tymes-Smyth knew where he was and what he was doing. Of course, when he had thought more on the issue, he grew to realize that *only* Tymes-Smyth knew where he was and what he was doing. What if something had happened to Tymes-Smyth?

The appearance of Leila Jallud and about a dozen of the guards down in the warehouse compound had interrupted this unpleasant thought. All of the men were carrying weapons of one sort or another. As the Mercedes roared into life and pulled out of the complex gate, two small trucks came around the corner of the warehouse and joined it in convoy. When the vehicles had taken the road eastward toward the capital of Nicosia, all appeared to be quiet in the compound.

Even with his binoculars Hawkins couldn't see any guards on duty down there. He swept the horizon and caught a glimpse of the convoy on another road now, headed north toward the western end of the Kyrenia Mountain chain. It appeared they were headed somewhere with a purpose and would not be back for some time.

Hawkins realized that this unexpected appearance of a clearly free and in-control Leila Jallud cast an entirely different light on this situation. This possibly meant that the Cypriots—or at least the Turkish Cypriots, from whose community the police chief was selected—might be guilty of complicity in this affair. Yes, it was entirely reasonable that the Turks were trying to undermine the Greek-dominated administration by helping the terrorist elements in the region foment trouble throughout the area.

But this wasn't good enough evidence to get Military Intelligence off his back about letting the weapons parts slip through his fingers while he was worried about the welfare of a woman who probably was actually one of the terrorists. He needed to get in that warehouse to see if he could find any more clues to the duplicity of the Turkish Cypriots there. And he couldn't wait around up here any longer. He needed to get down there and back out before the Jallud woman and her gang returned.

Hawkins warily started working his way down the hillside. He didn't head straight for the warehouse compound but descended to the road at a point that was not observable from the warehouse. He then composed himself, strapped his pack on his back to give the illusion that he was hiking his way across the country, and headed back down the road toward the compound.

Although he appeared to be enjoying the countryside, he never took his attention away from the warehouse for very long. Good. Still no sign of life. As he approached the compound gates, he stretched as if the load of his backpack needed to be adjusted and laid the pack at the side of the road. Pulling out a water bottle that he knew to be empty, he feigned surprise to find it empty and made a great point of looking around for a possible source of water.

Ah, there's a warehouse; I'll bet there's some water in that warehouse, Hawkins's little scene spun out.

Slowly, but in as nonchalant a manner as he could muster, Hawkins took up his backpack and strode straight to an open door at the side of the derelict warehouse. The hand that was buried in his backpack as an apparent means to carry it, was wrapped around the handle of a handgun rather than an empty water bottle.

So far, so good. He was in the large, darkened central portion of the warehouse and still saw no sign of guards. Could it be that all of the personnel had been leaving for good when they had departed a few moments previously? Not likely, he thought, as he looked around in the gloom. Although there certainly was no sign of a large artillery gun here now, there were signs of continuing habitation. Several cots were strewn around and there were bedrolls and duffel bags in various stages of disarray around what must be the general sleeping area.

No, they must be planning to return. However, it did not bode well for the possibility of finding anything he could use for solid evidence here if they hadn't bothered to leave the warehouse guarded. He would take a look through some of the guards' stuff, but he probably would have more luck with whatever Leila Jallud had in her personal effects. And he could not imagine the Jallud woman sleeping where the men slept.

It hadn't taken any effort to see how sensual she was and that she herself had a roving eye. If she had been sleeping with the general population here last night, Hawkins was sure that some sort of fight over her would have been inevitable and that he would have heard it up on the hillside. No, she must have slept in some smaller room.

Hawkins looked around the periphery of the central space. There were several doors around the sides.

Upon opening the third door, Hawkins found Eric Koniotis. He just stood there, in total surprise, at having found a naked young may trussed up and lying on a mattress. Eric's muffled urgings snapped Hawkins out of his trance, however, and he quickly moved to the boy and untied and ungagged him.

"What? Who . . . ?" Hawkins stammered.

"We've got to get out of here and to a telephone," Eric broke in as he worked his numb jaws and wrists to bring the circulation back. "They had a big gun. Leila bragged that it was what had caused the three explosions here in Cyprus and that it was being tested to use against the Israelis. I think they moved it out last night."

The boy continued his babbling, not thinking to ask who his rescuer was or why he was here, as he pulled on his shorts, tank top, and sandals. "I've got to get to my father. He'll know what to do."

"Your father?" Hawkins asked dumbly. This was all moving too fast for him.

"Yeah. My father's Takis Koniotis, the UN security chief. He fights these kinds of scumballs every day."

"You're a son of Takis Koniotis?" Hawkins asked with disbelief. But the introductions went no further, as a shot was heard and both could see the running guards through the doorway.

Leila Jallud had, of course, left a couple of her men at the warehouse to guard it, and they had watched Hawkins from the protection of a small outbuilding with great curiosity as he had performed his water charade. He had confused them long enough to get into the warehouse and then they had had a fierce discussion over what to do when he had entered the building. Having decided that killing him was the safest response, they had not reached the warehouse door until Hawkins had entered the smaller room and found Eric. They then saw the two moving around the smaller room and started firing and running.

They weren't being careful about who they were firing at. The woman hadn't told them to keep the boy alive. To the contrary, she had told them to kill him if he gave them the slightest trouble.

Hawkins dove for his backpack and came up shooting himself, which made the two guards seek cover and reassess their position. At a signal from Hawkins, Eric slammed the door, and Hawkins forced the lone chair in the room under the door knob. This was answered by three shots splitting the door's flimsy wood. Hawkins looked wildly around the room and spied the small window near the ceiling. He motioned toward the window and Eric reacted immediately. Hawkins positioned his hands in the form of a stirrup, and Eric stepped into this stirrup and bounded up to the window. It pushed out with ease, and the nimble youngster pulled himself up into the frame and found, to his great thankfulness, that the roof over the room was flat. He was easily able to swing up onto the roof and then turn around and bend his torso back through the window to pull the Britisher up and out.

But at that moment the guards burst through the doorway in a hail of gunfire. Hawkins went limp, Eric lost his grip, and the British spy's body slumped to the floor.

Flipping back on the roof, as the guards charged the window, Eric ran across the flat roof to the other side of the warehouse and dropped painfully to the ground. He was over the compound wall and weaving between olive trees at a good distance from the building before the guard who came up onto the roof got a visual fix on the boy. By then he was too far away to catch. The other guard had run out of the warehouse building and around to where Eric had vaulted the compound wall. He was preparing to go over the wall in pursuit, when the guard on the roof called him off.

Eric had had too great of a head start and he was a very good runner.

The two guards stood there, eyeing each other, in despair and growing realization that they had royally screwed up their assignment. Neither thought of either the Hizballah or Leila Jallud as forgiving types.

Within minutes they two had left the compound.

Chapter Sixteen

Once the secret was out, the word spread like wildfire down the Paphos resort hotel coast that their community had been tagged to hold a major Middle East peace conference. All business interests in the ancient town, the locale of the world's first Christian-ruled state, well remembered the last major peace conference that had been convened on Cyprus, held two decades previously on the southern Amathus resort beach coast. They certainly remembered that the Amathus conference had been a political failure, but they also well remembered that it had been a financial bonanza for the Limassol area businesses during the conference and for many years to follow.

The news that Paphos had been chosen had first leaked out through the Cypriot Foreign Ministry. The family of a former Cypriot foreign minister, which had remained prominent in Cypriot diplomatic circles, owned the relatively old but trend-setting Paphos Beach Hotel, which was located at one end of the Paphos harbor and at the top of the main hotel beach spread.

While feverishly starting its own plans to upgrade its amenities and to send glossy fliers through the foreign ministry to the diplomatic ministries of likely conference participants, the owners of the Paphos Beach Hotel also slipped the word of the conference to the municipal authorities.

Information flowed through the Paphos municipal administration like water through a sieve. In short order the Archaeological Department had received the news, and its director, Andriko Visiliou, had enlisted Caitlyn Koniotis's Archaeological Institute to activate an excavation near the existing mosaic-rich exhibits of the Greco-Roman houses of Dionysos and Theseus above the new harbor area to mark the event. He also ordered further visitor preparation of the ancient acropolis area, the Byzantine castle ruins, and the Tombs of the Kings.

Next to learn were the hoteliers along the two resort coasts near the island's old cultural capital. The hotels stretching down Ayiou Antoniou Street from the Paphos Beach Hotel to the south of the harbor quickly noticed the unusual, unannounced construction activity at the Paphos Beach. Thus, it did not take them long to launch into upgrade plans of their own when they first heard the rumors of the approaching conference. The Alexander the Great began refurbishing its rooms and the Phaethon and the Annabelle enlarged their discos and started looking for big-name talent for bookings around the time the opening of the conference was rumored to occur. The Imperial Beach and the Cypria Maris, located at the far end of the beach, hired new chefs and improved their approach drives and the front-elevation lighting. The lesser hotels off the beach, including the Theofano and the Veronica, started making their hotel rooms into small flats to try to entice the large contingents of conference staff that were sure to arrive early and leave late.

The most impressive hotel on the resort strip, however, the Paphos Amathus Beach, took the most ambitious action. Exercising its long-standing option to purchase the large Sodap wine factory on the adjacent parcel of land, that five-star hotel brought in a bevy of architects and construction engineers to turn the winery into a major conference center. The other hotels had thought of inventive ways to book their rooms; the Paphos Amathus Beach was determined to be the conference host.

The seaside hotels to the north of Paphos, and, in particular the Coral Beach Hotel resort, were every bit as impressive as those located just to the south of the harbor. They coalesced their efforts to form a lobbying group to harass the UNICIS chief, Ellen Larkin, and the UN's Cyprus-based under secretary for security affairs, Takis Koniotis, to pick their coast for the conference venue. They had remembered, as the hoteliers at the other end of Paphos had not, that the UN had picked the venue for the last conference on Cyprus and that Takis Koniotis had played a key role in that conference. They, however, would ultimately prove to be beaten at the game by the management of the Paphos Amathus Beach. The summit meetings for the Amathus Coast conference had been held at the Paphos Amathus Beach's sister hotel, Limassol's Amathus Beach, and when it came down to a selection, only the Paphos Amathus Beach could offer a major conference center for the venue.

Everyone in the country knew what was happening once the Paphos mayor became involved, because he publicly announced the intention to spruce up the tourist zone around the harbor area—probably the hundredth time this had been announced over the previous 2,000 years—and revealed the municipal cultural society's plans for a cultural festival to accompany the conference, complete with an open-air performance of a major opera by an international cast in the shadow of the Turkish fortress guarding the entrance to the new harbor.

Even the Greek Orthodox church got into the act. The plans for a week of church activities at the Church of St. Paul's pillar, located where St. Paul was said to have been scourged before converting the Paphos governor to Christianity and before leaving Cyprus while traveling on the first of his famous journeys, were moved back three weeks to coincide with the rumored dates of the conference. Although the original dates of the festival, designed to mark the 1,970th birthday of the Christian church in Cyprus, had been carefully worked out through painstaking research, the local bishop changed the date at the stroke of a pen. What was three or four weeks, anyway, when you were talking about a period of nearly 2,000 years?

Although the Western-leaning Middle East nations already knew about the conference plans, it now didn't take the more troublesome regimes and the interests of terrorism and fundamentalism any time at all to learn of the conference and of its planned venue at this point and to start making plans of their own.

Meanwhile, back in Nicosia, Takis Koniotis, the man who had been charged to set up the conference but who had only heard about it two days previously himself, was not nearly as concerned with planning an international conference as he was with recovering his kidnapped son and preventing the powers of evil in the Middle East from blowing half of the region up with nuclear devices.

* * * *

It was all going to pay off for him. All of the expense of buying up property to ensure the privacy of the operation, all of the deceit of President Ioannou, all of the efforts to keep the Archaeological Department out of the Morphou Canton, and even the deal he had made with the terrorists for their mutual benefit to help keep the Morphou area relatively deserted.

It had hurt him to back away from his cooperation with Chrystalla Ioannou, whose efforts to unify the ethnic communities of Cyprus met with his approval.

It hurt him even more to look the other way while Leila Jallud's people were testing a long-range weapons system on the plain below, especially after they had blown up the Turkish community of Gunyeli with an errant firing of the weapon. But Vice President Lala Hatan's primary loyalties had always gone to personal greed. They always had and they very likely always would.

Hatan walked to the entrance of the facility that tunneled into the southern slope of the Kyrenia Range above the Morphou Canton village of Sisklipos and lifted the pure copper sheet up to reflect the late morning sunlight. It was a beautiful sight, well worth having had to endure the charges leveled against him of sabotaging planned archaeological projects, buying up Morphou land to keep the economy of that region of the country depressed, and not supporting his president's agenda for national unity and progress. All of this was true to a certain extent, although he had not done it all by himself. Leila Jallud and her minions had done most of the work. And right now, he thought, as he fondled the first Cyprus-produced copper extraction in fifteen years, he didn't much care.

Copper mining had been a Cyprus mainstay since 1000 BC. Historically concentrated solely in the Troodos mountain range, the raw ore had been trundled down the slopes from the main mines at Skouriotissa to the Xeros jetty on Morphou Bay for many hundreds of years. The ore wasn't refined in Cyprus; it had been sent elsewhere to be smelted from greenish ore into bronze-colored sheets. By the early nineteenth century, however, the mines at Skouriotissa were being played out, and it was almost an anticlimax when the Turkish invasion of 1974 cut the rail link from the Troodos to the Xeros jetty near the town of Karavostasi.

The copper-extraction business in Cyprus was considered dead for the following more than twenty years, while the island remained politically divided. Not only was the traditional delivery route not possible during these years, but the ancient extraction methods for copper ore in Cyprus had also proven to no longer be profitable.

In the mid 1990s a British firm joined with an Australian venture to try a new extraction method, a technique called Solvent Extraction Electro Winning, which took the ore all the way to the copper sheet stage and which was having good success in the European mines. They bought the Skouriotissa mines for this purpose. This process did not require heavy-duty transport systems, as the finished copper sheets, not the raw ore, were being shipped, and the extraction company didn't have to share the finished-product profits with any other company.

The venture was perhaps too successful, however. In the difficult years in the late 1990s that led up to the country's unification, the forces, both in Cyprus and from abroad, that wanted to prevent the country's unification for reasons of their own, were looking for good terrorism targets of opportunity.

The copper venture, which would revive a major industry in Cyprus and strengthen its economy was a perfect target. On one cool autumn evening in 1997, a band of Hizballah guerrillas swooped down on the Skouriotissa Mines, killed everyone at the site, and blew up all of the tunnel entrances. The international joint venture company was not interested in digging with one hand and firing a rifle with the other, so it abandoned the project in Cyprus. There were other locations with equal promise of profitability and far less personal risk.

The wealthiest financier in the Turkish Cypriot community, Lala Hatan, had been watching the activities of the British-Australian copper venture for some time with great interest. It had always been a wonder to him that copper had only come from the Troodos Range. Why, he thought, could it not be found in the Kyrenia Range, then under Turkish control, as well? For nearly two decades, before Hatan became a politician and eventually the country's vice president, the financier had a small team of mining experts on contract to quietly test around the Kyrenia Range for evidence of a copper ore vein. After considerable time, they had found such a vein on the southern slope of the range, above the Morphou plain.

The mining engineers had told Hatan that ancient extraction methods would not have worked at this site, which probably explained why they had not been attempted before the advent of the Solvent Extraction Electro Winning method.

And the rest, as the man said, was history. In an attempt to keep his find a secret until he was able to establish a monopoly on the resurgent copper extraction industry in Cyprus, Hatan started buying up all of the land around the Morphou area and discouraging development of the region. In a drunken stupor he had stupidly revealed his plan to Leila Jallud during an unlikely sex orgy, and she had folded her own need to help find a remote site somewhere in this area of the Mediterranean for the testing of the Homewrecker weapon system into Hatan's efforts to keep the curious out of his own hair.

Now, however, he had produced his first copper sheet and his venture was off the ground. He could now go back down to Nicosia, settle the paperwork that would protect the mine and its process, and quietly betray Leila and her activities to the authorities.

As he was standing at the tunnel entrance and celebrating his success and his impending end run around the terrorists, he was much too slow to assess the danger posed by the cloud of dust being raised by three vehicles approaching the secret mine from the direction of Morphou on the plain below. He did spy the hated Mercedes sedan before it reached the entrance to the tunnel and he did manage to raise the alarm and drift back into the tunnel behind the Turkish guards who were running for their defensive posts. But the terrorist band had very sophisticated and very powerful explosives. Following a brief fire fight to force the defenders further into the interior of the mine, Leila's men set the explosives, which presently brought the side of the mountain down on Lala Hatan and his dream.

Initially in Nicosia and Morphou, the explosion was taken for the type of summer thunder caused by heat that is not being graced with life-sustaining rain. Eventually, however, the explosion was registered as one of the periodic earthquakes that plagued the eastern Mediterranean. Everyone was thankful, however, that it had occurred in one of the more remote and least-populated areas of the island.

The disappearance of Vice President Lala Hatan made headlines for several weeks, but, since he was known to be involved in many shady dealings and was loved and respected by few, his failure to turn up anywhere became just one of those little mysteries in Cypriot folklore. Perhaps the only one who truly mourned his absence was President Chrystalla Ioannou, whose life he had once saved, who had talked to him in depth and in mutual understanding on the future of Cyprus and of its needs and potential, and who had counted on him to help her bring the Greek and Turkish communities together.

Hatan indeed had been a smart man and one who could see the need to bring the communities together and who had the unique power to help do so. His downfall was that he had one uncontrollable vice, personal greed, and had been unlucky once in his life—his celebration of the success of his project to be followed by the destruction of Leila Jallud was preceded just a bit earlier by Leila's celebration of the success of her project and the destruction of Hatan.

* * * *

Sergey Stepanov was wracked with mixed emotions as he watched the unloading of the Homewrecker components on the pier below from the Tripoli seaside mansion owned by a major financial backer of the Hizballah terrorist movement. He had done it. He had landed the components in Lebanon ahead of time, and they were already being carefully loaded in the camouflaged trucks for the journey across Lebanon and into Syria. For that he had every reason to celebrate. He had fooled the Israelis. But he could take no comfort in that, because it was equally obvious that the Israelis had taken his son, Pavel. And if Pavel was in the Israelis' hands, then God rest his soul.

To avoid the wrath of the Israelis, Sergey had simply extended his transport switching technique in his personal travels to that of the weapons components. While actually transporting the parts from Cyprus to Tripoli, Lebanon, on the *Daphne*, he had prepared a cover story for anyone curious who was not directly involved in the transport that the components were being carried to Beirut on the *Alethia*. When the Israeli jets had flown over the *Daphne* and headed further along the coast of Lebanon and when he had heard the artillery fire in the distance, he had known that they had found the *Alethia* and that the *Alethia* had been their primary target. That probably meant they had leveled that oasis near Damascus where the UN refugee camp was located, as well. The change in the weapon's operational site had also been part of the cover story. He'd enjoy reading about the hell the Israeli's would go through for bombing a UN camp.

That also meant that the Israelis or their friends had seized Pavel and made him tell them about the shipment—because as chance would have it, Pavel was the only one who had been given the cover story.

Sergey had liked Pavel. He almost could say he had loved Pavel. Almost. Although most of the world thought that Pavel's father was Irina's husband, the Russian diplomat and spy Mikhail Lukenov, Sergey, Irina, and Pavel had known otherwise. And Sergey couldn't imagine why more people couldn't discern

Pavel's true parentage. The young man had been so much like him in so many ways.

"But why am I talking about him in the past tense?" Sergey admonished himself as his eyes started to tear. "Maybe the Israelis don't have him. Maybe they figured it out some other way or maybe they haven't killed him."

But Sergey didn't wallow in "maybes," and he was sure that his son had been lost to him. But why was he crying? He was supposed to be tough. But maybe he just wasn't tough enough anymore. Maybe it was time to get out of this business. But he had to steel himself. He was deeply involved in a very important contract. He could consider his future later. For now, he had to get these components to the Golan Heights.

As he raised his hand to wipe away the tears, he caught the slight movement in the dense foliage at the cliff top near the villa's upper terrace. Screaming for assistance, he managed to reach the young man, dressed as a simple peasant, as he was trying to bury his sophisticated communications device. As he held the frightened youth to the ground while two Hizballah terrorists smashed at his head with the barrels of their rifles, Sergey's mind was already racing over the possibilities of what this man had been reporting, and to whom.

* * * *

An angry, confused, frustrated, and frightened Leila Jallud was also going over her plans as she returned to the test-site warehouse from the wholly satisfying tunnel-closing expedition to the Kyrenia Mountains. Up to now, all of her plans had been going well. The weapons components had been tested and shipped out successfully, she was tying up loose ends nicely, Ismail and the rest of the Hizballah test crew and guards were scheduled to be picked up in the new harbor at Kyrenia for transport back to Beirut tonight, and she, herself, had prepared her alibi for her husband. One of the in-place women Hizballah agents who lived in the hills above Paphos was prepared to attest that Leila had spent the last two days with her and that her telephone had been out of order. A weak excuse, but Ahmad was gullible concerning his wife's activities.

However, she stood here in the small room off the warehouse central space, seething. She was angry because the Koniotis boy and the two guards she had left behind while she was away moving a mountain were gone. She was confused because, in their place, she had found the corpse of that fat little artist, Trevor Hawkins, with three bullet holes in his back. She was frightened because, if the Koniotis brat was still alive, she no longer could go home and pose as the respectable wife of the national police chief. And she was frustrated, because she couldn't get her hands on either the boy or the two guards to vent her anger.

She had to think quickly. And, being a quick thinker, she had a new plan ready before she reached the Mercedes. She certainly didn't want to leave through the northern port of Kyrenia with the Hizballah band. She—and only she—knew that her Iranian superiors had planned a little accident at sea for these men in order to keep the project tidy. But there was no reason why she could not activate her own long-standing escape plan through Famagusta harbor on the east coast via the fishing boat being operated there for the purpose by an agent who, like her, was an Iranian pretending to be a Turk.

But she would still need more clothes and some money. Fortuitously, she had a supply of both at Demetris Mattas's flat. Hopefully the sad drunk would be off writing another luscious hate column and wouldn't be at the flat. But, if he was there, she'd give him another lay, fill him with liquor, and he'd be in no condition to remember she had been there let alone that she had cleaned out her clothes.

Leila's one lingering regret as the Mercedes sped back toward Nicosia was that the Koniotis boy had escaped. Now what had she told him about the weapon project? She must learn not to pop her mouth off to every stud who passed by. Oh, well, learn by doing—and maybe, just maybe, they would catch up with the little creep on the road to Nicosia and she could snip off that little loose end.

＊＊＊＊

A strange sensation settled over Inga Hartzel as she walked out of the French restaurant on the Beirut seafront and waited for her limousine to pull up.

She felt a chill and pulled her wrap closer around her shoulders. The chill wasn't caused by the breeze coming in from the Mediterranean, however. That air was warm and soothing. It couldn't be responsible for what Hartzel was feeling.

It felt almost . . . almost like she was being watched. Yes, watched. And not just observed out of curiosity or awe, either. Inga was quite accustomed to being the center of that sort of attention. No, it felt like the glare of accusation and hatred.

Inga slowly turned her head and carefully examined every nook and cranny that was within her field of vision. There, what was that vendor looking at? Oh, he had been looking beyond her to one of his regular customers who was now starting to haggle over the cost of the produce even before she reached the cart.

But, there. What was that? Back in the shadows. There's something there.

Mercifully, the limousine had arrived and the chauffeur was patiently holding the door open for her. Inga was surprised at the relief she felt as she entered the limousine and it roared to life. She wasn't accustomed to backing away from danger. There would have been a time, and not too long ago either, when she would have strode into that alley and confronted the danger, if, in fact, that had been what was waiting for her back there.

As she settled into the plush seat, Inga realized how old and tired she felt. Maybe it was time for Wegner to show a little more interest in the operation and for her to retire, or at least pull back from the business. But that was all wishful thinking. Wegner wasn't about to take a more public interest, and where could she go? So many doors were closed to her and those who wouldn't close the door on her would expect her to continue furthering their interests. How did she get into this situation? Life had been so much simpler once.

Well, two more days on the Homewrecker project, and then perhaps she would have built up enough credit with her protectors to start scaling down her activities—and still be permitted to live.

Chapter Seventeen

If the scout who had spied the landing of the Homewrecker weapons components at the old Pierre Piccard villa near Tripoli, Lebanon, had been correct, they should see evidence of the convoy any time now. Joseph MacAlister and company had taken up positions on the rim of the wadi just where Lebanese territory shifted into Syrian territory. There were no border posts or border guards here, even though this was one of the only roads linking the two countries. The region was just too remote and the relations between the countries were just too good for either Beirut or Damascus to waste good men patrolling here.

Sergey Stepanov had surprised him. And he had surprised the Israelis, as well. That didn't happen very often, and it made them mad as hell. Joseph MacAlister would not want to be the Russian mercenary just now. The Mossad had been on the edge of taking Stepanov out for many years, ever since he had stuck with the capitulationist prime minister Rachel Gilat two decades earlier. His latest embarrassment to the Israelis had doubtlessly marked him for death.

MacAlister had been so sure that Pavel Lukenov had not been dissimulating when he had told them, after he had been worked over good and properly, that the components were on the *Althea* bound for Beirut and the operational site was at the oasis to the west of Damascus. He was still convinced that Pavel had thought that was the case. This, of course, only identified Sergey Stepanov as a very worthy opponent indeed.

The Israelis had, at first, been smug with the Lebanese and the Syrians concerning the targets they had wiped out. It had only been hours later when they started hearing the screams of the Greek shipowners of the *Althea*, complete with ship manifests and impartial-observer pictures of the flotsam that came up from the freighter, and after the United Nations itself had protested the bombing of the UN refugee camp in an oasis outside Damascus that they had begun to suspect that Stepanov had duped them.

Their first reaction was to go berserk with plans for a full-scale attack on Lebanon and Syria, but MacAlister and his Texas backer had convinced them to let his own mercenary force have a go at stopping the shipment. He revealed that he had some information on where the shipment had landed and where it was now headed, but he refused to tell them because of their extreme reaction to having been fooled. The Israelis had given into his plan quickly—suspiciously quickly, MacAlister thought—and thus he and his people were now waiting at the best ambush spot they could find along the path the spotters had told him Stepanov's camouflaged trucks had taken.

The sun was going down when they heard the sound of trucks in the distance. MacAlister peeked over the rim of the wadi with his field glasses and confirmed that a convoy of camouflaged trucks was approaching. He passed the word that the explosives at the Syrian end of the sandstone gully were to be set off at his signal, but none of his men were to shoot unless he ordered it. He wanted the weapon components and Sergey Stepanov undamaged, if at all possible, and, although he understood there were more than a dozen armed men in the convoy, he thought they probably would be willing to give up without a fight if their progress through the narrow canyon was irrevocably impeded.

At his signal the explosives went off and stone and rock tumbled down in the wadi. What happened afterward, however, stunned him. The drivers of the convoy, almost as if the attack had not surprised them at all, jumped out of the truck cabs while the dust was still settling on the floor of the canyon and scrambled over the still-falling rock and into the evening shadows of Syria.

MacAlister's second thought was that this probably was just as well. It was Stepanov and the men inside the trucks he wanted, not the drivers, and, with the drivers gone, there would be no movement of trucks without MacAlister's permission.

Before MacAlister could issue follow-up orders, however, the chatter of automatic weapons fire was audible from the Lebanese end of the wadi and Israeli troops surrounded the trucks and made mincemeat of them.

"I should have known," MacAlister muttered angrily to himself. They had acceded to his plan entirely too quickly. They had been following his own group to the wadi and had preempted the action as the Israelis knew how to do so well.

But then MacAlister's anger drained when he saw that there had been no answering fire from the trucks and that, when the Israelis had reached the vehicles and pulled back the camouflage canvas, the trucks proved to be empty. No men, no Sergey Stepanov, and no weapon components. Stepanov had fooled them again.

And indeed he had. After discovering the agent and his mobile telephone at the Tripoli villa and fearing the youth had called in his report, Stepanov had quickly realized that their primary plan had been compromised. He immediately switched to his secondary plan, which was to deliver the weapon parts in normal delivery trucks, traveling separately and straight to Damascus on the main highways.

By the time MacAlister and the Israelis were discovering that Stepanov and his precious cargo had slipped through their hands again, the last truck had made its uneventful delivery in Damascus and Stepanov had left for the airport to attend to the other problem he had discovered when he landed at Tripoli. So, the Hizballah had refused to curtail Irina's activities in Beirut. He would do that himself. And he'd best do that before Irina found out about Inga Hartzel.

* * * *

Demetris Mattas's apartment was dark when Leila Jallud arrived there to retrieve her clothes and some money. She had left her two men down in the Mercedes, which was parked some distance away. There had been no lights on in the windows of the apartment when they had driven up, and she didn't want to make a commotion while here that any of the neighbors would hear and remember.

"Good," she thought as she entered the foyer and started back to the bedroom. "It's just as well he doesn't know I'm leaving either."

But as she crossed in front of the double doors into the study, a desk light was switched on and there he was, sitting at the desk, staring at her. He was as disheveled and as drunk as usual. Leila caught a very brief hint of malice in his eyes, but this was quickly replaced by a welcoming smile, one of his million dollar smiles, so that she immediately decided she must have been wrong about the first look. And, anyway, he had probably reacted to an unexpected intrusion without realizing at first that it was her.

He motioned for her to come into the study and waved a half-empty scotch bottle in an exaggerated sign of hospitality. His exuberance nearly brought him off the chair and onto the floor.

"Great!" Leila mused. "He's in fine form again. It will take me longer to get out of here than I had thought. I hope the men downstairs don't get worried and come looking for me."

"Leila, my love. Just the person I wanted to see," Demetris announced with a sweeping gesture of his arms. "Haven't seen you in days. Come, come, come. Don't be shy."

"Plotting in the dark?" Leila asked with a bantering tone.

"You could say that," was the reply. "I've just finished one of my columns. One of my best columns, if I do say so myself. Come take a look." He pressed the computer screen on, retrieved his column, and turned the monitor screen toward her.

The column had resorted to another use of one of the analogies he liked best, that of the Cypriot Turk, personified by Shakespeare's Othello, and the Cypriot Greek, personified by Desdamona. As usual Othello was the villain of the piece, although for a change Desdamona was describe as a tart. The character of Iago was equated with the British, who were painted as usual as being full of duplicity. All were intent on tearing Cyprus apart.

This was not, in fact, one of his better columns. He had used this theme before, too many times, and it was beginning to wear a bit thin. Her disdain showed in her face, and he noticed it.

"No, no. I know what you are thinking. Read further into the piece. There's new material here."

That's when the name of her own husband, the police chief Ahmad Jallud, jumped out at her. And, for the first time, President Ioannou was identified with Desdamona.

"Surely you don't think I am concerned at you pillorying my husband, are you?"

"No, not especially, my pet. But I'm sure you would have been disturbed by my first draft. I had you, yourself, as Desdamona and Andre Piccard as Cassio, who Othello was falsely led to believe was your lover. And you'd never guess who walked in as Iago."

"Andre Piccard as my supposed lover?" Leila nearly screamed out.

"Ah, yes, you do know Andre, don't you? In the biblical sense, I mean? Ah, yes, I thought so. Is that where you've been the last couple of days?"

Leila was angry. "No I do not know Andre Piccard in that sense. He's now a married man. What is this nonsense? I am not having an affair with Piccard."

"Whatever you say, my love," Demetris responded sweetly. "The column was just a joke, anyway." And he reached over and deleted the piece from the computer.

"I wonder what this is all about?" Leila's mind was racing as she started to devise a plan for a quick exit. "I've just stopped by for a dress I want for tomorrow."

"No reason not to have a few for old time's sake, is there?" Demetris encouraged her.

"No, of course, not," she responded cheerily, while she was refilling his glass with scotch. She decided that this wouldn't take too long after all. He was already pretty far gone.

As Demetris swigged his scotch, Leila went around behind him and started to massage his neck. Within minutes, his head was down on the desk, and he was snoring loudly. Not long after that Leila had cleaned out her side of the closet and returned angrily to the lounge and shook the newspaper publisher violently.

"Demetris. Demetris, wake up. I wanted to take some of my money as well, and it's all gone. Where is my money?"

"Just a little loan, darling. I'm getting it back tomorrow."

"Tomorrow? Tomorrow's too late." Then she let it slip out of the bag. "I'll be in Famagusta tomorrow and I need the money."

"Thas just perfect," Demetris seemed only half awake and was slurring his words badly. "I'll be in Famagusta tomorrow too. I can give you the money then. How about two in the afternoon? And," he chuckled, "How about at Othello's Tower? Just for the right effect, of course."

Leila was livid, but she was careful not to show it. Demetris couldn't be toyed with when he was in one of his moods. That would only make matters worse. "If you must be so dramatic, then all right. But just you be there."

Demetris muttered an "Of coursh, t'will be delightful," and his head hit the desk again.

Leila lingered for a moment. He had her in his grip. She worried briefly whether he would remember the appointment, so she wrote a note to him and taped to the edge of his screen. Anyway, she didn't have any more time here. She needed to get to Famagusta and make the arrangements. Leila sighed, picked up her suitcase, and clicked the front door behind her.

As the door shut, Demetris's head lifted. There was a very satisfied smile on his face. He turned to the telephone and started tracking down Ahmad Jallud.

"Just thought you might want to know where your wife has been," he said in a very clear, decisive voice. "She's been with Andre Piccard. If you want to see for yourself, they will be at Othello's Tower shortly after 2:00 PM tomorrow. Oh, and I've sent an envelope over to your office that you should find *very* interesting." And before Jallud could do more than growl down the line, Demetris had disconnected.

Yes this was far better than merely revealing her murky past and naughty present in print.

* * * *

As luck would have it, Sergey Stepanov and Inga Hartzel met in the Damascus airport VIP lounge. Stepanov was headed for Beirut and Hartzel was returning from Beirut. Inga asked Sergey why he was leaving Damascus so quickly. She was worried that something was going wrong with the Homewrecker components delivery. Stepanov assured her that all of that had gone fine and he regaled her with the ploys he had used to circumvent the Israelis.

"Well, then, why are you returning to Beirut so soon?" Inga pressed through her tears of laughter. "The project isn't finished until it has gone operational, you know."

"Ah, yes," Stepanov responded. "But the Syrian end of the operation is yours. I wouldn't think of interfering."

The remark sounded sarcastic to Hartzel and she gave her Lucerne office manager a sharp look. He was getting just a bit too big for his britches.

"You're evading my question. Why are you going back to Beirut now? I need you here in Syria. I myself have business in Beirut I have to return for. I doubt I'll even be able to be in Syria for the launch."

And so Stepanov told her that he had been informed that his common law wife, the former Hizballah fighter Irina Lukenov, was now in Beirut and was looking for both of them.

"Looking for both of us?" Inga asked in disbelief. "What would she be looking for me for? Why, I've kept my distance from her all the time you have been in Switzerland. She doesn't even know I'm alive?"

"Don't be too sure that she doesn't know you're alive and isn't a threat to you," Sergey responded ominously.

"And what set her off, Sergey? Why did she pick just now to return to Beirut and to stick her nose into our business?"

When Stepanov was finished telling Hartzel about Irina's disapproval that their son, Pavel, was mixed up in the Hartzel-Wegner business and that Pavel probably now was dead, Hartzel exploded.

"You've gotten your own son killed?"

"You've just now been laughing about how I duped the Israelis. That happened because I fed Pavel false information and they caught him. I didn't offer him up or plant the information on him specifically so that they could seize him and wring false information from him. That's the cast of the lots. Pavel chose to be involved."

"You're a bloody son of a bitch!" Inga charged for all of the VIP lounge to hear.

"And you're the bloody bitch who made me that way!" Stepanov stood his ground.

The others in the VIP lounge were beginning to remember appointments elsewhere and the attendants were looking very worried. They couldn't just break this fight up. Everyone knew that the Hartzel woman had the very highest protection level for some reason.

The two sat, glaring at each other for a long moment, and then Hartzel delivered a tension-breaking horse laugh. Or at least it had been meant to break the tension. She would take care of Stepanov in good time, but now was not that time.

Stepanov didn't take the peace offering. Instead he moved to another one of his pet concerns. "I want more money for this job, Inga. This is the big one, and both of us will have to lay low for a very long time after this operation has been completed."

"You have your contract, Sergey," Hartzel's voice went to hard-edged steel. This was business she was talking about now, and she took her business very seriously. "You knew what was at stake when you signed your contract, and you knew the risks as well as the rewards. As you yourself have indicated, there aren't many places you can work at all. You get paid well for these jobs, and you are stuck with the deal."

"But the Iranians moved up the delivery date to three days, and I delivered. That should be worth more."

Hartzel merely stared at him contemptuously.

"You yourself have just said that I am still needed here, that my work is indispensable."

That got a rise out of the woman. "No one is indispensable in this business. You are useful, but you are not indispensable."

"I am," the man declared, as he stood up at the announcement that his plane was ready to board. "Even more than you can know at this point. But just maybe you will find out and we will talk again about this."

"I don't think so," Hartzel delivered to his back. "One day, Sergey. You do whatever you have to do and you be back here by late tomorrow. We still face a successful installation."

In his wake, Inga lost some of the assuredness she was trying to convey to him.

"I wonder what he meant about me finding out he was indispensable?" she mused. And then her thoughts went to Irina Lukenov, and she shuddered slightly. "Could it be that it was Irina stalking me back in Beirut when I felt the hostile eyes on me? What if it was? Irina is just an old, useless woman. No one to be afraid of." But Inga shuddered again, which belied her introspective bravado. You can't fool yourself for very long. Perhaps she didn't really care if Sergey made it back to Syria the next day. Perhaps she preferred that he did take care of the Irina problem before turning to any other activity. And perhaps he *was* more indispensable to her than she had said. She would take another look at his contract tomorrow. Maybe a healthy bonus for this job would bring him back in line.

Unfortunately, Sergey wasn't privy to this changing sentiment in Inga's mind, and his unsatisfactory encounter with the Hartzel-Wegner partner had caused a change in his own sentiments. Rather than going directly to catch his departing flight, the Russian headed toward the ticketing counter, intent on changing his own direction to match his new sentiment.

* * * *

The Mossad colonel walked out of the examination room, pulled the rubber gloves off, and reached for a cigarette. There hadn't been anything more to learn from the Russian arms merchant. The colonel didn't know if that was because the young man didn't know anything useful and had been planted to give them disinformation or whether he had been very good at holding what he had known back.

The colonel's anger had not dissipated over the day. Not only did he have the prime minister and the air force on his back concerning the attacks on the Greek ship and the refugee camp, but he had also just learned that the shipment of the weapon components had slipped through their fingers again en route from the Lebanese coast to somewhere in Syria.

The prime minister's reaction had been the worst, and the colonel had to recognize that the situation had been made very bad for the politicians. The leader had ignored the screams and threats of the Syrians and the Lebanese, but he had not been able to ignore so easily the righteous indignation of the United Nations secretary general and the admonishments of the leaders of the major Western nations. In order to mollify these leaders, the prime minister had had to promise to seriously take up the challenge of attending another Middle East peace settlement conference. The prime minister had not appreciated having his hands tied in this fashion, and the colonel was appalled that the Israeli armed forces had had any part, as unintentional as that was, in forcing Israel to the negotiations table.

All the colonel could do under the circumstances was to continue to concentrate on the knife being held to their throats. Well, there couldn't be all that many places where the weapons system could be sited in Syria and still be a threat to Israel. The Mossad would not permit itself to be duped. Flipping the cigarette in a metal bucket, the colonel proceeded to set two very important missions in motion: the continuous flying of spotter planes over Syria until the weapons site was found and the tracking down of that other Russian arms dealer, Sergey Stepanov.

"Let's just see if we can wring more information out of him before he dies than we managed with this one."

Chapter Eighteen

Irina Lukenov was still in shock and was only going through the motions of enjoying this evening out in Beirut with several of her Hizballah comrades of previous days. She had seen her. She had actually seen her.

Even though the papers Irina had found in Sergey's secret compartment in the cottage outside Lucerne had alerted the Russian to the surprise of the continued existence of the Austrian and it had been this very information which had drawn Irina to Beirut, she hadn't fully believed it until she had seen her with her own eyes, walking out of the restaurant just a stone's throw from this open-air café.

Ingrid Bittmann Isaksen was alive. Although she was now calling herself Inga Hartzel, she most definitely was alive and was still busily ruining the lives of Irina and many others. This was the same Ingrid Bittmann Isaksen who, as the UN under secretary general for Middle Eastern affairs, had sold out to the terrorist forces in the region and had been decisive in the undermining of a Middle East peace conference when final settlement of the festering issues in the region seemed assured. Irina had thought Ingrid a heroine in those days, of course, because this was during the period in which Irina herself was hiding from her family and her tragic past and was working with the Hizballah guerrillas.

But later, when Irina was souring on the Middle East terrorists and longing to escape to a simpler, less hateful life, Ingrid Bittmann Isaksen had left the United Nations and had become the CEO of one of the world's fastest-growing companies, which had stolen the formulas for compact solar energy storage and use, and which also was a front for the spread of counterfeit Western-nation currencies into the marketplace on behalf of the Middle Eastern terrorists.

At this time, just when Irina was trying to withdraw gracefully from her involvement with the Hizballah, Ingrid Bittmann and her cohorts had forced the Russian woman to serve as a courier of counterfeit currency from Lebanon to Europe through Cyprus. This forced assignment, plus the affair Irina had only then discovered had been going on between Bittmann and her own former lover and the father of her youngest son, Sergey Stepanov, had pushed Irina over the edge. Upon reaching Cyprus, she had melted into the village population rather than continuing with her assignment and had spent several harrowing weeks evading the wrath of Ingrid Bittmann and her partners.

And then Irina had thought the nightmare was over. Her son, Uri, had found her in Cyprus and had spirited her away to Switzerland under the protection of the French shipping magnate Andre Piccard. En route, they had coincidentally met up with Sergey Stepanov, also claiming to be escaping the control of Ingrid Bittmann, and a family had been reunited and set up in Switzerland. Immediately thereafter Bittmann's counterfeiting operation had been exposed and shut down and she herself had been believed to have died in a massive earthquake on the eastern coast of Cyprus.

But it had all been a lie. Bittmann obviously hadn't died. She was here in Beirut and back to her old tricks of catering to the lowest designs of dissension in the Middle East. And Sergey too, who Irina had joined with again as wife in every sense except in terms of a legal document, had been deceiving Irina all of these years. For he must have known soon after the earthquake incident that Ingrid Bittmann had not died, and he must have been maintaining close contact with her.

Irina now knew this had been so because very soon after the family had been settled in Zurich and Andre Piccard had brought her youngest son, Pavel, from the United States to join them, both Sergey and Pavel had left the employ of the Zurich branch of the Piccard shipping company and had joined another business, the Hartzel-Wegner brokerage firm. And Irina now knew that company's business was that of an international arms merchant and that the Hartzel connection of that business was none other than Ingrid Bittmann, now operating under the name of Inga Hartzel.

As an old friend tried to press a beer on her, Irina was trying valiantly to hold back the tears of frustration and betrayal. Not only had Ingrid Bittmann come back to wreck the possibilities for peace in the Middle East, a peace Irina now longed for, although she could not reveal this change in attitude to her old friends around this table, but the woman had also wrecked the only home that had given Irina any happiness, even though it had been short lived and she had not been blind to Sergey's faults.

For this, Ingrid Bittmann, or Inga Hartzel or whoever else she may imagine herself to be, would die, Irina thought bitterly as she lifted the beer bottle high. Ingrid Bittmann would die and Sergey Stepanov would have to die too. And then Irina could die as well.

It was the only way to peace for her now. And she had been guilty of more than her own share of sin as well. Maybe if she helped give peace a chance she could find some peace and atonement of her own.

Maybe when her friends here at the table became drunk enough, she could slip in the question of when and where Ingrid

Bittmann could be located alone and off her guard and they would not become alarmed at her question. Although she had been able to keep from them her true feelings about the situation in the Middle East, she had not bothered to keep from them her seething hatred of Ingrid Bittmann.

*   *   *   *

Just seventy nautical miles away, in Cyprus, the national police chief, Ahmad Jallud, was also getting a shock about a loved one. To be precise, he was getting shocks two and three of the last ten hours, all thanks to that drunken nemesis of a newspaper publisher Demetris Mattas.

Jallud hadn't wanted to believe Mattas the previous night when he had called and venomously blurted out that Leila was with Andre Piccard. He hadn't wanted to believe Mattas, but the claim was so far-fetched that it had a certain ring of authority and truth to it. And Ahmad was so beside himself about Leila's continued disappearance that he was willing to grasp at and accept any indignity as long as she turned up alive.

Well, almost, he had to admit to himself. He had to acknowledge that he was fiercely jealous of his wife, and he wasn't at all sure if it was better for her to be alive or dead if she were with another man. But Andre Piccard? Surely not Andre Piccard. He had just seen Andre and Ellen Larkin together the other night shortly after their marriage, and, if ever two people were in love, it surely was those two.

Still, he had to know. But it took him two hours after Mattas's late-night telephone call to build up the courage to call. When he did connect to the Piccard mansion on the Limassol seafront, it was a very sleepy Ellen Larkin who came on to the telephone. But Jallud produced an immediate sigh of relief when her voice was quickly replaced by that of an equally drowsy Piccard. Ahmad had to think fast to dream up a reason for having called, and the only thing he could think of was to update the two on the search for the Koniotis boy.

At the separation of the connection, the Piccards were left wondering why the police official had contacted them to pass on no new developments, and Jallud was left cursing the troublemaking *Semerini* publisher. Someday Mattas would go too far in his strange little games, Jallud declared as he switched off his light and tried to go to sleep, completely forgetting that Mattas had also promised that he would find further interesting information waiting for him at the office.

And this time Mattas had carried through on his promise. When Jallud arrived in the office in the morning, he found an envelope from the *Semerini* waiting for him, and his world collapsed. The envelope contained very carefully documented evidence that Leila Jallud was not Turkish, as she claimed, but an Iranian, and that she was connected to the

303

Hizballah terrorist organization. It also contained speculation that she was somehow tied to the recent bombings of villages and the British base in Cyprus. It didn't take Jallud long to confirm via informed cross-checks through the UNICIS computer system that most of the information about Leila was true. There was nothing in the system to corroborate the speculation that she was involved in terrorist activities in Cyprus, but Jallud had no trouble understanding the implications.

The last sheet of paper in the envelope was a copy of an "In Your Service" column by Demetris Mattas, dated the following day, in which he exposed Leila's background and charged Jallud himself with being an accessory, at worst, and a dupe at best. Jallud couldn't see any way out. His professional and personal lives were now over. There wasn't much point in life at all. Mattas was going to wreck his home. Or was it really Leila who had wrecked their home? Or maybe he himself had done so in his blindness to her true personality.

What galled him the most was that her nationality and terrorist activity weren't what really were eating at him. What actually consumed him, even now, was the probability that Mattas was right and that Leila was being unfaithful to him. Possibly, as Mattas claimed, with Piccard. Possibly not. Possibly she had been unfaithful with Mattas himself and this was some sort of revenge game. That was very much within Mattas's pattern. But, whoever it was it didn't matter.

Only one thing mattered now. Now, there was no doubt that Ahmad would be at Othello's Tower in Famagusta this afternoon.

* * * *

The impeccable timing of Takis Koniotis's aunt, Irene, had always been legendary, and she didn't lose any of her reputation when she invited—separately invited—both Takis and Caitlyn to lunch that afternoon. She had been watching the two for months, and she sensed that their individual hurts were just about ready to play the course.

When Takis's parents died in an automobile accident many years previously, Irene had been his closest living relative. And when the couple married and subsequently had their twin boys, Irene virtually moved in with the family so that both Takis and Caitlyn could pursue their individual high-powered careers and still have time for being parents without being burdened with the full load of running a household.

Whereas Takis's more-distant relatives had disapproved of his marriage to the American with an international career and no sense of the natural pecking order in a Greek family, Irene had come into direct contact with the two. She had never in the years before Takis moved the family to New York known a single moment's hesitancy that this had been one of those rare marriages that were blessed by heaven.

It had broken Irene's heart when Eric's antics had caused a rift between the parents—both because she adored the twins and because she saw in the marriage the same solid commitment and love that she had enjoyed in her own marriage up until her husband went missing, presumed dead, in the 1974 Turkish invasion of the island. When the marriage between Takis and Caitlyn went aground on the shoals, it was as if the memory of her own marriage was being assaulted. And, in contrast to the more distantly related Koniotis clan, she had determined to do everything that was in her power to get her nephew's family back together again.

Thus, when she heard of the possible kidnapping of Eric here in Cyprus, she called the two separately and begged them to come to lunch at her village house. They had each accepted without question, as they each loved and respected Irene deeply. And, although they were both surprised to see that the other had been invited to lunch as well, they each bided their anger and bile out of respect for Irene. With Irene as a catalyst, Caitlyn and Takis were finding over lunch that they were very much in accord in their concerns and their feelings when they didn't let their individual hurts get in the way.

It was during the dessert course that fate stepped in to dramatically bring Irene her wish. Maria Solonos called with the news that Eric had been found. She had been trying everywhere to reach Takis and Caitlyn. Eric was with her. He was well, although he had escaped from a very serious situation and was a little shook up and very much chagrined with himself. She would have him driven over to Irene's.

Takis, who had gone to the telephone when Maria called, was so ecstatic with the news and focused on Eric's welfare that he barely noticed Maria's question of whether he knew where Ahmad Jallud was, and he certainly didn't notice the worried catch in her voice when she had asked. Not wanting to ruin the Koniotis family's moment, Maria did not go into details on who Eric had been kidnapped by. That could all come to Takis's attention later, although she herself would have to get busy immediately, and she would need the help of the UNICIS computers. This she could, of course, get directly from the UNICIS director, Ellen Larkin.

Having worked her magic on the luncheon terrace, Irene left Takis and Caitlyn celebrating in each other's arms and went to wait for Eric at the entrance foyer. One look at Eric when he arrived, told her all she needed to know. This family would mend again quickly. And it would be stronger now than it had ever been before.

* * * *

In the absence of Ahmad Jallud, Maria Solonos led a full-scale police raid on an old, derelict warehouse compound outside of Morphou. They were, of course, too late to seize anything of importance, although Maria was sure that enough evidence had been left to link this warehouse with the reports the UNICIS computers had been compiling on the Homewrecker weapons system design and components accumulation and transport. She also found what she didn't really want to have found. She found a silk scarf that she had known was one of Leila Jallud's favorites. It was a Thai silk design that would not normally have been seen on Cyprus, and it was the only present Ahmad's merchant uncle in Damascus had ever given Leila that she had liked. In fact, it had been the only connection Leila had tolerated between herself and the uncle.

It was quite ironic, Maria thought to herself, knowing as she did how much Leila and the uncle had disliked each other, that it had been the uncle's present that was now linking Leila to this weapons test site. Ahmad, if he ever showed up again, would now have a hard time not accepting Leila's complicity. Maria had had no idea how she was going to tie Leila to this terrorist band besides the charge of the Koniotises' delinquent son. She was very happy now that there would be no need to strain the relations between Jallud and his old friends, Takis and Caitlyn, on that score.

The only real surprise to Maria was finding the body of the quirky painter Trevor Hawkins in the small room in the warehouse. Eric had led them to expect to find a body, but she was flabbergasted that it was someone she actually knew. But, upon reflection, she realized it shouldn't have been that much of a surprise for her. Everyone had known Hawkins was a British spy. Only the British themselves had been impressed with his itinerant painter ploy. She wondered how British Military Intelligence would explain his presence here to the Cypriot authorities. She would normally have considered having some fun with the possibilities if she wasn't so worried about where Ahmad Jallud was and what he was doing.

* * * *

At that particular moment Ahmad Jallud wasn't doing anything at all. Just an hour previously, however, he had been stalking his wife around the battlements of the ruins of Othello's Tower.

Othello's Tower received its name from the Shakespearean play. Built in the sixteenth century by the Venetians, it was the fortress protecting the harbor of the walled city of Famagusta, famous for having a church for each day of the year. The Bard's inspiration for the tragedy, which claims within its own dialogue to be set in a Cypriot harbor town, came

309

from the records of a dark-skinned Venetian governor who was said to have arrived at his posting in Famagusta with a Venetian wife but, mysteriously, was pointedly recorded as having returned home without her. From this fragment of historical record, Shakespeare had constructed the classic tale of deceit and mistaken belief of betrayal of the dark-skinned Othello who murdered his wife on the malicious rumor that she was someone else's lover.

It was thus that the fortress of the Venetian governors of Famagusta subsequently received the name of Othello's Tower and it was a case of fact mimicking fiction that saw the jealous, dark-skinned Ahmad Jallud moving stealthily around the fortress battlements to intercede in the presumed tryst of his fair-skinned Leila with the lover whose name had been whispered in his ear by the venomous Demetris Mattas.

Leila's guilt was proven to Ahmad when he found her there, at the appointed location and on the appointed hour, at the upper-most tower walk overlooking the commercial port to the east and down into the castle courtyard to the west.

He didn't bother to say a word as he rushed her, impatient in his wait for her lover to show up and fearful from her nervous and angry demeanor that she was about to abandon the meeting. Still and all, it was purely an accident when his hand caught in her scarf and she stepped back and over the side of the walkway in shocked response to his appearance.

Ahmad stood there on the walkway, in stony silence for the longest moment, as the body of Leila was suspended below him, out over the void, her neck entangled in the scarf that he still held. He could not bring himself to haul her still-twitching body back onto the walkway. Neither could he bear to let loose and watch her crumple to the courtyard floor below. So he did the only thing he could. He stepped up onto the wall and accompanied his beloved wife on her last, flashing journey through space.

Chapter Nineteen

The rumor of the Middle East peace conference had only been launched a few days earlier and already the town of Paphos was well on its way toward reconstructing itself for the event.

Municipal cleaning crews from throughout the town had descended on the harbor front the previous night, and now the promenade in front of the old Turkish fortress was spotless. The boats in the small marina had also been culled during the darkness, and now there wasn't a single hull in the small harbor that would not appear pristine on a postcard.

Scaffolding had gone up on the Annabelle Hotel, the façade of which was already receiving a new coat of paint. The private beach at one end of the harbor, which was owned by the fine old Paphos Beach Hotel, had been closed to all, including the current hotel guests, and beach boys were sifting the white sand, itself imported from elsewhere, to ferret out all impurities. The Imperial Beach at the other end of the resort coast had closed altogether, and its manager was nervously striding up and down in front of its entrance waiting for the refurbishers to arrive.

Next door to the Paphos Amathus Beach, a fleet of trucks had pulled up to the old Sodap wine factory to clear everything left on the premises off to another site, while architects watched from the roof of the large five-star resort and argued over how strong a wine festival theme they could build into a conference center whose first planned users were primarily totally—at least professedly—abstemious Muslims.

The three restaurant workers who were known to have an Arabic ancestry were being scuttled back and forth, all across the seafront, consulting with chefs on the eating habits and preferences of their countrymen and providing rough translations of menus that were then rushed off to the printers to obtain pride of place in production queues.

Even the countries of the Middle East and the Western guarantor nations were already picking up on the rush. The king of Jordan had booked the top floor of the Paphos Beach already, the British had let an old mansion in upper Paphos, the Americans had booked a good portion of the flashy Paphos Amathus Beach, and the Libyans, ever suspicious and less than total in their commitment even though they supposedly had recently celebrated a democratic revolution, had merely reserved a boat slip in the harbor marina. They planned to house themselves on one of their coastal patrol boats off the Cypriot coast and come in by skiff when and as they wished.

Even the hotels on the "unlucky" coast to the north of the town were not to lose out on the opportunity.

The Saudis, also wanting some distance between themselves and the proceedings but unwilling to travel anything but first class, had put their bid in for a wing of the Coral Bay resort hotel eight miles away from the center of the action.

Takis Koniotis's assistant could feel the expectation and frenetic activity of the town when she arrived under the bright afternoon sun, supposedly to quietly research the various options for a conference site. The research would not be necessary. She could readily see that and, in fact, found herself grateful for this as she exited her car only to be greeted by name and with a bouquet of roses by the beaming mayor of Paphos. Takis had told her it would be touch and go to have the conference venue ready in time. It was quite evident that the industrious Cypriots had already cut several of the corners for her. There was nothing wrong about that—provided their choices could be secured against possible terrorist attack. With one eye on the armed attempts that had been made to close the last Mideast peace conference down early, Takis had warned her that there could be no corners cut on the safety of the participating leaders.

Demetris Mattas should have been crowing with victory when the printer in his flat's study starting spewing out the Cyprus News Agency story of the day. But somehow it didn't matter to him that much anymore. He felt completely hollow inside. This despite his valiant efforts from just before the 2:00 PM bewitching hour into the gathering twilight to fill every nook and cranny in his tortured body with scotch.

He couldn't keep his mind off what he had done to Leila Jallud, how he had set her up for whatever had happened at 2:00 PM at Othello's Tower in Famagusta. He had no idea whether an angry Ahmad Jallud had shown up and confronted his wayward wife, who, if not technically guilty of having had an affair with Andre Piccard, most certainly was guilty of having had an affair with almost every other man on the island. He didn't even know if Leila had shown up at the tower herself.

What he did know was that whatever had happened with or to Leila this afternoon had been his doing. He had set her up, and he hadn't even shown up to give her her money back or to be at least fair in telling her husband that the charge of an affair with Piccard at least was just a vengeful joke.

For a brief moment he thought of what he might have done to Andre Piccard with his lie. What if, in his anger, Jallud had gone after Piccard instead—or as well? Demetris worked

315

this scenario over in his mind for a while, but he found that it didn't cause him any concern. No, for some reason, it was only what he had done to Leila that caused him concern. And he didn't know why this was so. He had been betrayed by Leila. And not just betrayed, but used. There was no reason for him to feel remorse. Why did he care what happened to her and what role he had played in that?

Demetris sat down at his desk and screwed his eyes shut. He was trying to conjure up a picture of Leila. Perhaps that would help explain this unexpected feeling of guilt and despair. Ah, yes. She was sitting at a table, her face turned from him, brushing her luxurious dark hair. Her shoulders were bare. Beautiful shoulders. Demetris found himself wanting to reach out and touch her, but no matter how close he walked toward her, when he reached out, she was just beyond his grasp.

That was when his Cyprus News Agency printer dinged its notification of delivery of an important, fast-breaking story, and Demetris's blood-shot eyes opened to the spectacle of the mess about him. He looked over at the printer with dulled eyes and barely became cognizant of the story of the century for the island. An event that he had been working for most of his literary life.

The first line of the item that was rolling up from the printer was reaching out to Demetris with its message of personal victory:

Dateline Nicosia. 2 July 2014. British High Commissioner E. Stanley Gates announced at 5 pm today to a quickly assembled press conference that, due to the redesign of the structure of the British armed forces, the three British military bases on Cyprus of Episkopi, Dhekelia, and Akrotiri would be closed over the next four years. Gates went on to say that the closing of the bases would obviate the need for Britain to maintain its historical and legal sovereign presence on the island of Cyprus and that negotiations would begin immediately on the possible transfer of territory to the Cyprus Federated State.

Contacted at the Presidential Palace a short time following the press conference, the spokeswoman of the government of President Chrystalla Ioannou said that there would be no comment at this time. However, the spokeswoman did add that negotiations for reversion of the three parcels of territory to their rightful sovereign was expected to proceed smoothly, as the agreements on Britain's use of Cypriot territory was predicated on continuous need for the basing of troops that aided in the defense of the island. Whenever the British forces have no longer had a need for one of their installations on Cyprus, the facility and the land have always reverted to Cypriot ownership.

Long a bone of contention between . . .

Being one of the last persons on the island who needed a tutorial on the background of the struggle between the British and the Cypriots for control over territory the British had forcibly retained in the country's independence settlement some fifty years earlier, Demetris willed his eyes shut, and he drifted off into his alcohol-soaked melancholy once more.

Gathering all of the powers of concentration the scotch had left to him, he was able to return to his reverie of Leila at the boudoir table. Maybe with just a little more effort he could touch her, and she would turn. If she turned to him, he knew he would be able to understand why he felt this total sense of having betrayed and wronged her. And then, in his misty dream, he did touch her shoulder. It was warm to the touch and sent a sensuous thrill through his body. And then she turned.

"Maria," Demetris moaned aloud. It wasn't Leila's face he saw, It was Maria's. It wasn't Leila he felt guilty about. It was Maria. It had always been Maria, and it would always be Maria. How could he have screwed up his life so badly? He had had the love of his life.

Life had been perfect. How could he have let her get away from him, and how had he sunk to these depths?

Demetris looked around the disheveled flat. No solace there. He rose and walked to a mirror. Certainly no solace there either. He returned to the desk and unrolled the CNA story, which the printer continued to spit out for all the world to enjoy.

Strangely, there was no comfort there, either. He picked up the scotch bottle. It was empty, but even if it had been full, his revelation that he continued to carry the burden of guilt for his treatment of his estranged wife would have assured him that there was no comfort there. No solace anywhere but in Maria. And he had screwed that up royally.

He had wrecked his own home. He had once had a perfect home with Maria. And then his resentment of her success and his love for the cards, the booze, and the dangerous liaisons had taken over. He had been blaming Leila for wrecking his home, but that wasn't true. He could see that now. He had wrecked it himself.

No comfort anywhere for such as he.

* * * *

The news of the death of Ahmad Jallud and his wife reached the Koniotises while they were still at Irene's house, celebrating both the escape of Eric and the change in all of them in attitude toward their relationship with each other and their feelings toward family bonding. As shocking as it was, the news was not a total surprise.

Eric had told his parents of his encounter with Leila Jallud. Takis and Caitlyn had known Ahmad was deeply distressed about the disappearance of his wife, and Ahmad's

319

temper and his strong sense of justice had often been exhibited to both of them, more often than not to their benefit.

Takis did not want to cut short his reunification with the family, but Maria Solonos needed him now. Cyprus was without a police chief when it perhaps needed one most. The news of the Jallud murder-suicide—although it was being treated in what was being released to the public as a tragic accident—had broken at the same time as Britain's announcement that it would be withdrawing from the sovereign base areas, a development for which the country had not been prepared and which had resulted in anxiety as well as public jubilation and in various factions of political interest groups taking to the streets.

There, further, was still a race to neutralize the Homewrecker weapon system, which, if it was to deliver a nuclear payload as was suspected, would have tragic consequences for Cyprus whether or not the system was still here in Cyprus. And, with Cyprus quite obviously having been a staging area for this weapon and the wife of its highest police official having been implicated in the project, the Cypriot government had to show to the Israelis and the Western powers every effort to help close this operation down before it had done further harm.

While talking with the interior minister, who had brought him the sad news about Jallud, Takis had pledged to help her in every way he could. Then, after a short discussion with his family, he telephoned the UN secretary general and asked for a short, formal leave of absence. Under the circumstances, the secretary general concurred that Takis could be better used just now to help within the Cyprus arena of the events that were unfolding across the broad political spectrum. But he requested that Takis consider himself as remaining in charge of the preparations for the coming Middle East peace conference in Paphos, which the secretary general was going to optimistically assume would still come off until unless the situation in the area deteriorated further.

With Caitlyn standing at his side and Eric and Irene sitting close by, Takis telephoned back to Maria Solonos and offered to take up Ahmad Jallud's responsibilities until the situation settled down and the government was able to bring in another national police chief. He would still informally oversee his UN security duties, as well, but he would formally be returning in the short term to national duty for Cyprus.

Solonos, of course, accepted the offer with alacrity and with a deep sense of appreciation. The ethnic-strife-producing bombings, the anti-British campaigning culminating in the abrupt British announcement to leave Cyprus, the unexplained absence of the Turkish Cypriot vice president, and, now, the suspicious death of the nation's police chief were putting considerable strain on the unity government of Chrystalla Ioannou. Takis Koniotis, who had risen to international prominence, was a hero of virtually legendary proportions in Cyprus. His willingness to dedicate himself to the Ioannou government might prove the difference between the continuance of a strong unity government and the sinking of the country into divisive factionalism and violence.

As Takis hung up, he turned and said to his wife and son, with considerable evident regret, "Well, that's it then, I guess. Maria accepted the proposition. I'm afraid I'll have to be leaving now to go back to the acropolis house. You probably don't know it, but we've set up a temporary UNICIS command post there, and, although I will go into police headquarters occasionally, it would probably be best for me to work from UNICIS until the Homewrecker aspect of the situation is worked out."

He had, of course, weighed the effect of leaving Caitlyn and Eric again to concentrate on his work so soon after they had begun to reconcile, but he was now finding it hard to put what would likely be seen as just another rejection of his family obligations into words.

"I guess . . . I guess the two of you will be going back to Famagusta. Hopefully . . ."

Caitlyn placed two fingers on her husband's lips, wrapped her arms around him, and smiled through tearful eyes.

"No, I don't think so. Do you, Eric?" Her son shook his head solemnly.

"No, we'll come home with you," she continued. "Eric can start to learn a little more about just how complex and sophisticated the UNICIS research process is. I'm sure you can use an extra pair of hands and another good mind in the temporary watch office. As for me, the center's in my home, and I'm sure no one has bothered to organize meals and rest periods properly."

"But your job. The archaeological institute and excavation projects. The new ecological center at the Bogaz exhibit site . . ."

"History won't go away. The projects have been waiting for us for thousands of years. A few more days or weeks won't matter. I won't ever say my work doesn't matter, of course. But you and the boys matter more, and I can readily see that your work is a greater priority—for all of us—just now."

Takis absorbed this, and eventually managed to stammer out, "I appreciate that, Caitlyn, and after this and the Paphos conference are over, I promise I'll take a leave of absence and we'll take Eric back to the States to find a good school for him and visit Ahmad and then we'll come back and stay in Famagusta until you can reestablish the threads of the institute's work."

"Thank you, you know I'd appreciate that," Caitlyn responded, fixing her husband with a steady stare. "But we'll see.

I'd rather you didn't make any promises just now that you can't keep."

As the three said their good-byes to Irene and headed toward the door, Takis's mind was racing. He couldn't say more to Caitlyn just now. He had said the same things before and had not come through for her. But he resolved to come through this time. He wasn't the same self-centered Greek husband who Caitlyn had left. He understood better now what she and the boys were worth to him, and, as important as the professional demands on him of trying to maintain world peace and security were, he was not the only one who had concerns for and skills in his police work.

"Home" and "family" had once just been abstractions for Takis. Now they were everything to him. He would not have appreciated that if he had not lost them. He was determined not to blow his second chance.

* * * *

Gerhard Mueller cursed the Israelis for the third time that day, as the quiet warning buzzer sounded that enemy spotter planes were up and headed for the Golan Heights. At the push of a button, the camouflage netting zipped across its frame and the sliding rock doors closed in above that, hiding the gully that had been carved out of the rock of the heights to accommodate the Homewrecker's long barrel. The barrel itself had been painted in camouflage paint as well. The Syrian Air Force had assured Mueller and the crew he had working around the clock to have the gun assembled and ready to fire tonight that the site couldn't be picked out by even the lowest-flying spotter aircraft with the most sophisticated detection devices. For this to be so, however, the site had to be secured and the crew had to be positioned, motionless and silent, in the side tunnels.

Gerhard Mueller took little comfort in the fact that, as promised, they hadn't been detected despite several Israeli sorties directly overhead. Each time they had to break off their work meant precious delays, delays that he could ill afford if the gun was going to be assembled in time.

He was irritated at his firm's director, Inga Hartzel, for having decided, apparently on her own, not to permit the crew that had tested the gun in Cyprus to survive to be here to advise the operational crew in any idiosyncrasies they had detected in the tests. When confronted, she had claimed, rather unconvincingly he thought, that she hadn't had anything to do with the demise of the test crews and that, anyway, there wasn't anything esoteric about the gun components that had been tested and that the strategic component, the sophisticated triggering device that they had stolen from the American lab, hadn't been included in the testing. Still, what did she know about the intricacies of launching a low-altitude rocket, especially one with a nuclear payload? He knew better than she whether the testing crew had already outlived its usefulness to them.

Mueller's respect for his boss had been shaken on another front as well. She wasn't here for the launch. She had told him that she was needed elsewhere, but he suspected that she even now was speeding back to Switzerland to be well clear of the nuclear cloud that would result from this launch.

Mueller was just as irritated with the Lucerne office manager, Sergey Stepanov. Where was he? He was supposed to be here now, helping Mueller complete this installation. But he wasn't here and no one seemed to know where he was. He didn't seem to be in Syria at all. Mueller was actually grateful that Hartzel wasn't here. That bossy bitch would only get in the away. But he had thought that Stepanov would be here to help.

The all-clear buzzed gently, and Mueller began to move out of the side tunnel, trying to remember where he had left off in the calibration sequence. But, just as the rock ledges had slid open and the crew could see to resume their work, the warning buzzer went off again and the ceiling panels began to close.

Damn those Israelis! Mueller was really going to enjoy triggering the Tel Aviv- and Jerusalem-directed nuclear bombs now.

* * * *

Inga Hartzel sensed something was wrong even as she entered the door to her sixth-floor Saladin Intercontinental Hotel suite overlooking the Beirut seafront corniche. It was too dark. The chambermaids always left a lamp burning for her somewhere in the suite and she always kept the draperies open to the view of the sea. But now it was dark beyond the threshold and someone had closed all of the drapes.

She hesitated to go in, but she quickly realized that she was vulnerably exposed in the light from the hallway as long as she stood on the threshold. She slid into the room and clicked the door shut behind her. She reached across the doorway and flicked the light switch. Nothing happened. Had the foyer light burned out or was there an isolated power failure in the building? Or was her intuition spot on and someone was in the suite, waiting for her?

Inga's first reaction was to slip out of the door again and seek help, but, as she placed her fingers on the door knob, she realized that she would be exposing her silhouette to the dark room if she opened the door to the hall light once more. She tried to slide to the side of the room, seeking shelter, only to bump into a table. Someone had moved the furniture as well.

Someone didn't want to leave her with any of the advantages. But she wondered if that someone was aware that Inga was armed. She pulled the small revolver from her hand bag. She was ready and she was a good shot.

That's when Inga heard the ragged breathing. Someone indeed was in the darkened room and was stalking her. There. Was it by the door into the bedroom or the one into the small kitchenette. No need to differentiate. Inga fired off shots in both directions and then instantly let off two more shots toward a form she could now see moving in the dark. Toward her. In a rush.

Before Inga could fire again, Irina Lukenov was upon her, knife slashing and curses flying.

Chapter Twenty

They had made the deadline, and Gerhard Mueller was triumphant. Technically the system should have been installed and armed three hours earlier, before midnight, but the Iranian himself had decided, quite sensibly, that they would now have to fire in the darkest of night, because the gun barrel still had to be elevated above the level of the man-made gully rim on the edge of the Golan Heights cliffs. If they were to show the roving Israeli air patrols the profile of the gun during the day, the Iranian knew the site would be destroyed before they could fire—and certainly before they could launch the second nuclear warhead.

They had worked inside the closed gully since dark had fallen, showing only the minimum of light required to ensure all of the components were together properly. The first of two warheads had taken an hour to maneuver onto the tip of the rocket being launched. This first one would land on Tel Aviv. They were hoping that they would have time to place the second rocket and warhead, directed at west Jerusalem, before the Israelis recovered from the shock of the first detonation. Anyone left alive within thirty miles of the Tel Aviv missile landing would certainly have their hands full just trying to stay alive in the short term, having already been doomed to death by the nuclear fallout from the low-grade, but nonetheless very lethal, warhead.

The stolen triggering device turned out to be the easiest component to install. Stepanov had given it to them as a closed-system box that just needed to be locked into place and switched on. When turned on, it hummed along quietly as its small systems' lights blinked on and off in the sequence that indicated, according to the instructions that had come with it, that all was well.

At 3:05 AM on 3 July 2014, Gerhard Mueller of the Hartzel-Wegner arms broker firm proudly turned control of the Homewrecker low-altitude rocket launcher gun over to the control of an Iranian businessman, a Syrian general, and the Hizballah envoy to Damascus, as representing the financial sponsor, the system host, and the operational planner, respectively.

At 3:10 AM, the Syrian general accepted operational control of the site, and, upon reconfirmation of orders from Damascus, ordered the rock ledges above the gully to be slid away and the camouflage netting to be retracted from the long gun barrel.

By 3:18 AM, the gully was open to the sky, and the Syrian general ordered the raising of the barrel.

By 3:25 AM, the barrel had raised to its precalibrated level, and Mueller's technical crew began swarming around the gun's carriage to make last-minute checks on the accuracy of the trajectory settings.

At 3:36 AM, the warning buzzer of aircraft in the vicinity began its quiet but persistent sound. The Syrian general looked at Gerhard Mueller, who returned a challenging and insistent stare.

At 3:36 AM and ten seconds, the Syrian general screamed the order to fire, and the gunnery officer flipped the firing switch on the triggering device.

There was a click and then a pregnant silence.

The lights of the triggering device were gaily blinking on and off in their "every part of the system is just fine" sequence. The gunnery officer madly clicked twice more, without result.

At 3:37 AM, silent, dark-clad figures with lashing knives flowed over the rim and into the artificial gully, quietly dispatching everyone in their wake except those who obviously were part of the technical crew, while being very, very careful not to touch the Homewrecker gun or its nuclear warheads.

* * * *

They hadn't touched a thing. They had just made sure that there was no reason for heroics and then had closed off the flat and awaited the arrival of the interior minister. It didn't take Maria Solonos too long to reach her former husband's flat. For some reason, she had always assumed it would come to this—to her being called out in the wee hours of the morning to identify the alcohol-soaked body of Demetris Mattas at his home or the newspaper offices or in some alley behind a nightclub or in some other woman's bed. It had been somewhat of a surprise that he had died from suicide rather than from alcohol poisoning, from setting himself afire in a drunken stupor, or from drug-related heart failure.

As she entered the flat and walked over to his body, which was slumped over the desk in his study, she was wondering what could have possibly caused him to take his own life. She would have thought that someone would do that when they had sunk as low as they could get, and Demetris had dived to the depths of his degradation two years ago and had stayed there. He should have been used to coping with the depths of despair. Just what had caused him to kill himself now? He had won his campaign to expel the British, if the jury was still out on his other campaigns of the month. Was it success that he couldn't face?

Looking down at her husband's face, Maria suddenly found she could look through all of the filth, unshaven whiskers, and haggard lines and see the handsome young idealistic newspaper columnist who had swept her off her feet with his brashness and zest for life. She hadn't thought the encounter would be like this. She had thought that she hated him so much that she wouldn't feel anything for him at all when she saw the body.

But she was wrong. It had been a mistake to come here. She found she couldn't gloat over his departure from life and from a career of running her and her government down. She couldn't even remember now how she had grown to hate him. It was a lot of little things, she decided. And she wondered if there was anything she could have done to prevent the trail having led to this small pistol in his lifeless hand.

Maria reached out and patted a strand of Demetris's hair back into place. He had always had trouble keeping that lock of hair where it belonged. Then she bent down and kissed his cold forehead one last time. Turning to go, she noticed that his computer screen was incessantly flashing at her. "Press any key," it kept saying. So, she pressed the "G" for "good-bye," and Demetris's last message scrolled across the screen. He had also set it for voice message.

"I love you, Maria," the screen and his voice passionately declared to her. "I am so sorry. It was always you. It was always you."

As the message scrolled away into a whisper, Maria collapsed unto a chair and cried all of the tears for her marriage and for her lost love in death that she had been unable to cry for him for years in life.

The private message was not to be Demetris's last act of atonement. The morning's edition of *Semerini*, which was just beginning to hit the news kiosks as Maria arrived at her former husband's flat, carried the last column of the publisher in which he apologized to both Maria and to President Chrystalla Ioannou for having preached a line of hatred for so many years in his paper when the events of the world required all Cypriots, Greek and Turk alike, to unify their efforts toward peace and mutual trust.

It would be two more days before the note that had been taped to Mattas's computer monitor was brought to her and Maria began to understand both what had led her husband to suicide and why the Jalluds had died. The note had reminded Mattas to meet the writer at Othello's Tower in Famagusta within the time frame that Leila and Ahmad Jallud had died there, and the handwriting had eventually been identified as that of Leila Jallud. A recovery program on Mattas's computer had surfaced three pieces that he had tried to destroy: a column that laid out the analogy between Leila and Shakespeare's *Othello*, the note to Ahmad on Leila's murky past, and a column implicating Ahmad Jallud by way of his wife in the explosions that had occurred in Cyprus.

* * * *

The nationalistic Texas oil tycoon and computer chip king was nothing if not neat. He also was too well connected and resourceful to let the UNICIS computers, the heavily guarded and encrypted single largest data bank of personal, corporate, and national data, remain closed to him. For these combined reasons, his "arm of personal justice," Joseph MacAlister was once more standing in the subterranean vaults of Tehran's Ghasr Prison and waiting to complete his assignment.

The tycoon had been furious that his personal force had not been able to interdict the Homewrecker device before it reached Syria, although the Israelis did credit him and MacAlister's people with enabling them to neutralize the threat themselves. And, if truth be known, the Israelis preferred having done the final work themselves rather than having it done for them.

I wasn't good enough, however, to MacAlister's sponsor for the threat itself to be ended. He wanted to pull the evilness out by its roots. And the UNICIS computers had finally put together the Homewrecker plan, piece by piece, and had produced a name list. The tycoon was only sorry that there were so few people left alive to root out on that list. Major Syrian and Hizballah players had been killed by the Israelis at the Homewrecker launch site, and the tycoon had special plans for the Syrian president and a few other leaders of the Hizballah. The Russian nationalist political leader who had provided the nuclear material had already had an unfortunate accident while being detained on charges.

Of those involved from the Hartzel-Wegner arms broker firm, Inga Hartzel, Gerhard Mueller, and Pavel Lukenov were already dead. The elusive Sergey Stepanov would be found one of these days. The tycoon was conducting an intensive search of the Middle East, Europe, and Russia for the man, and it would be his special pleasure when that man had been brought to justice.

Of the Iranians, the woman who had coordinated the weapons testing in Cyprus was gone. But the one behind the whole scheme, the Iranian ultimately responsible for the whole project, was still alive. But it was his turn now, and MacAlister's force had been set in motion. His death would muddle up one of the tycoon's other important projects, but there were more people available besides him for that purpose.

The Iranian had now shown his hand. He would have completely betrayed the American's program for Iran someday anyway. Indeed, the continuance of the Homewrecker project had been just such a betrayal.

Iranian prime minister Assadollah Egbal was bundled into the small cell in the depths of Ghasr Prison and thrust before Joseph MacAlister. The two members of MacAlister's squad who had virtually carried him into the room withdrew to the doorway. Egbal did not honor the situation by revealing any sign of fear. He defiantly stood there, openly glaring his hatred at the American mercenary.

"You were going to miss our appointment, Mr. Prime Minister," MacAlister calmly stated. "You had said you would meet me here, but my friends found you preparing to leave for the airport instead."

Silence.

"I suppose you know why you are here," MacAlister continued.

Egbal fixed the American with a look of contempt.

"I thought so," said MacAlister just as if Egbal had answered in the affirmative. He then proceeded to read the charges on Egbal's role, extending from the time of the ayatollahs into the current regime of the shah, in the plans to destroy Israel with nuclear weapons. When he was finished, he asked Egbal if he had anything to say.

This time the prime minister answered. "Nothing you have said puts me in contradiction to the feelings of the Iranian people. This is our legitimate policy no matter whether we are being governed by Islamic fundamentalism or the ancestors of ancient Persian dynasties. I have nothing to fear from the shah or my people for the policies I have pursued against Zionism. The shah will not countenance your harming me for these activities."

"Unfortunately, that is undoubtedly true," MacAlister said with a sigh, as he closed the book of charges. "But just as unfortunately for you, I'm sure, we've reached the ear of the shah and explained to him all of the little ways you are undermining his rule and lining your own pockets at his expense and that of the Iranian people."

"Lies! All lies," sputtered the angry Iranian. "I have done nothing against the shah or the Iranian people."

"True perhaps," MacAlister smiled, "but that's not what the shah thinks. And you have become very inconvenient to my employer and entirely too self-willed as a partner in the Iranian program. You may have died for the wrong reasons, but justice does, after all, work in strange ways."

Egbal was still sputtering his innocence and screaming his curses upon all Americans when the appointed Iranian guards came in and dragged him further and permanently into the depths of Ghasr Prison.

* * * *

As he cast out his trout line, Jim Mikelson cooled his toes in the fast-running waters of the upper reaches of the Snake River in the Rocky Mountains of northern Colorado. Each time he brought out a rainbow trout, he reached over into his tackle bag and took out a little metal object, chuckled, and put it back again. This had become a ritual, one he apparently never tired of performing.

He had bought this isolated stand of ground in the mountains near the little town of Dixon more than a decade previously and had built a small but luxurious cabin near the Snake River. He had figured that he would need to retire here sooner or later, and he had established an identity and presence here that were entirely separate from his life in Europe as Sergey Stepanov. He was content that he wouldn't be found here as long as he remained where he was, and he had established enough of a nest egg to keep him in very respectable gentility for the rest of his life. And if this hideout and identity didn't hold, there was another one waiting for him. He always had a backup plan.

He just didn't know whether or how long he could manage without the thrill of the game or on his own. He was already beginning to miss the presence of Irina and of Pavel and Uri. It had been entirely too late for them when he began to realize just how pleasant family life in the cottage near Lucerne had been.

Ah, well, there are other compensations, he thought, as he reached into the tackle box one more time, extracted the little metal object and laughed heartily. Insurance. Insurance came in all sizes, and this had been Sergey's insurance. They hadn't believed him and they hadn't even deigned to discuss with him the possibility of paying him what he was worth for the Homewrecker project. The Iranian, the Syrian president, and Ingrid. They had all just laughed at him. But, even though he wasn't any richer, he was now the only one among them who was laughing.

He would have enjoyed being there when they switched on the Homewrecker triggering device and nothing happened. He had known nothing would happen, because he held the triggering clip in his hand now. He had had the entire voyage from Marseilles to Cyprus to Tripoli to work with the triggering component and to extract the actual trigger and then bypass the circuitry so that the maintenance system of the component was fooled into thinking the trigger was still in place.

An expensive joke and one that those Islamic fanatics would not have appreciated. But his old Russian friends would have seen the humor and would have laughed with him. Jim Mikelson cast his line into the burbling brook again. The trout were running, and they barely had enough water depth to keep their gills wet. Playing these trout was almost as easy as playing Islamic fundamentalists. He couldn't wait to make another strike. He wanted to feel his insurance policy again and enjoy his joke one more time.

Epilogue

Zurich was snowed under during the Christmas of 2014. This, in itself, was not unusual. But the snow was falling more frequently now than in years past and was drifting much higher. This was an indication, the scientists were saying, that the deterioration of the earth's protective ozone layer was continuing despite the advances that had been made in clean and efficient energy of late. Uri had moved out on the countess, although it was more of a case of the countess's husband having shown up and leading to Uri's departure. There hadn't been a scene, and the husband would have really preferred that Uri stay, but that had actually been the problem. Uri believed in mixed pairs, not mixed triples.

Uri had moved just to the other bank of the Limmat River, to the commercial center of the city. He had purchased a small, second-floor apartment overlooking the Limmat and opening directly onto the Lindenhof gardens, which occupied the highest point in the city and had been the site of a Roman customs post in the first century BC.

Although he still worked for the Zurich office of the Piccards, Uri was now spending much of his time continuing the investigation into the Hartzel-Wegner firm and its involvement in Mideast terrorism. He had lost his mother and brother in that fiasco, and he would never rest until he found everyone who was responsible and brought them to justice. Stepanov thought he was safe, but Uri had found him and was just waiting for the convenient moment to call in that debt. He would have done so earlier, but the memory of his mother kept staying his hand. Even at the end she had voiced her love for Stepanov.

Uri took the now-yellowed and brittle letter from his desk drawer and moved over to the window to read it once more in the light reflecting off the ice-covered Limmat. Of course he didn't actually have to read it. He had memorized every word.

His mother had written it to him not long before she had found and confronted Ingrid Bittmann, who had been passing herself off as Inga Hartzel. The letter spoke both of the sins and mistakes that his mother had committed and how she knew she hadn't been a good mother to him and Pavel, especially in view of her desertion of her young sons when she had defected to the Hizballah cause. But she went on to ask him to forgive her and to learn by the mistakes she had made.

Nothing she had done in the choices she made, she had stated, had lessened her love for her sons and her respect for family. What had undermined the family, she believed, had been the fact that she had loved Pavel's father, Sergey Stepanov, rather than her own husband and Uri's father, Mikhail Lukenov. She had loved Sergey first and had been more or less forced into marrying Mikhail. All had been bearable until she and the boys were trapped alone and abandoned in Grozny for several weeks under bombardment by Russian artillery. She had scrabbled like an animal to keep her family alive and safe during those weeks, and something inside her had snapped. Her search for Sergey and Ingrid Bittmann to put a stop to their project of destruction had been an act of atonement for her sins and a renewed commitment to her family. In conclusion, she begged Uri to create, honor, and cherish a family of his own.

Uri refolded the letter and gazed up at the little yellow palace on the hillside across the Limmat. Yes, it was time for him to give up married countesses and to settle down. He loved his mother more now than he ever had before, and he no longer held her accountable for all of those years he had been left dependent on his father. He didn't even resent his father anymore. Lukenov had done what he could for his boys. At least he had thought in his own eyes that what he was doing was for their good.

No, perhaps the secret of making peace with life was to take responsibility for your life and not to blame anyone else, and especially not your parents, for how things turned out. Uri certainly knew he couldn't criticize his parents for the choices they had made until he had faced raising a family of his own. And, as his mother begged, he was about ready to take on the responsibility now—right after he finished with his investigation into Hartzel-Wegner.

As he pulled away from the window, Uri was considering again his coming meeting with Andre Piccard. He was here in Zurich and had asked Uri to meet him in the park area behind the Schweiz Landesmuseum, the national museum. A strange place for a meeting in winter. Andre must not want anyone to overhear their conversation. Maybe he had some important information on Hartzel-Wegner to share.

Uri and Andre had not met face-to-face since Uri had gone to Cyprus in search of his mother the previous summer. Uri could only guess at what was really on Andre's mind, although he had alluded to another assignment he might want Uri to take up. But it didn't matter what business the Piccard shipping magnate had; Uri had wanted to see Andre again for some time.

So many things to do before he could get on with his life, but he was not blind to the thrust of his mother's letter—

that you couldn't keep putting off the things in life that were important.

* * * *

The Christmas of 2014 was the most joyous one thus far on record for the Koniotis family even though the temperature had hit record highs in Famagusta. This was caused, scientists were saying, by the continued deterioration of the earth's protective ozone layer despite the recent improvements in the use of energy. Everyone in the immediate family—Takis, Caitlyn, Eric, Ahmad, and Irene—were wedged into the old Turkish-style courtyard house with the burbling fountain.

Ahmad had come over to Cyprus for his winter break, and Eric was preparing to leave to start his premed courses at Johns Hopkins University, where Takis and Caitlyn had managed to win his place back for him by going back to the United States with him and sitting in the university president's office until they had convinced him that Eric had managed a significant change in attitude and was now ready to take his studies seriously. The entire family was spending the holiday helping Caitlyn and Ginger Patterson put finishing touches to their plan to add an environmental dimension to the archaeological exhibits at the Bogaz site.

Takis was there working on the project with just as much attention and dedication as any other member of the family. The situation in Cyprus had calmed down within a month of the British announcement of withdrawal, which now was proceeding with good will on both sides. The successful conclusion of the nuclear bomb threat to Israel had also helped to ease tension in the region significantly. The Middle East peace conference in Paphos, which had been held in October, was a success in that all major participants showed up, did not throw chairs at each other, and concluded the meeting with the setting of a date for deeper level talks based on meaningful agreements on important issues. Takis and UNICIS had considered the conference particularly successful, as the security measures that UNICIS chief Ellen Larkin had laid on, in Takis's absence on other business, had prevented even the hint of threat to any of the leaders who participated in the conference.

The success of the conference administration and security with only a minimal amount of attention by Takis had convinced him that he had good people working for him— naturally enough, since he had handpicked them all—and that he could stop micromanaging the UN security programs and take more time off for his family.

Not so strangely, Caitlyn had found the same thing in her own professional life as she was playing mother, wife, and hostess at the temporary UNICIS headquarters in their Nicosia home. Even though she wasn't physically in Famagusta during this period, she found she was able to contribute significantly to the work of both the Archaeology Department and to her own archaeological institute without devoting every waking moment to the effort.

Takis and Caitlyn had found each other again, and they had also learned to take life a bit more slowly and to depend on their highly talented colleagues more.

Irene's conclusion and the thrust of her Christmas toast to the Koniotis family, one and all, was that they were all going to get along just fine now. They were quickly learning the Mediterranean lifestyle and its secret to a calm, yet worthwhile, life.

* * * *

Andre Piccard had promised his wife Ellen Larkin, glowing in full-blown pregnancy, the veal dinner of her life for their Christmas in Switzerland experience, and he was about to deliver on his promise as they swept in out of the blizzard on Zurich's east bank. He had chosen one of his favorite restaurants, one of the city's most elegant, which was housed in the early eighteenth-century carpenters' guildhall, the Zunfthaus zur Zimmerleuten. He had made reservations months in advance and, even then, he would not have been accommodated if his name had not been Piccard.

The owner of the restaurant had been at the door, greeting the exclusive clientele, when the Piccards arrived, and he literally showered the couple with attention.

"Where is Klaus tonight?" Andre inquired politely about the restaurant's legendary maitre d'hotel, who Andre had never seen absent from his post.

"Alas, I'm afraid the old age has taken Klaus away from us," the owner answered sadly. "It grieved all of our hearts to see him go, but he could hear and see no more, you understand. He was so good, however, that he was blind and deaf for two years before we noticed. He knew his clientele that well."

Andre, the owner, and Ellen all clucked appreciatively in unison.

"But, I am delighted to say," the restaurant proprietor continued to gush, "that we managed to steal Hans from the Lucerne Sofitel Hotel's Diff Restaurant. He will be along in a moment. Oh, here he is now."

Andre had stiffened at the information and had actually backed involuntarily toward the door, his right foot painfully finding Ellen's instep.

Hans bore down on the threesome, ready to show the extent of his talents. "Ah, Herr Wegner. How wonderful to see you in Zurich. And would this be Frau Wegner? But . . ." and here he stopped in great perplexity and embarrassment, ". . . I do not think we were expecting you tonight, and . . ."

"Mr. PICCARD and his wife have reservations for table number five, Hans," cut in the owner, his voice full of censure. "I will guide them to their table myself."

Hans was left, flapping his jaw in the air, and ready to engage in mortal combat with the proprietor upon his return. The questioning of a client's identity was a case of the most vile insult in his business, and Hans would not have it. He knew Konrad Wegner of the Lucerne firm of Hartzel-Wegner when he saw him.

As they proceeded through the restaurant toward their table, the owner was gabbling obsequious phrases in a concerted attempt to erase the past ten second's of Andre's memory, Andre was greeting friends left and right and pretending that all was right with the world, and Ellen was protectively clutching her developing child, feeling herself becoming more distant from her husband with each step, and trying not to scream out the collapse of her happy family and of her ordered world.

Gina Drew

Gina Drew is a retired American foreign service officer who specialized in investigating and countering international crime and espionage and who still travels the world in both the imagination and in fact.

Years spent working on Cyprus have left her with a deep love of this divided island and its people.

www.cyberworldpublishing.com